ANTHONY LE MOIGNAN

A LONG
GOODBYE

First published in Great Britain 2018

Anthony Le Moignan
www.anthonylemoignan.com

Cover illustration by Vanessa Mendozzi
Author photograph by Dan White

Printed and bound in Great Britain by Biddles Ltd, King's
Lynn

First Printing: May 2018

Paperback ISBN: 978-1-9995902-0-8
Hardback ISBN: 978-1-9995902-2-2

To Dad

For the many, many sufferers
One day, let there be a cure

1

Tuesday 09 May 2017 - Midday

Simon hadn't attempted a personal best on the way to Orchard. He was wearing a tracksuit as well, which wasn't optimum gear for a new record. It was also pouring with rain.

He was definitely the most athletic future care home resident that Emma had ever met.

He was also soaked, so the first thing she did after shaking his hand was locate a bath towel.

'You poor man, we could have picked you up, you know? Would you like to go into one of the bathrooms and dry off properly? We can give you some dry clothes too. Maybe take a hot shower? I'm Emma, by the way – I work here. It's a pleasure to meet you.'

It had been a long while since Simon had given a single thought to his appearance. Sure, he shaved every day and went to the barber's every three weeks, but his dark hair was short enough that it never needed any attention – it always looked the same, with maybe the additional grey hair or two. Yet now he was wishing he'd taken a taxi to avoid the drowned rat look.

'It's no problem, really, but thank you. Nobody ever died from a drop of rain.'

They looked each other in the eye, and there was an awkwardness tingling in the air. Why had he said that? What a fool he was.

'And I'm Simon, though I guess you knew that? I've seen you in your car a couple of times when I've been running around here.'

A glow of recognition sparked in Emma's face.

'*That's* where I know your face from – I never forget a face. You run very fast. Did you used to be an athlete? Oh, no wait, I didn't mean '*used to be*.' I'm so sorry; I meant that …'

'It's okay. No, I never ran at a club. I used to run for my school and to work and back most days in London, but after the diagnosis, I've begun to take it more seriously. I guess that sounds a bit weird, but it gives me a purpose trying to beat my best time – that sort of thing. Just something to do to keep fit. Well, you know, fit as in …'

The air shivered again as they both looked at each other's shoes. Water was beginning to pool on the tiled floor around Simon, who still hadn't thought to use the large towel in his hand.

'Hello, I'm Simon.' He looked up and smiled, extending his hand to shake hers.

'Hello, I'm Emma.' She smiled back. Emma was fluent and at ease with this type of dialogue – she had over 20 years' experience of it.

'I should say at this stage that I didn't accidentally repeat myself just then. I just felt the first exchange hadn't gone to plan so thought I'd have another bash at it.' He grinned, and Emma's jaw dropped. Then she laughed, despite herself.

2

'But I can't guarantee I won't repeat myself quite a lot in the future, and might not be able to apologise for it.'

Emma stopped abruptly in mid-giggle and coloured slightly.

'Sorry for the confusion there, Ella. It is Ella, isn't it? Don't tell me I've got that wrong already?'

Emma put a hand on his shoulder. 'Simon, it's anything you wish to call me. Sometimes I even forget my own ...'

But he interrupted her again.

'Gotcha! Just tricking. Oh God, I'm so sorry, Emma. I don't normally muck around like this. Let's put it down to nerves, eh?'

She feigned frustration and seriousness.

'Not a problem. I allow everybody two strikes, but then you're out. You've got one left, Mr Carter.'

It lasted less than a second, but Simon was taken in. Then they both pointed a finger at each other and burst out laughing.

And Maddy came out of Emma's office.

'Hey, good to see you guys have met. Simon, you're soaked! Tell me you didn't run here?' She grabbed the towel out of his hand and started to wipe the sides and shoulders of his sodden tracksuit.

'Thanks, I probably shouldn't have run. Maybe I'll take up that offer of a hot shower if it's no trouble? I don't fancy sitting through lunch like this.' He took the towel from her and started to rub his face and hair.

Emma had the solution. 'Why don't you go with Maddy. She'll show you where a bathroom is, and there'll be a dressing gown there to get into. Pass her your clothes, and I'll put them in a dryer – they'll be dry in half an hour. Then we'll meet back here and go to lunch. Fair enough?'

It made a lot of sense to Simon who was beginning to shiver despite the warmth of the environment.

'Okay, it's a date. Make sure you don't iron creases in my tracksuit bottoms, though. That would be *really* naff. And what colour dressing gown, by the way? I'm quite fussy about that sort of thing.' He winked at Emma and followed Maddy down the hall.

Emma watched them go and smiled to herself. Simon Carter was going to have quite an impact on life here.

2

Wednesday 27 July 1988 to Tuesday 09 May 2017

Emma Thornton was fully aware of her responsibilities. Substantial responsibilities they were too. 18 years ago, she'd started as a junior carer with Orchard Residential Home in the village of Histon just north of Cambridge. It was anything but a financial decision. She'd achieved a First Class Honours degree in Psychology and could have commanded a very attractive wage in a variety of other careers.

Her first year after university was spent gaining the specific qualifications necessary to care for people much less fortunate than herself. It wasn't a vocation – at least she didn't think it was. Emma traced it back to when Nan, already in her 80s but still fiercely independent and living on her own in Newmarket, had taken a tumble at the supermarket.

It was near an ice-making machine in the height of a long, sweltering summer. Cubes lay scattered on the linoleum floor, forming miniature lakes in seconds. Nan had slipped while lugging her groceries out to the car, landed badly, then passed out from the pain. Rushed to the hospital, the x-ray had shown a hairline fracture of the hip.

The injury wasn't uncommon for elderly people, but that made it no less serious. With age came the brittleness of bones, and Nan was never the same again. She missed her car more than anything, her independence snatched from her. Physiotherapy had helped, but her mood grew darker. With her parents' blessing, Emma, then only fourteen, had moved in with Nan for the rest of the summer holiday. She lived in a cottage in Cheveley, some three miles away from Emma's family home.

What started out as errands and companionship turned into something much deeper and more meaningful. Through that autumn and winter, she formed a bond with her grandmother which never previously existed. Three years later, she was living at Nan's cottage permanently, now able to personally drive her around the town.

The old lady's fighting spirit had dissipated over the years, and her mind had started to wander. Emma was initially unable to deal with the same questions being repeated over and over again. She gently reminded Nan how repetitive she was becoming, but it seemed to make no difference. If anything, it began to antagonise her gran, so Emma adopted a different approach and constantly refined her ways of communicating. It brought them both much more happiness, and Emma began to engage with her grandmother in a way she'd not thought possible.

Whether Nan felt the same way towards her granddaughter would never be known, but to Emma that wasn't important. Nan's happiness was the only thing she focused on, and the present was the only important time. Yesterday was old news, and tomorrow was the future they'd reach later. *Now* was all that was relevant.

*

It was the first family funeral Emma had experienced. She'd never forgiven herself for not being with her gran at the end, but Fresher's Week at King's College in Cambridge was something her parents had not wanted her to miss. Nan had been in hospital for a few days, but the prognosis wasn't bleak – the antibiotics seemed to be working. Then she'd suddenly gone downhill with pneumonia. Nan passed away overnight.

Although Emma hadn't discussed it with her parents, she knew her future lay in the care industry. Through choice, her psychology degree had dealt extensively with diminished mental capacity in an ageing society. She'd excelled, though refused to apply the letters after her name that announced her academic status, much to her mother's disappointment.

She'd met guys and had good times during her years at university, but there was nothing serious. A couple of relationships had continued long enough to leave her miserable for a while after they ended, but she readily accepted it was all part of the learning curve. She was prepared for her career to produce much more heartache than she could imagine, so the end of one or two college relationships was nothing to get too morbid about.

In Emma's first year at Orchard, a senior carer had taken more than a passing interest in her. He'd been with the company for three years and was her immediate boss, though they both answered to the Home Manager. Michael Lowry was 25, a year older than Emma, on the fast track to managing a residential home with The Collins Knight Young Care Homes Group in the not too distant future. It was hardly an inspiring name for a care home group, and he'd never met any of the founding partners who insisted their names be included, but the title didn't seem to stop them from becoming a considerably large company.

Michael was from Liverpool – a dynamic guy with a broad scouse accent and a wicked sense of humour. She wondered why these two traits often seemed inextricably linked. He was a natural with the residents who all adored him. He was always cheerful with everyone and regularly teased residents and carers alike, though in the gentlest of ways.

Of average build and height with a permanently cheeky expression, his dominant feature was a shock of grey hair – something he'd developed whilst a teenager. He constantly took the mickey out of himself, telling people he'd rather ridicule the colour of his hair than have others do it for him. Emma didn't believe the explanation – Michael had the appealing personality of someone who was genuinely self-deprecating.

Their courtship was the best thing she'd ever experienced. Friends told her how lucky she was, and she knew it. They'd honeymooned three years later in the Maldives. Michael was now manager of Orchard, and although not earning a fortune, with prudent saving and booking far enough ahead to get a great deal, he was able to give her the most amazing two weeks of her life.

The couple decided early on in their marriage that they wanted children. More than a decade later, they'd come to terms with the stark and painful reality. Neither openly admitted their feelings to each other, but it was a devastating blow.

By then, they were seeing less of each other because of Michael's promotion to Collins Knight Young head office in London. Emma had taken his position as manager at Orchard. They were apart during the week, but he would come home for weekends, or she'd occasionally travel down to his rented flat in London. It was far from ideal, but they still loved each other and were determined to make things work.

For Michael's 40th birthday, they returned to the Maldives, to the same hotel they'd stayed in during their honeymoon. It was another wonderful fortnight, and they convinced themselves they could still have a child. Emma was nearly 39, and perhaps time was running out.

The following days were torturous. The home pregnancy tests had always been disappointing and painful, but they'd pinned all their hopes on this month. The eventual outcome was soul-destroying.

Michael's work schedules proved more and more stressful, resulting in more weekends apart. The couple made love less and less frequently, though never argued – neither had that type of temperament or personality.

By the time of Emma's 40th they'd discussed and decided against adoption. It was the obvious way forward, and their friends knew they'd make wonderful parents, but it wasn't to be. Michael and Emma's life goal had been their own biological children – there could be no substitute for that.

A few months later, Emma was offered a position at head office. It was a chance to live with her husband again, and the company would provide accommodation in London as part of the package. It was a substantial salary rise for Emma, and they had the opportunity to rent out their own apartment in Cambridge.

Emma turned the offer down. She'd managed Orchard for five years, and it was more than a job to her – much more than that. Orchard Residential Home was now the focus of her life, the residents more important to her than anyone or anything else.

*

The weekends Michael and Emma spent apart began to escalate. Their lengthy daily calls became shorter, and there were occasional days where they had no contact at all. A text message started to replace a short conversation, and eventually, a month went by when they didn't see each other.

There was no suspicion during their times apart, and no jealousy felt by Michael or Emma. This was understandable as neither had eyes for anyone else – they just didn't seem to have eyes for each other.

By now the Collins Knight Young Group had become the largest care home provider in the UK. Michael had been offered a directorship and a substantial salary increase. He'd never set out to be financially successful. Nobody who dedicates themselves to being a carer ever does. But against all the odds, Michael was now a success.

He spent much of his time in Ireland where the company was currently expanding, and latterly on the west coast of America. He was required to manage delicate negotiations for the takeover of a large Californian care home group – a far cry from his first days as a junior carer at Orchard.

*

Emma didn't count the hours she worked – it was irrelevant to her. Her team looked after 96 residents at full capacity, and Orchard was always at that level. Not only that, but there were always people on the waiting list. It was rare for any space to become available before the funeral home had been called.

The property had three floors divided equally, with 30 rooms on each level, two larger ones dedicated for couples. The top floor housed people with medical problems, and this carried the biggest age range – from mid 60s to late 90s.

The middle floor was dedicated to people with dementia-based issues, while the ground floor looked after elderly but still mobile residents with less severe memory problems. Orchard had a slightly higher carer to resident ratio than most homes, with nine full-time staff on each floor. Four worked the morning/day shift, three the day/evening shift, and two stayed overnight.

Apart from the carers, Emma had someone at reception, a bookkeeper, and four kitchen staff. There was part-time staff who helped with auxiliary duties, plus two maintenance handymen who doubled up as gardeners.

The logistics involved in her job were substantial, but it was Emma's interaction with the residents that meant far more to her than anything. As often as possible, she made it her duty to visit all the residents and spend some time with them, however brief that may be.

That some of them may no longer be aware of her presence made no difference – they all deserved her individual care and attention. And love. She wouldn't let these people down the way she felt she'd let her Nan down 25 years ago.

*

Death was a tragic but unavoidable part of her routine, but there were always new faces to welcome. Many of these residents were moving to a care home for the first time, and special help and affection were needed.

Where possible, Emma would always stay with these people as much as she could for their first week or two. At 43, she had always been considerably younger than all the people she looked after, but this was about to change. Someone was moving in today to the 1st Floor, with the start of one of the cruellest of all diseases – early-onset Alzheimer's.

Simon Carter was just 40.

It was rare that she didn't meet all the residents before their arrival at Orchard. There were preliminary procedures to make sure everyone was suitable for the environment. Just as important, to make sure the new residents were happy living there too.

Emma had been on a rare weekend break with Michael in Ireland when Simon was due to visit Orchard. Having read his notes, she was keen to greet him, but this trip had been planned for weeks. It would be at least a month before she saw Michael again, due to yet another lengthy business trip to the States.

She'd only met one other person suffering from early onset Alzheimer's. It was at a home in Southampton whilst Emma was on a three-month course. Lisa was in her early 40s and a beautiful person, both physically and spiritually.

Emma had kept in touch with her for a couple of years, either by telephone or the occasional visit when she could. The two of them once had a memorable weekend in Brighton before the disease took its inevitable hold.

Lisa died three years after she'd first moved to the home. At the funeral, apart from staff of the care home, there was only one relative in attendance. Emma had wept for days.

*

Emma was unaware of Simon Carter's appearance as photos weren't used in a potential resident's application. Maddy, the senior carer and 2nd in command, had seen Simon in her absence and was full of admiration for the man. He was cheerful and initially shy but had a lovely sense of humour. He came on his own and wished to admit himself while he could still make rational decisions.

Simon was due to arrive at midday. Emma had set time aside to welcome their new guest and show him his allocated room. A lunch would follow in the main dining room. She was already aware of his change of address since his initial visit with Maddy – he was now only a few miles away from Orchard. Studying his notes once more, Emma could see that Simon had been diagnosed with his condition eighteen months ago.

Unfortunately, this never represented the start of Alzheimer's. In every case, the diagnosis always lagged behind the earliest signs. The average period between the initial symptoms and a formal diagnosis was nearly three years, so it was fair to predict that Simon had probably been suffering with the illness for five years.

*

Among Simon's indicators were the classic memory problems interfering with everyday life. He was a successful accountant and a partner in his practice. His work was always excellent, and his calculations were faultless. However, messages relayed to him were sometimes forgotten, and occasionally he'd forget a client's or even a colleague's name.

He'd also had two incidents on the road – one as a driver and one as a pedestrian.

Both occasions related to a failure to judge speed correctly. Walking across a road near his home, a car had come close to hitting him. The irate driver screamed abuse before driving away in a squeal of tyres. A neighbour who'd witnessed the incident confided that although the driver displayed appalling behaviour, Simon had actually stepped out into the road almost right in front of the guy's car.

A few weeks later whilst driving, Simon had pulled out of a junction into the oncoming traffic. On this occasion, the driver was unable to avoid him, and there'd been damage to both cars, though thankfully nobody was hurt. He'd gone to court and pleaded guilty, losing points on his licence and being fined.

Simon's doctor had referred him to an ophthalmologist – the diagnosis was posterior cortical atrophy. After jokingly clarifying that it wasn't a problem with his backside, he'd been informed it was an inability to judge speed correctly.

Further tests followed, and second and third opinions were sought until his GP eventually had to conclude that Simon was regrettably suffering from early onset Alzheimer's. The following day, Simon handed in his driving licence to the authorities and started planning for the future.

He'd been separated from his wife for some time, and they had no children. There'd been the occasional relationship since then but nothing serious. He still saw her occasionally and got on well with the new partner.

An amicable divorce had taken place before he'd received his diagnosis. Simon intended that his ex-wife should never learn of his illness.

He called a board meeting at work and shocked the whole practice with the announcement of his early retirement, though he was careful not to divulge the true reasons for his decision.

His parents had both passed away when he was in his mid-30s. His mother died from Alzheimer's and his father, another successful accountant, from a lifetime of smoking. Simon chose to believe his dad had passed away from a broken heart, and not broken lungs.

He'd met his brother only once, and for just one brief afternoon. Simon had a photo on a wall of his drawing room to prove it. Paul had lived for 23 weeks inside their mother and twelve days in an incubator. He missed him now even more than he missed him then.

The substantial house in London didn't need to be put in the hands of an estate agent. Rarely a month went by when a hastily written note or letter didn't arrive through his letterbox, guaranteeing a higher price than anyone else if he ever wanted to sell.

Home was a three-storey Victorian house in South Kensington, very close to The Victoria and Albert Museum. He'd inherited it from his parents who'd bought it for £400,000 more than 30 years ago. It was now worth at least twenty times that.

With all the spare time he now had, Simon did what he presumed everyone would do after being handed a medical death sentence – he studied his disease online. For many weeks it became his obsession.

There were times when he became deliriously excited and optimistic about moving to America for a pioneering miracle treatment, but then he depressingly came to his senses with a bump. He had a prison sentence that ended in death. A death which often involved the inability to swallow or cough, the brain having given up barking out orders to even the most basic of functions.

Simon now knew more about early onset Alzheimer's than most doctors. The information he'd gathered helped him formulate some logical conclusions. He'd move into a care home before he physically needed one. It would be somewhere his few friends, colleagues, and any distant family would never find him – nobody should have to deal with this except him.

The thought of people feeling obliged to visit him as he gradually forgot them in front of their eyes was deplorable, depressing, and disgusting. The thought of them seeing him die was worse still.

And on that subject, he also reserved the right to take his own life, illegal or not. If need be, they could prosecute his ashes. With that in mind, he gained a similar level of knowledge on how to commit suicide.

The consensus was that his illness would grant him between three and twenty years from the first symptoms. He'd already had a good five of those since first noticing people staring in an unfamiliar way, wondering why he'd repeated himself or didn't know their names. His last relationship had ended after forgotten dates and '*being weird*'.

He'd assume there were five years left, the latter half veering towards an unacceptable standard of life. For the moment, he was still healthy in his body, if not in his mind. He intended to keep that level of fitness up for as long as possible.

Simon had always run to and from the office every day, come rain or shine. There were very few days when he deemed the weather to be too inclement. Now he ran twice a day and twice as far. He kept a log which told him he covered about half a marathon every day. He wouldn't increase on that distance but would work on the time it took.

When selecting the care home where he'd spend his final days, he put emphasis on one that had a gym. This narrowed the choice down enormously - nonagenarians and running machines were rare partners. Most of the places offering this facility were in London, so immediately ignored. He didn't want to run the risk of someone from his past coming to visit.

He found a healthcare group that seemed to be dominating the British market – Collins Knight Young care homes. He dimly remembered reading about them in the Financial Times when they were floated on the Stock Market a while back. With their head office not so far from his own company in West London, he'd decided to contact them to see if he could bag their accountancy requirements.

But then he'd forgotten – he chuckled at the irony.

He studied their website and found just one residential care home outside London which offered a small gym and indoor hydrotherapy pool. It was even in substantial grounds which could afford him some running space when he felt unable to face the roads any longer. There was a waiting list for a room, but this was hardly a surprise – he made the call and arranged a meeting.

He was invited to have a look at the home and enjoyed the time he spent there. The staff he met were friendly, the residents seemed happy, and the facilities were just as described. He particularly got on well with a senior carer called Maddy – a delightful woman and clearly dedicated to her work.

He knew he'd found the place he needed to be and told her so before he left. Sure, he'd be the youngest resident by a good twenty years, but that didn't trouble him if it didn't trouble anyone else. He knew that was almost certainly going to be the case wherever he ended up. Maddy said she'd discuss it with her boss, and they parted, already good friends.

He received a letter a couple of weeks later to confirm he was on the waiting list. She reminded him that once on the list it could still be up to a year before he joined them, but sometimes it was less – she could make no promises.

*

With the swift sale of his house including all the contents, he moved to a pleasant rented apartment within running distance of the place that would one day be his final home. He brought few personal belongings with him – if he were short of anything, he'd buy it.

He left no forwarding address for anyone, and there were no leaving parties. He owed nothing to anyone and had more money than he knew what to do with. It would be fun deciding who he left it all to over the coming months and possibly years.

Sure, any private detective worth his salt could find him in a very short period through a credit card trail, but he hoped nobody would want to get in touch with him that badly. He *really* hoped that wouldn't happen.

Time passed slowly, which to most people was a drag. To Simon, it was a joy. If two and a half years ended up feeling like a lifetime, that worked for him. He never veered from his routine, running past Orchard care home twice a day, pushing himself harder and harder as his times came down.

Some of the carers had noticed him over the past few months, and occasionally one would wave as he passed the car park on his regular route. A couple of times he'd seen the manager of the home driving out of the entrance, though she would have had no idea who he was. He recognised her from the photos of all the carers displayed in reception on his visit. He thought the name below her picture was '*Emma*' but couldn't be sure. She was an attractive woman with a lovely smile. Simon was looking forward to meeting her when a place became available.

He'd moved to his little apartment in November and spent a first Christmas and New Year on his own. It was much easier than he'd feared. He took pleasure in seeing the happiness on other people's faces as they went about their daily business. It was as if he was in the middle of a never-ending film, an invisible voyeur watching all the actors play their respective parts. Nobody saw him, nobody noticed him, nobody knew him.

In the middle of January, Simon celebrated his 40th birthday. He worried that a birthday card may arrive in the post, but there was nothing. He went to a local wine bar and got quietly and effectively drunk on two pints of Guinness, a bottle of Champagne, and a dozen oysters. Rarely drinking alcohol anymore he slept for 12 hours, missing his morning run for the first time. He ran that afternoon and evening to make up for it.

He set himself tasks to test his mind – to check the deterioration. He completed the crossword in his daily newspaper on most occasions, plus the fiendishly difficult Sudoku puzzles. He bought an almost impossibly difficult double-sided five thousand piece jigsaw puzzle and completed it, then started all over again. And he read avidly, spending hours of his day at the local library between his runs.

Winter turned to spring, and his running times continued to improve. Simon thought he may be running faster than he'd ever managed before, but he didn't let his achievements bubble over into optimism for the future. He was *very* careful not to allow that to happen.

His mantra was '*Seize the Day*'. He tried not to look back nor wonder about the future. And as a reminder, he had '*Carpe Diem*' tattooed on his right forearm – his first and his last tattoo.

In May, he received the call he'd been waiting for – it was Emma Lowry. She had some positive news for him and would he like to meet with her next Tuesday for lunch at Orchard.

She asked if he'd require transport as he was a few miles away, but he'd declined the kind offer. Was it okay if he was in shorts and a T-shirt or should he dress more formally? She'd be delighted to meet with him in whatever clothes he found most comfortable and looked forward to welcoming him at midday.

He wrote down the day and time of the meeting immediately.

3

Tuesday 09 May 2017

'That was really tasty – who do I pay?'

'Nothing to pay. That's our pleasure, right Maddy? Our cook's a bit of a company celebrity at the moment – he's just won the 2017 Chef of Collins Knight Young.

Maddy stood up. 'That was a treat.'

Simon looked at both women with an expression of surprise and delight.

'Cocky twat.'

Maddy grimaced and moved to go as Emma put her hand gently on his arm.

'Everyone's entitled to their opinions, but I should tell you that Mr Patel, our chef, is a very quiet and mild-mannered man. I'd go as far as to say he's actually a little bit shy, and definitely not cocky as you sugges…'

But Simon had put his hand on hers and interrupted her, still grinning.

'I'm sure he is, and I'm looking forward to meeting him, but I have to take my hat off to yours and Maddy's acronym teamwork. Just fantastic.'

Emma was looking puzzled, and Maddy had stopped and turned around.

Simon continued to grin, and Emma wondered if he might also suffer from Tourette's disorder, which could be a little disturbing for the other residents.

'You said *'Chef of Collins Knight Young'* and Maddy said *'That was a treat'.* It's honestly one of the best examples I've ever heard. Sorry for the confusion – I do a lot of crossword puzzles and love playing around with words.'

Simon's grin morphed into a loud chuckle as Emma's jaw dropped, and Maddy burst out laughing.

'Strike *three*, Mr Carter.' Emma attempted a stern face but fell woefully short. Here was a person of rare wit and humour. There was only one other man Emma knew like this – she was looking forward to introducing her husband to Simon one day.

'Let's go back to the first floor where your room is. We always have lunch down here in the main dining room, but breakfast and supper are taken in smaller dining rooms on each floor. I'm sure Maddy's already been through this with you?'

'She did, but it was a few months ago, and I hate to admit it, but it's only a vague memory now.' He looked at Emma and put on a sad clown's face that made her want to smile and sympathise at the same time. What a bastard this disease truly is, she thought, as she led him to the ground floor lift.

Simon turned and winked at her as she pressed the button.

'I think I can manage the stairs on this one occasion.'

'Oh. Yes, good point. Sorry about that – habit.' Emma wasn't sure why she was feeling a little flustered as they walked up the stairs.

'If you're able to move in with us by Friday, Mr Patel is putting on a big spread for all the residents, families, and friends that day. We're having a guitarist come and join us as well, so people can dance and sing along. We want to celebrate his success.'

'Sounds good to me. Who's Mr Patel?'

Emma was confused – was this another joke? Things were getting awkward. She decided it was far better to be fooled yet again than to upset him in any way.

'Mr Patel, our award-winning chef.'

'He must be a great cook – did he cook lunch today? It was really good, but I hate to admit I can't remember what we had. It's so damn frustrating.' Simon was staring down the corridor, but Emma could see his focus was on nothing.

'How are the carers meant to handle that? Will they try and help me remember or just tell me again as if it's the first time? Or just ignore the question and move on to something else?'

Despite all her experience, this was getting to Emma in a way she always managed to compartmentalise. She felt the presence of someone special beside her – a rare person damaged beyond repair.

She put a hand on his shoulder and brought him back from where he'd briefly gone. He turned around and looked at her – there was a very slight sheen in his eyes. 'I was soaked when I arrived here today, but now I'm warm and dry. How did that happen?'

Emma smiled as she led him further down the hallway to his room. 'All part of the care package, Simon. We aim to please.' He put his hands in his tracksuit bottoms, and she linked an arm through his.

*

The room was perfectly clean and looked brand new – as if nobody had ever lived in it before. Simon guessed the previous resident had just passed away. He wondered if he or she had actually died in this room. There were two large windows which faced the back of the property, looking out onto the expansive grounds where Simon would soon be running. May was a lovely month to be moving into somewhere new.

The en-suite bathroom had a bath and shower, the latter with a sit-down facility for when he could no longer manage. He shuddered involuntarily. He must have been shown a room like this when he visited before, but he couldn't remember it now.

'Would it be alright if I moved in tomorrow instead of Friday? I only have one suitcase – there's nothing else.'

Simon already had a plan for his apartment. It was something he'd been looking forward to for a while and would only take a couple of hours to implement.

'That's fine with us, but there's no rush. This is *your* room now – nobody else will be taking it.' Emma knew there'd be a huge period of adjustment for Simon – she'd do everything in her power to make that transition as smooth and calm as possible.

'Who used to live in this room?'

'Mrs Morin. Margaret, or '*Margie*', as everyone called her. She was 92 – a very dear lady.'

'How long had she been here?'

'Seven years. Her husband was with her for five of those years. This is one of the larger rooms, built for couples. There's only two on each floor, so you're lucky – they're quite a bit bigger than the single rooms. Oh, but don't worry

– you'll only be paying single occupancy rates. Luck of the draw and all that.'

'Oh, I'm happy to pay the normal rate – more than happy. I find myself in the strange position of having a lot more money than I'll ever need. More than enough for a lifetime. A normal lifetime I meant – not a short one like mine. Damn, I've done it again – misappropriation of words. I should stick with slightly humorous acronyms, eh?' He looked at her, and they both put on brave smiles.

'Don't stick with anything, Simon – just be yourself. I can already tell you're kind and funny by nature, and that'll do just fine for me. I mean for all of us,' she added quickly.

Emma felt her cheeks glow ever so slightly and hoped it didn't show. This was an unusually personal thing to say to one of the residents, especially one she'd known for only a couple of hours and who didn't even live here yet.

'I think you're a lovely person too. Just from your photo at reception, I knew you'd be like this. And when I forget your name, there it is under that picture – 'Emma'. Or was it Ella?' He grinned, and she watched the corners of his eyes crease and his blue eyes light up.

'Or perhaps it's plain '*Ms. Lowry*' to you?'

But her mock stern face wouldn't fool him again.

'Or is it *Mrs* Lowry?' The blue eyes didn't blink.

Emma tucked a non-existent wisp of hair behind her ear.

'Yes, it's '*Mrs*', though we sometimes have to reintroduce ourselves to each other lately.' Emma heard the words but wasn't quite sure she'd spoken them.

'What I mean is, Michael, that's my husband, he's so busy travelling at the moment that we don't spend much time together.'

'Lucky Michael.' Simon bit his tongue.

'I mean, not lucky that he's away travelling instead of being with you. Lucky, as in, well, you know? As in being Mr Lowry. Not that he hasn't *always* been Mr Lowry. But husband of, you know? You.'

Simon felt himself blush. And Emma had noticed, bugger it. When one's had a lifetime of blushing, one gets to know whether others have noticed or not.

'I'd try the '*Hello, I'm Simon*' routine again but ...' He shrugged and grinned at the same time. Emma nearly gasped aloud at the expression – the similarity of mannerism between this man and her husband.

She put a hand to her face, ostensibly to wipe the corner of her eye but mainly to break eye contact and potentially cover at least one swiftly colouring cheek.

'Thank you, I think. How about we wander down to reception and fill out some dull and boring forms? It shouldn't take long, and there won't be any more after that. Then you're free to move in whenever you want.'

Normal service had been resumed as she fell into her regular work spiel.

As they walked down the stairs, Simon couldn't resist the question – he didn't know why. 'Did Margie die in the room – my room? I just wondered.'

'No. She had complications. She had to go to hospital, and at first, we thought she was going to pull through, but then ...'

'I'm sorry. I'm sorry for asking, and I'm sorry for Margie. How do you deal with it? How can you cope with the sadness all the time? You're surrounded by it – don't you ever want to go and just be with healthy people? Happy people?'

Emma ushered Simon into her office and closed the door.

'Don't mistake illness for sadness. Nearly everyone here is happy for most of the time. That's a fundamental part of my job. Happiness breeds happiness, and you coming to live here is going to be a real bonus. For everyone. And as for the first question, well that's a very simple one to answer, and one I see you've already answered yourself.'

Simon looked confused.

'Look at your right forearm, Simon. There's your answer.'

*

There was almost nothing to pack at his flat. It had come fully furnished, and he'd added very little in his time here. He'd had to rent it for a year and set up a direct debit for the monthly payments. There were five months remaining on the lease, but that was perfect. He also had direct debits set up for electricity and council tax.

He didn't have a television which had suited him perfectly, but which he now regretted. He'd passed an electrical store on his way back and bought a reasonably sized one, together with a satellite TV package. He paid for the annual TV licence at the same time. He was also able to set up the regular instalments for the satellite channels with his bank details while in the shop.

The only other stop was to his bank where he withdrew £5,000 in twenty-pound notes. This required five bulky envelopes instead of only two if he'd withdrawn fifty-pound notes, but he thought the higher denomination might cause problems.

He looked around the flat one last time – not quite as perfect as his new room, but he wasn't a professional at this sort of thing. The bed was made with clean sheets, and the spare bedding was in the dryer, already washed. The extra set of door keys were already on the kitchen table along with the five envelopes. He left a note he'd written some time ago and placed it under the keys. Then he wheeled his suitcase out of the door and double locked it, heading for the supermarket.

The rain had thankfully stopped as he walked towards the bus shelter on the high street. Not for his own comfort as he wasn't really bothered by the rain, as his new friends in the next and final stage of his life had already discovered. However, Amy and her cat, Amba, would be very grateful for the dryer weather.

He didn't know much about either of them, even though he'd seen them every day for the past six weeks. Amy was anything between eighteen and mid-20s – he wasn't sure and felt awkward asking – and had clearly enjoyed a very good education. She was a bright and well-spoken girl.

Her cat, a Bengal, was expensive and well groomed, though a little less so more recently. Life on the street had not been so kind for Amy, either. What would her parents think, if she had any? He felt certain they'd be out of their minds with worry. Yet all he could do this past few weeks was keep her cat fed with the best cat food he could find and present her with what he felt was a decent array of food from the local supermarket – anything fresh which didn't require heating. He always left a £20 note in the bag as well.

He was desperate to help but wanted to avoid making her nervous. If she'd fallen out with her parents, then she might put all people of his age group in the same category and disappear somewhere else if she felt he was prying. Histon was a peaceful town, and Amy and her constant companion could be in many worse places than here.

Similarly, he also worried what she may think about his regular gifts. He prayed she wouldn't think he had any ulterior motives – the thought made him shudder with revulsion. He hoped, in the nicest and most positive way, that this would be the last time he ever saw the girl and her cat.

The cat was remarkable – it had no lead or any form of restraint, yet it stayed glued to Amy's ankles at all times. It was also her only form of income. Apart from the beautiful Bengal golden markings and wide hypnotic green eyes, Amba never stopped meowing. Passers-by could be forgiven for thinking she was talking to them, and the little box next to the cat was a handy receptacle for spare coins.

'Hello Amy, hello Amba. The sun shines for you guys at last.' He smiled and stroked the cat's head.

'Hi Simon. Yes, it's a little warmer too, thank God. I'm hoping my sleeping bag will dry out before tonight.'

'I think you'll both be okay.' He passed her a supermarket bag. 'I've put a couple of different things in there today, and I also need to hand you this.'

Simon gave her two keys attached to a keyring and a piece of paper.

'That's the address of my flat and those are the keys.' Amy's expression was one of confusion, which quickly altered to suspicion.

Simon held his hands in the air. 'Please don't worry; I've left the place. That's why I have this suitcase with me. I'm moving to Orchard care home.'

'I don't understand.' The girl was still wary – six weeks living on the street had changed her perceptions.

'Why don't you and Amba go there now – it's less than a mile away. There's a £20 note in the bag so maybe take a taxi? And there's some steak as well, and greens and potatoes. The rent's covered until the end of October, plus the electricity and everything else. No bills to pay, I promise you. It'll give you a chance to sort yourself out and look for a job or go back home perhaps? Whatever you want. It's on the ground floor so Amba can come and go as she pleases too. I have to go now. Bye-bye Amy. Bye Amba.'

Simon smiled and walked away. After a few paces, he looked back – the girl and her cat were staring at him. He waved once and then turned around again.

4

Friday 12 May to Sunday 21 May 2017

The guitarist was very good – he was a tribute act and really did sound like Glen Campbell. Simon wondered if the staff member who booked the musician was aware of the irony – the country singer was suffering from the advanced stages of Alzheimer's, having checked himself into a treatment facility three years ago.

Simon had learnt of this during his exhaustive study of the disease online. His focus was on early onset, but he'd also Googled a list of celebrities currently suffering from the more common form of the disease. He wasn't sure why, but he vaguely remembered getting some crumb of comfort from it at the time. If *they* have it, who am *I* to complain?

He'd gladly have swapped all those useless facts for the knowledge of what he'd eaten for lunch today. At least he could go to reception and see the day's menu on the board – that would jog his memory. He dreaded the day when the menu could no longer prompt his memory into remembering.

But when that day came, would he be bothered by his lack of memory? He hoped so, however painful it may be.

Simon joined in with the spirit of the day. All the carers were there, whether off-duty or on-duty. It was free food and wine, but he liked to believe all the staff would have genuinely come of their own choice. It also meant a huge amount to the residents. Most of them had a favourite carer, and by the end of the evening, everyone seemed to have danced or had a drink and a chat with their special one.

Simon took to the makeshift dancefloor on a couple of occasions. He'd also had one slow dance at the end with Maddy, who'd come up to him and taken his hand.

He wished it had been Emma.

*

Life fell into a routine over the next week. He'd now established his new running route within the grounds and started logging the times on his laptop. He'd borrowed a measuring wheel from the gardener, and his track was precisely one mile long. He also went swimming in the small therapy pool every day – a hundred laps sounded a lot, but it wasn't that far. Any more and he'd have started feeling giddy, so close were the turns at each end of the pool. Emma gave him a time before breakfast where nobody else was using it, as he tended to cause a bit of a tidal wave in such small confines.

Any spare time he spent reading in the main lounge, where a substantial array of books was always to be found. He still read a daily newspaper and tackled the Sudoku puzzles, but the crosswords were becoming a little more difficult to complete. He'd looked at all the jigsaws, but they were too simple – Simon hoped there wouldn't be a day when he couldn't complete them if the mood took him.

On Sunday, he was about to leave his room for an afternoon run when one of the carers popped her head in and told him he had a visitor. The news stunned him – how was that possible? He was sure he'd been so careful in making sure nobody knew of his whereabouts. Maybe he wasn't as thorough as he'd thought?

'Do I have to see visitors?' He couldn't remember the name of the girl and glanced at her name badge.

'Would you be able to make up an excuse for me, Sarah? I was just about to go for my run.'

'No, of course you don't have to see visitors. This is your home, and you can do anything you want. I can tell her you're not here if you like?'

Simon was baffled. 'It's a woman? Did she give her name?'

'More a young girl, really – still in her teens I'd say. Her name's Amy. Is she a relative, perhaps?'

Simon didn't have a clue. He put a finger to each temple and pressed, making small circles. He'd begun to do this recently, normally when attempting crossword puzzles.

'She was carrying a present and seemed really keen to see you. What do you say? Maybe a quick cup of tea and a chat with her, then off for your run?'

Simon felt like he was sweating, but when he wiped his brow, there was no dampness.

'Sure. Of course. Will you stick around and show me who she is?'

They walked downstairs and into the lounge. A girl he recognised jumped up from her chair and ran towards him. She threw her arms around him and buried her head in his chest. He looked at Sarah who was beaming. She winked and left the room.

Amy pulled back and stared at Simon. 'I'll never be able to thank you enough, Simon. You're the kindest man in the world. Look, I've brought you this – I hope you like it.' She picked up a large thin parcel from against the chair.

'Please, open it now – I so hope you'll like it.'

She was a beautiful young girl who looked vaguely familiar. Her happiness was infectious, and he began to smile too.

'That's very kind of you. I have no idea what it could be.' He carefully removed the plain brown wrapping paper and discovered a large, framed photograph.

'Oh wow, it's Amba. She looks so gorgeous. And her eyes – I can almost hear her meowing.' He laughed and looked at the girl. The sight of the cat had triggered his memory.

'Amy, you … You've changed. You look younger. Oh, maybe I shouldn't say that? And thanks so much for this – it's going on my wall right away. No hang on; it's far too good for just me to see. I'll have it put up in here, so everyone can admire Amba.'

They both smiled, as did Emma who had watched the whole scene unfold from just outside the door.

'It's a pleasure. And it's nothing – I'll never be able to repay you for what you did. Not just for me, but for Amba. She's so happy again.' Amy leaned up on her toes and kissed him quickly on the cheek.

Simon was lost for words. His eyes stung, and he didn't know where to look or how to behave.

'Why did you move here, Simon. Do you work here now?'

That was a good question. He wished he had a minute or two in which to compose an answer. He worried that he'd appear stupid in front of Amy and frighten her.

'He's just come to stay with us for a little while, dear. I'm Emma, one of Simon's friends.' She warmly shook hands with the girl. 'Shall we all sit down and have a cup of tea?'

'Oh I'd love to, but I have to get back. My mum and dad are coming for an early dinner tonight, and I have to start cooking. I'm doing a roast chicken, and I'm hopeless. But I'll come and see you again if that's okay with everyone? Is that alright, Simon?'

'Oh, that would be great. I'd like that.' It was all flooding back now — wave upon wave of glorious technicolour memory, crashing over his brain and flooding his mind with warmth.

'Your mum and dad are coming to see you for dinner?'

Amy looked at him sheepishly.

'I owe them an apology — a really, *really* big one. I'm so nervous.' She paused, and her head fell, then she looked at him and her face lit up again.

'But hey, I have a job interview tomorrow. I saw an advert in the local post office. A lady has a business looking after pets in people's houses when they're away, and she needs help. I bet she'll have loads of replies, but she's agreed to see me. I have to go — I'll see you soon, okay?' She hugged Simon again.

Emma stood up with her. 'I'll see you out.'

They walked out of the lounge. Simon went to the window and watched the two women in the car park. They seemed to be talking for a long time.

He went back to his room to put on some running shoes.

*

Simon was studying running times on his laptop after dinner. He'd used spreadsheets all his working life, and it was second nature. The first three days, Friday 9th to Sunday 11th May, didn't really count as he was still discovering and then tweaking his route around the grounds. He'd disregarded that data and started from Monday 12th, then left a space for two times each day until the end of the year.

Thanks to the gardener, his circuit was exactly a mile, so he ran six laps per session. He'd run fourteen sessions so far, and tonight's was the best of the lot – 41 minutes 47 seconds. He wanted to try and run his age if possible – 40 minutes. That was his new goal, and he warmed to goals. Running 41 minutes when he was 41 years old didn't count, so he had about eight months.

He was moving over to the Sudoku puzzle when there was a knock on his door.

'Only me,' Emma called out. 'May I come in?'

'Of course, one second.'

Simon scanned the room for any clothes lying around or plates of food and drink – the bed had already been made. He wasn't sure why he was doing this, or why he looked at himself in the mirror on the way to the door.

'Simon, sorry to disturb you in the evening – I know you have plenty to do. I just wanted to mention something to you.'

'Sure, come in. It sounds ominous. Have I done something wrong?'

'On the contrary, you've done something right – very right.' Emma sat on the chair by his computer, and he sat on the edge of his bed.

'A lot of people do kind things, and nobody ever notices. It's almost as if part of the generosity seems to be the anonymity that goes with the gesture. Do you agree?'

'I'm not sure I've ever thought of it. I'm sure you're right, though. In my old profession, I knew little about people's personalities or the way they behaved. I just knew how to check their accounts and sometimes save them from paying too much tax. I imagine you'd know a lot about how people tick – what makes them who they are?'

'Some people do very kind things. Special things that make a whole world of difference to a person or persons' lives. And in my humble opinion, when that goes unnoticed, it's a crying shame.'

She looked into Simon's eyes, long enough for him to turn away. That wasn't in any textbook on how to handle dementia, and she scolded herself, but she couldn't help it.

'Do you know what I'm talking about, Simon? Do you understand?'

'I think I understand, but I'm not really sure. You'd tell me if I'd done something wrong, wouldn't you? If I have, I'm sure I can make it better. I've only been here a little while, and I'm still getting used to things.'

In all her years as a carer, Emma could only recall shedding tears at a resident's funeral or their death bed, and then only after they'd passed away. What was happening to her now was uncharted territory.

She stood up and walked towards Simon with stinging tears welling in her eyes, soon to spill over. She asked him to stand up and hugged him hard, and for far longer than could ever have been appropriate. Her tears were absorbed by the shoulder of his tracksuit.

'You're a dear man, Simon Carter. A very special man.'

She felt him hold her and then pat her back gently as if trying to console her.

Emma stood back, wiped her eyes, and put on her bravest smile again. His face was blurred in her vision.

She touched the side of his face then turned and left the room, shutting the door quietly behind her.

*

Emma had left for home earlier than usual that night, though her shift had officially finished a while ago. She needed to be away from Orchard to unwind and reflect. She needed a glass of wine and some music.

Home was a relatively new two bedroom apartment in a small block, very close to Cambridge train station. Emma and Michael had bought the place together a couple of years ago. Lying on the sofa with her playlist set on shuffle, she listened to Randy Crawford singing her version of Imagine. These were the types of song which Michael had no time for – 'sentimental crap' was a favourite musical critique of his.

She wasn't thinking about her decaying marriage tonight, though, or what she could do to make it right again. She was thinking of Simon, and not in a way she'd contemplated any resident before. He was twenty years younger than any person she'd cared for in the past, but it was much more than that.

He was so like Michael in so many ways. His personality and sense of humour. Even his mannerisms. And yes, there was more than a passing physical resemblance too. But as she was making these comparisons, she realised Simon wasn't like the Michael she knew now, but the Michael she'd first met and fell in love with.

She poured herself another glass of Sancerre – a larger one this time.

Did she feel attracted to Simon, the man? Or was his tragic disease the driving force? Was the desperate sympathy she felt for him being misinterpreted by her heart? How could she fall under the spell of a man whose time left was so short, yet why should that have anything to do with her feelings?

What rules was she breaking when she held him and hugged him this evening? If this carried on, should she request a move to another home? And what would she tell Michael if she did that?

In her heart, she realised leaving Orchard was now impossible because she knew she couldn't leave Simon. Come what may, she had to be near to him, to care for him until he died.

And with that thought, tears streamed down her face as she sobbed.

5

Sunday 21 May to Saturday 27 May 2017

Michael seemed to spend the majority of his life on planes nowadays, or at least that was how it felt. Not that he was complaining – there was a time when he'd look forward all year to a two-week holiday. One with Emma, involving a long flight to somewhere warm in the middle of a bitter English winter.

It's just that too much of a good thing could ruin it. He sipped a glass of chilled Sancerre as he sat at the bar of the Virgin Atlantic Upper-Class deck. It was a far cry from their honeymoon in the Maldives, packed in the back of the plane with a screaming baby in the next row. How ironic that they'd have given everything and more for those screams to have come from their own baby, but they were blissfully ignorant of the problems in those days.

His problems, it turned out. The only secret he'd ever kept from Emma, but he had to know why they couldn't conceive. He *had* to know.

It was soon after their trip back to the Maldives for his 40th when the pregnancy test had shown the same old familiar result. He'd had tests in London away from their family doctor and discovered his sperm count was the problem.

Why he hadn't told Emma in the following three years was a mystery to him. Perhaps a combination of ego, embarrassment, and a belief that it didn't really matter who was at fault – they were never going to have a child.

Michael wondered what Emma would be doing now. He hadn't set his watch forward yet – L.A. was eight hours behind, so 10.30 p.m. in the UK. She probably stayed on at Orchard until far later than she had to, and was now sitting in front of the telly at home, sound asleep with a cold cup of tea in front of her.

A few days ago when they'd last spoken, she'd told him of a new resident. A man, younger than himself, suffering from early onset Alzheimer's. What an awful situation – the poor guy. Apparently, he was a successful accountant but had sold everything and closed his life down after diagnosis, then applied to stay at Orchard.

Michael asked Emma how long she thought the man had left, but she didn't want to talk about it. She was quite short with him for asking, actually. Perhaps that was insensitive of him. He knew how close Emma was to some of the residents – too close in his opinion. She became too emotionally involved with them, and only heartbreak followed.

He'd always given his level best when caring. Like Emma, he'd never been a clock watcher and liked to believe he made a lot of people much happier in the later stages of their lives. He'd always drawn a line at genuine emotional involvement, though, because he didn't want to expose himself to the inevitable pain.

He remembered Emma telling him of a resident she went to Brighton with a long time ago. The poor woman had

41

early onset as well. The funeral a couple of years later had left Emma utterly bereft – she'd been inconsolable for days.

His bed had already been prepared by one of the cabin crew. A brandy seemed a sensible idea for a nightcap, even though his body clock was still in the afternoon. Then some shut-eye, so when he arrived in London in the morning, he might not be too jet-lagged. He had a full week ahead with these never-ending negotiations, but he promised himself he'd do his best to get up to Cambridge for the weekend.

If Emma could spare a day or two for him, maybe they could do something nice – a quiet country hotel perhaps? He could always make it a surprise visit. He'd done that a couple of times in the past, and she'd always managed to get Maddy or someone else to cover for her. He'd hire a car on Saturday morning and drive up to Orchard, then take her somewhere relaxing – maybe the Cotswolds or somewhere like that.

*

The crossword was proving more difficult than usual. Simon normally took less than an hour and had a 98.5% completion rate. Tonight looked as if it would fall into the remaining 1.5% of failures. He screwed the puzzle up into a ball and threw it in the bin. There was a time when he'd keep his failures and check where he'd gone wrong in the next day's paper, but his new mission statement drove him only to think of the present.

Time for bed and a read of a magazine he'd been receiving in the post since he was 17, but this would be his last. Along with all the other direct debits he cancelled when moving to Histon, The British Milers' Club News was amongst them. This last issue was from months ago and picked up on the very last day before he left his London home. He'd packed it still sealed, but not bothered to open until this morning.

Simon had been a member of the BMC since running the 1500m in a senior school record time. The sports teacher had been in contact with the club to give details of his record, and Simon had been invited to join. Since then, he'd paid his annual membership and received the club magazine every six months.

By the time he'd finished university and qualified as a chartered accountant, his running times were way behind his early successes at school. Even so, he still took an interest and went to BMC athletics meetings every now and then. He was drifting off as he scanned through the fixtures for the forthcoming season – there was a championship coming up this weekend at Sportcity in Manchester.

How he'd love to have gone to watch. For the first time, he wished he wasn't living at Orchard. He guessed he could simply sign himself out of the place and then sign back in on his return, but he sensed that wasn't really the correct protocol. But he also knew that a carer couldn't be expected to go with him all the way from Histon to Manchester and back. He took a pen from his bedside table and put a ring around the meeting this coming Saturday, then turned the light out and eventually fell asleep.

*

Emma couldn't sleep. It wasn't the temperature, which was a little chilly if anything – perfect for snuggling up in her bed. Nor was it the alcohol, though it was unusual for her to have two glasses of wine during the week. It was a clear night, and the stars were sparkling. Somewhere in that vast sky, Michael would be flying home. But was it really home to him anymore?

She looked for her special constellation. Ursa Minor – the one like a saucepan with a wonky handle. Emma's mum had pointed it out to her when she was very young and unable to sleep one night. It always took a little while to find, but that was part of the fun. Like unwrapping a present when you knew what was inside.

'It's easy when you know what to look for, sweetie. Look, there it is. Now close your eyes and make a wish. Don't tell anyone what you wish for, though, or it won't come true ...'

'Where are you tonight? Where are you when I need you, wonky saucepan ...'

*

Simon had woken late. He hadn't slept well and had a vague recollection of pulling a pillow over his eyes to keep out the dawn light. The dreams had tumbled around in his head after that. He was running in dark woods – running as hard as he could, looking for his watch to see how he was doing. But his watch had gone, replaced by a tiny calendar seemingly stuck to his wrist. Little pages rhythmically and continually flew upwards and away, day by day by day.

He headed for a light at the end of the woods, but the faster he forced himself to run, the slower he seemed to travel. He looked down and could see his school running strip. A small rectangular piece of blue silk was smartly stitched on his white vest, proudly announcing the school house he represented. He remembered watching his mother sew it on, making sure it was dead centre and dead straight.

Bursting through darkness into blinding light, he found himself in an empty athletics stadium. He attempted to sprint but was spent, his pace down to a jog. He slowly rounded a bend and saw a white ribbon in the distance, fluttering between two poles. His jog became a walk, and his walk became a crawl as the finishing line moved further and further away.

Simon woke up in a sweat, hearing himself cry out. He took a second or two to establish his surroundings. It was after ten o'clock – he was normally out on his morning run by now. He looked around the room and saw doors in two walls. He was bursting for a pee but couldn't remember which door was the right one. It hardly mattered as he'd try them both, but he hated the fact he didn't know – didn't have a clue.

Finally showered and dressed in shorts and a T-shirt, he went downstairs to the dining room. There was nobody there, and the tables had been cleared. A carer walked past in the hallway and greeted him.

'Morning Simon, did you miss breakfast? It's no problem – shall I bring something to your room? Bacon and eggs with toast and marmalade, or porridge and fruit?'

'That sounds good, but what do I normally have? I feel stupid, but I'm not sure. I think I overslept.'

'A lot of people are a little confused in the morning. It doesn't matter at all. Sometimes you have a cooked brekkie, and sometimes you go for porridge, so whatever you fancy. And tea with no sugar, right?'

'Yes please, that's definitely how I have my tea. I think I'll go for bacon and eggs if that's okay. I should be running by now, you know? I'm afraid I overslept.'

'No problem at all. I'll bring it to your room in a jiffy – see you in a few minutes.'

Back in his room, Simon sat at the desk and moved his laptop to one side. He picked up the running magazine and saw an ink ring on the page.

Saturday 27 May – BMC Championship – Sportcity, Manchester.

It was an evening meet starting at 5 p.m. Different age groups ranging from Under 17 to Seniors, and a variety of heats from 800m to 5,000m. Simon would have loved to go. He made a mental note to go and have a chat with Emma after his run. He was about to write it down as well when a knock at the door drew his attention.

'Dah Dahhh! Welcome to The Orchard Hotel – Histon's very own five-star resort. Would sir care for a sprig of parsley on his eggs? Perhaps a little freshly ground black pepper and crystal sea salt?' Emma walked in with a tray in one hand and a white tea towel over her other arm.

'Oh, my word – the boss delivering breakfast personally because the lazy resident overslept? It's the kitchen floor and the dishes for me after lunch, right?'

'Just the kitchen floor. I can't possibly trust you with the bone china.'

'What? You're kidding? I haven't got Parkinson's, you know. The worst I can do is put your precious china in the deep freezer.'

'True enough. Maybe I'll get Mr Parkinson to mop the floor. He won't cover the whole kitchen, but what he does cover should have a hell of a shine.'

They both cracked up laughing, and Emma wondered how many other company rules she'd broken in the last few seconds. If any of the staff had just heard her … It didn't bear thinking about.

'Please, five minutes of your time – have a seat. And thanks very much for breakfast.'

'I'd love to take the credit, but I just took the tray from Pauline in the hall outside your door. So what can I help with?'

'I don't know how the rules work here, but there's something I'd really like to see, and I know if I go out you'd like a member of staff to be with me, right?'

'That's right. You remember when we filled out those documents when you moved here? You agreed you wanted company when you were off the premises? It's entirely your choice, and you can revoke it whenever you like, of course.'

'No, I don't think so – I'd rather be safe than sorry. I really don't want to be causing any problems in the future for anyone.'

'It shouldn't be a problem at all. If you want to go out to town today, I can organise that for you.'

'It's not today – it's Saturday.'

'Yup, that's fine – I'll sort something out. Morning or afternoon.'

'Errr, it's evening, actually.'

'Okaaay. Well, as it happens, I have a rare weekend off. I wasn't going to bother with it and just catch up on some paperwork here and maybe take some of the residents out in the minibus, but I've agreed to nothing yet. Actually, I'd be happy to help out.'

Emma smiled, and Simon would love to have returned it, but the timing was bad, and he had a mouthful of egg, bacon, and toast.

'Don't worry – keep eating. So where are we going?'

Simon wiped his mouth and had a gulp of tea. 'Manchester. I'll book the train tickets today.'

'Ahhhhh. Aha. Manchester?' Emma fidgeted in the chair and straightened her skirt.

'What's happening in Manchester? I'd take a guess at football, but the season's over, I think? I'm not sure Michael would allow me to go and watch a football match in Manchester, anyway. Coming from Liverpool, that is. It's a bit of a religion with him, I'm afraid. He's on the red side of the city.'

Emma wondered why she was rambling on and tucked a strand of hair behind her ear.

Simon handed her the magazine at the appropriate page while biting on a large piece of toast.

'Running. I see. On Saturday evening? In Manchester?' She tucked more wayward strands of hair behind her other ear.

'It'll be great. I've been to a couple of them before, and it's really exciting. You'll love it, I promise. I can't believe we're going – this is fantastic. Are you sure it's okay with you?' Simon couldn't contain his excitement and enthusiasm as he looked at her.

It was the creases at the corners of his eyes as much as the vivid blue pupils. And the mouth. Then there was his hair – very dark brown with slight flecks of grey – almost the polar opposite colour to Michael, yet so similar in style and length. Even the little blotch of egg yolk on his recently shaved chin.

Emma picked up the napkin and dabbed the egg off his face.

'Yes, I'm sure.'

*

41 minutes 13 seconds – 34 seconds quicker than his best time. Perhaps he should run a little later like this from now on? Simon followed his shower with just a salad for lunch – he was still quite full from breakfast. He brought his laptop with him and set about booking the trains for Saturday.

He'd like to be there an hour before the start, so needed a train from Cambridge at midday, with just the one stop in Birmingham. Annoyingly, the races finished a few minutes before the last train back. This presented a problem. He certainly didn't want to miss any of the events. It was really important to him – Simon suspected it may be the last time he'd ever go and watch an athletics meeting.

There was nothing else for it – he'd have to book a hotel for the night, and they'd get a train back the next morning. The Radisson Blu looked good. He'd always stayed in four or five-star hotels for business or pleasure – it was one of his few luxuries. He clicked on the site to book but couldn't get through. Again he tried, but with no luck. There was a direct line to the hotel, and he used his mobile to call them.

The hotel was very full with only business suites left on Saturday night. That was fine – he much preferred that anyway. Anya, the girl in reservations, was very helpful and kind. If she were on duty when they arrived, Simon would do his best to remember to thank her.

He booked for two people / two rooms and gave his credit cards details, jotting down the reservation number. Having already glanced at pictures of the suites and the facilities, two business class rooms for £335 sounded like decent value.

Later that afternoon, he went to the lounge to have a cup of tea and a chat with his fellow residents, many of whom he already considered good friends. They didn't seem to mind the age gap at all. In fact if anything, he thought they enjoyed talking to someone much younger.

As he walked back to his room, he spotted Emma at reception.

'I've booked up for Saturday. We need to get a train just after midday from Cambridge. Will that work for you?'

'Yes, that's fine. I can drive us to the station. I'll leave the car at home, and we can walk from there – it's very close. What time's the train back?'

'There's one at 11.15 that gets us into Cambridge by three o'clock.'

'What, in the morning?'

'No, the next day. The last train on Saturday night left before the end of the races, and I didn't want to miss it. I booked us into a hotel very close by. They were really full, but I managed to get two rooms.'

'Right. Ummm, fine … I guess. How much do I owe you?'

'Nothing, of course. It's something I want to do, and unfortunately, I need someone to hold my hand. It's more a case of me owing *you* something – a lot really. Thank you – you don't know how much this means to me. I'm off for a run now.'

His disarming smile was getting to her. She needed to go and have a cup of tea and a chat with the residents. A bit of reality and normality was called for at this moment.

Emma's hair was already tucked behind both ears as she walked into the lounge.

*

Friday was always a late one for Michael – the day when the lawyers in California always wanted to talk. With the

West Coast eight hours behind, if he could get out of the office by nine, he was doing well. Tonight, it was after ten o'clock.

There was a great wine bar nearby in Soho which he frequented now and then. Quite a few of his team were there, a little the worse for wear. He had a pint of Guinness handed to him before he'd managed to push his way to the bar.

'Come on Michael, get some down yer neck. Catchin' up time.' Jerry was a long-term employee of the company and a drinker of legendary status, as middle-aged Irishmen could sometimes be.

'We're off to that new club in Wardour Street at closing time – you're up for it, of course?' Although Jerry was shouting, it was only just loud enough for Michael to hear above the Friday night revelry.

'Nahhh, cheers mate, but not tonight. I'm on the red-eye back to L.A. on Monday and want to get up to Cambridge tomorrow morning. Surprise weekend for Emma – she doesn't know I'm coming.'

'Fair play, bud. I've yet to meet a man more devoted to his wife than you. Finish that up and let's get another one down you while you're here.'

Socialising was now as much a part of his job as caring had been a few years back. If he was lucky, he'd get out of the pub before 11.30. He'd then jump in a cab back to his flat in Islington, no more than four pints worse off. He'd already eyeballed Susie in the crowd, who'd be on his tail in a moment. She was a personal assistant and 11 years younger but seemed to have a thing for him. Much worse, she was always quite public with the flirting. It was very complimentary and all that, but he could really do without it.

He'd never once strayed from Emma and didn't intend to, however old-fashioned that sounded.

Michael had a strict Catholic upbringing, and although it was a while since he'd been to church, he was serious about monogamy. He knew Emma was too, and that held them together when other things threatened to prise them apart.

He was due to collect his rental car by eleven the next morning. By the time he'd sorted the paperwork out and crawled his way out of London, he should be in Cambridge by lunchtime. He'd already spoken with one of the carers at Orchard earlier that week and had her quietly check Emma's roster for the weekend. Emma was free until Monday morning – something that didn't happen too often nowadays.

The hotel in Oxford had already been booked, and they were due to have a long hike in the Cotswolds before eating at a Michelin-starred restaurant that evening. He fell asleep looking forward to a special surprise weekend with his wife.

*

'Tickets please. That's fine, thank you.'

'There's something about going somewhere by train that I've always liked. I've never had a great sense of direction, so the way a train travels on its rails really appeals to me – always has done. I remember wanting to be a train driver when I was a kid.'

'So when did your aspirations lower to accountancy?'

'When I was diagnosed with severe claustrophobia. I went on a school trip to a British Rail compound where they serviced trains. A teacher put me in the cab and shut the door, then couldn't open it again. I was screaming for ten minutes before an engineer managed to break the lock, then I had to be rushed to hospital in an ambulance.'

'Oh my God, you're kidding?' Emma felt dreadful.

'Yes.'

'Yes what?'

'Yes, I'm kidding.'

She punched him on the arm.

'I also like the peace and quiet – the solitude. Don't you find it relaxing?'

'Well, the first class coach definitely has the edge where solitude is concerned. You didn't need to buy first class tickets, you know. Oh, let me guess – you always travel first class?'

'Ummm, well pretty much, yes. But it's nicer, don't you think?'

'Well yes, *obviously* it's nicer. But then so's the first class cabin on a plane. And let me guess again – you always turn left when you walk inside a plane?'

'Guilty. Unless it's a client's private jet – then one turns right.' Emma looked at him to see if he was joking again.

He wasn't. She sighed and closed her eyes.

Ten minutes later, Simon felt her head resting on his arm. He looked at her face as she slept.

Then he looked out of the window and smiled.

*

Emma's car was in her space, but she wasn't in their flat. Michael was tempted to call her but didn't want to ruin the surprise. She was either in town somewhere or at Orchard, even though officially off duty. The chances of Emma working some extra hours were much greater than anything else, so he drove to the care home.

As he walked into reception, a new girl he didn't recognise was at the desk. Her lapel badge gave her name.

'Hello, Julie. Is Emma about at the moment?'

'Hi. Not at the moment, no. Can I take a message?'

She had a good smile and a pleasant manner, though Michael would have expected nothing less. Emma was an excellent recruiter of staff.

'If she's on duty I'd like to deliver the message myself if possible. It's a surprise – I'm Michael, her husband.'

'Oh dear. She's actually away with Simon at the moment. They've gone to Manchester.'

'What? Errr, what time are they back then?' He looked at his watch.

'Sometime tomorrow afternoon – she reckoned around four o'clock.'

Michael's jaw dropped, and Julie sensed the problem she'd just caused.

'Simon's a new resident here,' she added quickly, grinning awkwardly.

'Right. Good. Fine. Umm, perhaps I'll just give her a call then. Well thanks very much, Julie. Have a good day.'

Michael jumped in the shining Mercedes convertible he'd hired for the weekend and powered the roof up – it was starting to rain.

He called Emma's mobile but went straight through to her voicemail. 'Hi Emma, it's me. I'm at Orchard now, waiting to take you to Oxford and the Cotswolds for the weekend. A surprise weekend. Well, there goes the surprise. Catch you later, kiddo. Have fun.'

He couldn't quite hide the bitterness from his voice, which he was now ashamed of.

He thought for a minute and then went back inside, slipping on a damp step in his haste and scratching the leather toe cap of his new brogues. 'Fuck.'

'Hi again. Sorry, can you remind me who Simon is? You mentioned he was new here?'

'Sure. Simon Carter. He's only been here a week or two. He's such a lovely man.'

'And what's wrong with Simon? In his eighties? Nineties?'

'Ah. Err, I can't actually give out that information, I'm afraid – it's confidential.'

Michael sighed both audibly and visibly.

'Julie, I'm a director of Collins Knight Young, your employers. I was also manager here when you were still a child.'

'I understand, sir, but I'm still not at liberty to …' But she was interrupted.

'It's Michael, not *sir*. And I'm sorry, and you're right. I'm just concerned my wife isn't taking on a little more than she can cope with. Is Simon in a wheelchair?'

Julie burst out laughing, put her hand in front of her mouth and blushed.

'Sorry about that. But no, he's most definitely *not* in a wheelchair. He runs ten or fifteen miles a day, and I've never seen anyone run any faster. Simon is seriously fit.'

Michael's jaw threatened to drop again. His corporate identity was slipping a little too.

'So what the fuck's he doing in Orchard? Is he one of the carers?' He could feel a vein throbbing in his temple.

Julie was stunned by the outburst and began to well up. Michael ran a hand through his grey hair, while the other jangled the Merc keys impatiently.

'Sorry. Julie, please – I'm sorry.' He went to put an arm on her shoulder, but she quickly moved further back behind the desk.

'Christ. Look, I'm sorry, but this weekend was meant to be a surprise. I've just driven up from London. I was taking Emma to the Cotswolds and … Oh, never mind. Sorry.'

Michael held the palms of both hands up as he moved away, bringing them together in prayer formation and bowing slightly. He bleated another apology as he walked out of the door.

*

'Wake up, Ms. Lowry. It's time for your sleeping tablets.' Simon held out two small mint sweets in the palm of his hand.

Emma opened her eyes and found the side of her head pressed into Simon's shoulder. She shook herself awake and sat upright.

'Where are we?'

'All will be well if you'll just take these sleeping tablets. Open wide.' He pinched the two mints in his hand, and Emma felt obliged to continue the façade, opening her mouth.

'There. We're five minutes away from Birmingham. A quick platform change, and you can have another kip – we're due into Manchester at about four thirty.' He stood up and collected the two overnight bags above them.

Emma checked her phone while they were waiting for their connecting train. One text from Julie and one voicemail from Michael.

Hi Emma, I met your husband this morning, and it didn't go very well. I told him where you were and he shouted at me. I'm really upset as I did nothing wrong. I'll talk to you tomorrow or give me a call if you like. Julie

She listened to Michael's message, put the phone back in her pocket, and put both hands up to her face.

'Something wrong?'

'Yes and no sums it up nicely. Let's stick with the latter for now.' She put on a brave smile.

On the train to Manchester, she thought about his message and her blood boiled. Then she thought about it some more, and her temper cooled a little.

What had she physically done wrong to upset her husband? Nothing, nada, riens. Not guilty – absolutely – no question.

What about emotionally? Nothing? Not guilty? No question? The jury was out on that one.

*

'Good afternoon, here's my booking reference. We just want to drop our bags off in the rooms, and then we'll be back later.'

'Certainly, sir. Sorry to keep you waiting, but we're fully booked, and everyone seems to be checking in at the same time.'

'That's fine; we're still alright on time. We're heading for Sportcity but don't need to be there for another forty-five minutes.'

'So here we are, sir. Staying for one night – the room's pre-paid, and it's on the top floor – one of our business class suites. Will you be requiring one or two keys?

'Err, that's two rooms, right?'

'No sir. You made a reservation for two people in a twin-bedded room.'

'No I didn't. I said it was two people for *two* rooms, and mine was a twin – I prefer a smaller bed.'

'I'm terribly sorry sir. If you look at your credit card payment here, you'll see you've paid £335. That's the price of one business class room. You specified a twin on the telephone booking, and that's what's been allocated.'

'But we need two rooms. Okay, please debit another £335 from my card – here we are.'

'I'm afraid I can't do that, sir. We're fully booked and even have a waiting list.'

'Excuse me a minute.' Simon turned to Emma and led her away from the reception desk.

'I can't believe this, I specifically asked for *two* rooms. I remember asking for twin beds in both rooms, then thinking I'd better ask you if that was right, or if you'd prefer a double in your room. And I forgot. I'm such an idiot. I even remember thinking what good value it was – £335 for two suites. Oh, bother. What do we do now?'

Emma took a deep breath and counted to three. She looked Simon in the eye.

'A question and a statement. Here's the question – do you snore, Mr Carter?'

'I don't know. I don't think so. If someone else asked me that I'd tell them to ask you or one of your staff.'

'Hmm. Okay, here's the statement. I get to use the bathroom first. Today *and* tomorrow. Deal?'

They shook hands and returned to the girl at reception. She was experienced and already making two key cards by the time they got there.

As they travelled to the top of the building in the lift, Simon broke the silence.

'I'm sorry. I'm an oaf.' He was genuinely upset and didn't know what more to say or do.

'It's okay. Hey, it's alright.' Emma smiled, put a hand on his shoulder and squeezed it.

6

Sunday 28 May 2017

'Does this bar ever shut?' Emma definitely hadn't mixed her drinks but couldn't remember how many glasses of white wine she'd had. She didn't think they'd all fit into one bottle.

'Not for hotel guests. We keep drinking, and they keep pouring. Not to worry – we don't have too early a start in the morning. I'm up for one last tipple for the road. One more for you?'

'This goes no further than this table, right? What goes on in Manchester *stays* in Manchester. Shake hands on it and Scout's honour, then one last drink – a small one too.'

They shook hands and both did what they thought might be Scout salutes, then fell back in their seats giggling. Simon went to the bar and ordered a large Merlot and a large Chardonnay.

'This tastes like a large Chardonnay, Simon.'

'Yeah, and this looks like a delicious Merlot.' They chinked glasses and took generous sips.

'That five thousand metre race was so exciting. I couldn't believe how close it was – never seen closer than that. And the juniors were great. So many personal best times. Thanks again for coming along with me. I've loved every minute.'

'S'okay. I really liked it too. First time I've ever watched athletics, but I may go to another one now. Oh, my God.' Emma scrambled in her pocket.

'What? What's the matter?'

'I meant to phone Michael. Oh shit. Oops, pardon my French. Thank God he didn't try to call again, I'll call him now.'

'Is that a good idea? It's after 2 a.m.'

'Oh bloody hell. I'll be sleeping in the doghouse whenever I next sleep with him. Which could be quite a while, now. What a mess.' She sighed and took a gulp.

'Well, you certainly won't be sleeping in the doghouse when you sleep with me tonight. At least that's something.' As tipsy as they both were, an awkward pause clung between them.

'I didn't mean when you sleep with me. I meant when you sleep with me but in your own bed.'

He looked at her sheepishly, and the corners of his eyes crinkled again. Emma wondered if Simon had any idea just how attractive he was.

She touched the side of his face and grinned. Holding her glass up, she made contact with his again. 'Cheers. Here's to friendship.'

They downed their wine together, and both stood up a little unsteadily. 'Did you say first one to the room uses the bathroom first?' Simon stuck his tongue out and ran to the elevator.

'Hey you, not fair. You practice this running stuff too much.' Emma staggered after him, both of them laughing all the way into the lift.

61

*

The unrehearsed system worked well. Emma went to the bathroom first, having taken a pair of pyjamas and a washbag with her. While she was in there, Simon got out of his clothes and into his pyjamas. As she came out, he went in to have his wash, and when he came back, she was tucked up in bed.

There was a reasonable space between the two beds – about the width of another single bed. He switched the wall light off and turned in her direction.

'You asked me something a few hours ago – something very personal. I gave you my answer, but I should have followed it up with a question of my own as well. Is it too late to ask? Are you asleep or can I ask you now? It's an equally personal question, Emma, and it's going to have a big impact on our night in this room.'

Emma had wondered if this situation would arise. She'd feared it would, but she also wondered if she hoped it would, if for no other reason than to find out how she'd react. She had no idea what she'd say or do. A lot of the time leaning against his shoulder on the train had been spent thinking about this very subject. She had managed to get a little sleep but a lot of the time was spent pondering and enjoying the contact with him.

She could say nothing, and he'd have his answer about whether she was asleep. Another second or two of silence, and there would be her reply. The room was black just after the light went out, but her eyes were already becoming accustomed to the dark.

She had the advantage of a small amount of light escaping through the curtains behind her – she could make out the contours of his bed and his body. When they'd first walked into the room and she'd awkwardly broached the subject about which bed she'd sleep in, he told her that a man should always be nearest to the door entrance to ward off any form of attack. She'd laughed at the time, but with a straight face he'd informed her it was true, a basic form of etiquette, and he hoped most men would know this.

'No, I'm not asleep. What do you want to ask me?'

Her mouth had gone very dry, and she wanted to swallow but feared it would sound like a sitcom parody of the noise, emphasised by the darkness.

'Do you snore?'

*

They shared two paracetamol in the morning – it was all Emma had with her. Simon was already up and dressed by the time she woke. He smiled and watched her pad to the bathroom, which both pleased her and made her self-conscious in equal measures.

She was so relieved the night had gone by without incident, yet disappointment laced her relief. Emma thought her current emotional state might accurately represent that of a fourteen-year-old girl.

A long enough time was spent in the bathroom that Simon was prompted to ask if she was alright at one point. She was loath to admit to herself that there'd been way too much faffing on her hair and make-up.

'Wow, you look lovely. Different to when you're at Orchard. Are you meeting Michael when we get back to Cambridge?'

The hair didn't need tucking behind her ear, but she attempted to anyway.

'No, not at all. He'll probably be at the company flat in London, and then he's off again to the States tomorrow or Tuesday.'

No Simon, this effort is all for you. 'Wow' and 'lovely' are a good start, but I could take some more if pushed. Even a hand on my arm to lead me down to breakfast would be enough. Or just walk up to me now, put a hand behind my head, stare into my eyes and tell me you're sorry, but you have to ki…

'Doesn't he miss being with you? Especially on a weekend when you're off duty? I'm surprised he didn't want to be with you this weekend. Oh, not that it's any of my business, of course.'

Emma's thought bubble had popped. 'Don't worry; you're not saying anything I haven't wondered myself once or twice. Shall we go down to breakfast?'

'Yes, good idea. I'd have loved to get a run in before the train, but I don't think we have time. Besides, I'd get lost I suppose.'

She so easily forgot about his illness that any reference to it hit her hard. It made her think of another resident on Simon's floor. A sweet man of 96 suffering from vascular dementia. He was so fit that he looked 20 years younger. Every day he'd ask how old he was and all the staff were instructed to ask him how old he felt. He normally replied '64', and the carer would say *well there you are then,* and smile. But he knew his date of birth, and he'd see a newspaper in the lounge, look at the date, then ask a carer if he was really 96 – he couldn't believe it. He was so shocked and saddened, even though the emotion only lasted a moment. And it happened nearly every day, poor soul.

Emma wondered if she was experiencing some form of that same feeling. 'Of course you wouldn't get lost, but I just wouldn't be able to keep up with you. It's me who'd get lost.'

'Official face off and pretty face back on, please. Let's get breakfast.' He put a hand on her shoulder while opening the door.

'*Pretty*' and a hand on her shoulder – she could work with that.

*

The journey back wasn't quite as smooth. Simon struggled with the correct platform at the changeover in Birmingham and was forced to ask a member of staff. This upset him a little, and he was quieter on the journey to Cambridge. Emma had inexplicably left both her wash bag and make-up in the room. There was nothing of value, but it was a nuisance – she couldn't remember ever having done that before.

They walked to her flat, and she offered Simon a cup of tea and a sandwich, but he was keen to get back to Orchard – he wanted to have a run on his course. She excused herself after he'd got into her car and ran up to the flat to grab a couple of things, picking up a note from Michael at the same time and putting it in her bag. She'd tried calling him three times on the journey back, but there was no reply.

Back at the home, she met with Julie while Simon ran upstairs to get his shorts and vest on. He turned back at the top of the stairs – 'Thanks again, Emma – you're the best. And gorgeous too!'

Julie looked down at the floor then back up at Emma. 'He's right – you look lovely today. Errr, anyway, I've gone through the conversation in my head a dozen times, and I honestly didn't say anything wrong. He just got so angry with me. I'm sorry, Emma. Am I in big trouble?'

Emma had mostly recovered from Simon's public compliment.

'Thank you – just a little extra cover-up than normal. You've done nothing wrong, and you're in no trouble at all. On the contrary, I'm really grateful you were able to work this weekend. It sounds like *I* should be apologising for my husband's behaviour. Are *you* okay?'

'Yes, I'm fine. It's silly, really – some of the residents are much ruder and more aggressive than that, not that they can help it, but I guess I'm used to it and expect it.

I'm afraid I laughed at something your husband asked. I didn't mean to – it was just, you know, funny?'

'What did he say? He's a natural born comedian, so nothing would surprise me.'

'Well, he asked if Simon was in a wheelchair – he was worried you'd struggle to look after him on your own in Manchester. I thought that was hilarious and told him that Simon was like, well, a really fast runner and the fittest guy I know. Which he is, right? So I didn't see a problem in saying that. I wasn't giving any of his medical condition away by saying that, surely?'

Emma took a deep breath and sighed while attempting a smile. She'd better look at Michael's note.

'That's fine, Julie, you did exactly right. You go off home now, and thanks again for stepping in.' Emma disappeared into her office and shut the door.

Hi Em,

Well, there's a surprise to trump a surprise. I guess I should have called earlier and booked some time with you, but it wouldn't have been a surprise then, would it?

Well, as it happens, it was your turn to surprise me this time. I've seen Simon's record at head office and look forward to meeting him sometime soon. I'd have been concerned about his suitability at Orchard, what with being 23 years younger than the next oldest resident. Thought he may have got a wee bit bored with life there?

However, he certainly sounds like a very fit guy, and if he can make friends with people of his own age, that's the best therapy of all.

Must dash – need to get this new Mercedes back to the rental firm asap and see if I can get some money back. The hotel in Oxford was pre-paid so too bad about that, though Le Manoir were very understanding about the dinner reservation.

In LA for a week though may be longer this time. Who knows …

Much love,

Michael (hubby)

'*Fuck*! Fuck, fuck, *fuck*!' She screwed the note into a tight ball and threw it in the wastepaper bin.

Emma had never received something like that from Michael before. Not even remotely close. It was all too easy to become indignant and fume at his undisguised hostility towards her totally innocent and work-related actions.

How would she feel if he still ran a care home and went on an overnight journey with a female resident in her forties suffering from early onset Alzheimer's? The answer was that she'd have no problem at all. Not the tiniest sliver of a problem.

But the truth was that she'd want to know how ill the resident was. If she was currently suffering very few adverse symptoms, then Emma would be curious to know what the woman looked like. But even if Emma had driven some distance to see Michael for a carefully organised surprise weekend and she found he'd gone on an overnight trip with this mythical woman, she was one hundred percent certain she wouldn't have left him a note like that.

Indignation began to rise again as she picked up her phone to text Michael – she would *not* be calling him.

Hi Michael, I'll look forward to a call from you when you're ready to apologise for that note. Love, Emma x

There was another note to be written as well – the one that went in Simon's medical records. She would have to be a little economical with certain aspects of the trip. The amount of alcohol consumed would definitely need to be reduced. The sleeping arrangements would simply not be mentioned, and her own personal feelings and thoughts would remain exactly that.

She wished she didn't have to report the confusion Simon had experienced on the way back at the train station in Birmingham and didn't know why. Perhaps she imagined that if she didn't refer to it, it wouldn't exist. To deny the illness would be to ward it off for that much longer. After all, forgetting her wash bag and make-up was worse than mixing a platform up at a station.

Thinking about Simon made her want to be near him. To be with him, even if it was just having a cup of coffee in the lounge with the other residents. She looked out of her office window and saw him running in the distance. She couldn't tell the difference between the way he ran now and how they were running yesterday. He looked so fluid and at ease.

She'd write the report later. He'd be back in half an hour and would want dinner after his shower. Emma would go and have a wander around all three floors and aim to accidentally bump into him near the first-floor dining room in about an hour.

*

'What a nice surprise having dinner with you. The food's great, and I like living here, but I wish we were still in Manchester. Do you think we'd be able to do that again?'

'Yes, a pleasant coincidence. I was passing through on my way to the staff canteen, and there you were, sitting on your own and waiting to eat. Do you mean go to Manchester again or go to another athletics race?'

Emma wondered if Simon believed her pleasant coincidence.

'No, I didn't mean specifically Manchester. Just to go away again on an adventure somewhere. We've done the athletics trip – now what about something *you* really like? Do you have a favourite pastime?'

'I can't think of anything specific. I guess I like a much slower version of your area of expertise.'

'Slow motion accountancy? You'd earn a lot more doing it that way.'

'What? Oh. No, silly – I like walking. I find it very relaxing.'

'Yes, I guessed you meant that – only winding you up. You have a lovely expression when you're a little confused.

Let's go walking next time. If it's okay with you that there's a next time?'

Oh, it's so okay that there's a next time. I have no idea how it'll pan out and the problems and the pain it'll cause, just as long as there's always a next time.

'Well, let me know a date, and let's see if it's feasible, eh?' *Chicken! You complete chicken shit, Emma! What about 'Sure, Michael's bound to be away next weekend and I'm owed at least a year's worth of weekends off, so what about going to the Cotswolds this Friday?'*

'That sounds great – you're on. I'll check out some really good places to walk and look for a nice hotel that's convenient. And don't worry – I'll get two rooms this time.' *Or maybe I could use the early onset card and claim a booking error?*

Mehhh, not really necessary – a twin room's fine. 'You'd better – I can't be putting up with that snoring all night again.'

'Me? Snoring? Are you kidding? I didn't get a wink of sleep with all that noise coming from your side of the room. I'm almost tempted to book another twin room and record you just to prove it!' *But I'm a realist – who am I kidding? I'm riding on a wave of sympathy, and this beautiful woman is going to tire of it pretty soon.*

'Don't think you'll be the only one recording, Mister.' *Hug me. Please? I so want you to hug me.*

Cathy had been standing beside the table for a minute and decided to quietly clear her throat.

'Sorry to interrupt. It's just that Deirdre's called down to reception a couple of times now. She said you spoke to her earlier today about a new painting for her room? I wasn't sure if she'd imagined it, but ...'

'Damn, you're right – it slipped my mind. I'll be in her room in five minutes. Can you pop by and let her know? Thanks, Cathy.'

Emma couldn't believe she'd forgotten.

'I should be going, I guess. I'll see you tomorrow. Have a good evening, and thanks again for a great weekend.' They both stood up, and she touched his arm and smiled.

Simon smiled back. 'My best weekend in years — thank *you*.'

7

Monday 29 May to Wednesday 07 June 2017

Michael had developed a liking for gin. Bizarrely, this craving occurred only when in an aircraft. Even so, with the amount of air miles he was racking up with the company, it would have given him swift membership of the Betty Ford Center.

Before he moved to head office in London and started living in the capital, if asked to guess, Michael would have said there were maybe a dozen or so gins made, and perhaps half that which people had actually heard of or drank.

He'd now seen dedicated gin bars offering more than a hundred different brands. Not only that but at least twenty different styles of tonic, for God's sake. It gave him the potential to try over 2,000 G&Ts without ever repeating a particular concoction. It was both reassuring and daunting in equal measures – large equal measures.

The next up on this Herculean task involved Pink Pepper gin with Aromatic tonic.

'Do you think they taste different at thirty-seven thousand feet, Jake?'

'Probably not after the first three or four, sir.'

How terribly difficult pride and egos were. Together with jealousy, they basically ruled the world. He could nearly remember his note verbatim, and he could still read Emma's reply on his phone. She'd managed to convert what he genuinely believed were balanced words with a subtle hint of emotion, into a barbed and vitriolic attack. She'd somehow left him feeling as if *he* was the one in the wrong. That *he* should be apologising to *her*.

Luckily, the gin was helping to redress the injustice of it all. Who the fuck did she think she was, anyway? On his fourth or fifth double, he wasn't sure who Emma thought she was. Seeking the barman's wisdom on the matter, he'd found Jake strangely non-committal on the subject, whilst still managing to give the impression he was entirely on Michael's side.

It led him to wonder if barmen might make extraordinarily good politicians. Certainly better than the bell-end in charge of the country he was heading for now.

Something else was afoot too. For the first time in an age, probably since he'd first seen Emma, he felt his eyes roaming. There was an elegant older woman sitting at the bar on her own – he hadn't noticed her when first boarding. He'd made eyes at her, and she'd held his stare for a while before smiling and turning away. A little later, while Jake was replacing his Pink Pepper with a Monkey 47, he caught her looking at him. He raised his glass across the little bar and toasted her. The woman returned the gesture.

Michael decided he'd join her and introduce himself once he'd finished this latest tipple – there an empty stool perched tantalisingly next to the woman. Fortunately for all involved, the slight delay to build his Dutch courage allowed for a tanned Adonis in his late 20s to take the unoccupied seat his wife or girlfriend or mother had been keeping for him in his absence.

For a while, he'd convinced himself that this was fate – God giving him a helping hand when he was being a complete prat. However, towards the last hour and a half of the flight, a very cute flight attendant sporting a badge saying '*Penny*' had approached him at the bar and asked if he wanted her to turn his flatbed back to a normal seat. It was an Australian accent if he wasn't mistaken.

She was enchanting. Perhaps 30, about 5'4 and very short dark hair, a stunningly pretty face and a figure hovering between perfect and slimmer. He was now as drunk as he'd ever been on a plane, but a lifetime's experience of alcohol allowed him to still conduct himself in a vaguely acceptable manner.

'That's so sweet of you, Penny. But really, I insist – let's do this together.'

He lurched off the stool and followed her to his seat, his eyes transfixed on her backside. On his way down the aisle, he noticed the woman he'd been toasting at the bar. She winked at him and whispered '*Good luck.*'

'Don't worry sir; it's all part of the service. Just wait a moment, and I'll have it all tidied up for you. Would you like a newspaper or magazine?' She bundled the sheets, blanket and pillow up in an instant, and the seat hummed back to its primary function of a large, comfy armchair.

'Are you on the return flight or do you have some downtime in L.A.?'

'I'm here until Wednesday – a couple of days off and then on the evening flight back to Heathrow.'

'I'm sure you hear this all the time, but I'd like to give you my business card. I'm here for at least a week – I'd love to hear from you while you're here. Perhaps we could get a lunch together somewhere?' He was more than rusty and cursed himself, both for saying these things in such a hopeless way and for saying them at all.

'That's very sweet of you, Mr Lowry. Maybe I will.' The smile was blinding and took his breath away.

'Please, it's Michael. I'll keep my mobile close to my ear at all times during the next two days.' This was pathetic, and he needed to shut the fuck up. He attempted his best smile and awkwardly fell into his seat, which appeared to amuse her.

'I'll see you a little later in the flight, Michael. Not long to go now.' She reached over to the magazine rack and passed him a classic car magazine and the Financial Times. Thanking her profusely, he followed her arse with his eyes as she went back up the aisle. He half expected to see four torn pieces of business card flutter onto the floor before she reached the galley.

*

Simon had decided to formalise his swimming in the little indoor therapy pool. He made some calculations and increased his daily hundred lengths to 135. It was a twelve-metre pool, so he'd clock up 1,620 metres – a few metres over a mile. It wasn't just the physical exercise but the mental aspect of keeping the lap numbers in his head as he swam. There was nothing he could do about halting his condition, but where possible, exercise was always recommended. He loved the endorphin rush too.

He spent many of his exercise hours thinking about Emma. She brought a huge amount of pleasure and happiness to his existence, but she also reminded him of the hopelessness of his situation. Even without his illness, she was still a happily married woman. Well, a married woman at any rate. He chose to think that her willingness to go for another weekend with him somewhere was proof that something wasn't right with her marriage.

This was obviously delusional – deep down he knew she was just doing her job and was probably just relieved to be dealing with someone nearer to her own age for once. It made him physically wince when he contemplated her attention as purely professional. How could he find out her feelings without making a complete fool of himself? What could he say or do to discover if Emma had any true feelings for him?

When she had dinner with him last night in the dining room, was that a pure coincidence? Or had she planned to make sure she walked past when he was about to order his food?

Who did he think he was kidding? He shook his head and almost laughed at what he'd just thought. Perhaps this was another part of the illness he hadn't accounted for – one in which his time left was spent in pure fantasy?

On reflection, that wasn't such a bad frame of mind. It could be worse – he could end up dying a violent death, drowning in his own fluids as his lungs filled while he was unable to swallow.

Tears started to roll down his cheeks, and he was glad he was sitting on the side of the pool with his legs dangling in the water. He was on his own as was normally the case down here. If someone walked in, a carer or fellow resident, he'd jump back in the pool, and his tears would disappear amongst a trillion others.

Maybe he'd just sink to the bottom and stay there, just like in some of the dreams he had. Except in the dreams he was always able to breathe underwater. Always.

*

Emma was watching the CCTV of the pool from her office. She'd initially had someone by the pool as Simon swam, just as someone would always have been present if any of the other residents were in the pool. But they could all see that he was an extremely good swimmer. Why should she have ever thought otherwise? His rhythm in the water was just like his running – smooth, gracious and effortless. He mesmerised her.

This was why it took her more than a couple of seconds to react when he appeared to topple forward into the pool from his sitting position on the side. She peered closely at the monitor, waiting for him to surface. As the effect of the initial splash began to dissipate, she could just make out Simon through the rippled water. He was curled into a foetal ball at the bottom of the pool.

Emma jumped out of her chair. The castor wheels took it hammering back against the wall as she sprinted past Maddy at reception.

'Swimming pool. *Now!*'

Emma jumped into the pool and dragged Simon back up to the surface. She brought him to the side, and Maddy helped her pull him out and onto the tiles.

There was no resuscitation needed. Simon coughed, and some water came out of his mouth, then he rolled onto his side of his own accord.

'What happened to me?' He slowly got up with their help and sat down on a chair.

'Good question, and one I was about to ask. Are you okay?' Emma was trying to hide the shock and concern on

77

her face. Maddy passed Simon his towel and went to get a dressing gown from the changing room.

'I can't remember anything. I was sitting on the edge of the pool. I think I'd completed my laps, then nothing. I can't remember anything else. This isn't good, is it?' He looked dismal, but the colour had returned to his face.

'It's nothing. My fault if anything – there's always meant to be a member of staff here when anyone's in the pool. Because you swim like a fish, I didn't adhere to the rules. I'm really sorry, Simon – it won't happen again. I was really stupid.'

'Don't be ridiculous. I'm the only idiot around here. Is this the start of all the crazy things I'm going to do?' He looked at her pleadingly, water still running in rivulets down both their faces.

Emma felt her heart melting in her chest and rising up her throat. She was completely unable to resist her spontaneous reaction – she moved towards him, put her arms around his shoulders and hugged him as hard as she could, her wet face pressing against his. She felt his arms move around her, and she was hugged just as hard in return. She felt his whispered words in her ear as much as heard them.

'I'd love to say this won't happen again, but I can't do that, can I? I hope I never say this to you again, but please help me. I'm scared of lots of things, but more than anything, I'm scared I won't remember you one day. Please don't let that happen.'

Emma was grateful for the pool water still on her face. She noticed Maddy standing next to her with two white pool robes, and the words she was about to whisper back evaporated. Had she spoken them, there were probably good grounds for her to resign immediately.

She stood up awkwardly and took the robes.

*

In her office again after a change of clothes, Emma contemplated the enormity of the last hour. Simon could so easily have died in the pool. She would need to seek Maddy's advice on how they should play it. The incident must be logged of course, but what should they include? Emma wasn't technically on duty, and Maddy was therefore in charge, but Maddy had seen Emma watching the pool on the CCTV so had focused on other duties.

On a personal level, what if Maddy hadn't appeared with those robes? Emma knew what she was about to say to Simon. She could no longer deny her feelings, but did that mean she had a conflict of interest which wouldn't allow her to continue her duties effectively?

Emma wondered if Simon had any idea what she'd been about to say. Could he somehow sense or feel it through her body? Was she fooling herself when she imagined he felt the same way as they held each other?

When she'd first met Michael at Orchard, Emma had been bowled over by him. She was more than flattered by his attention and found him mentally and sexually attractive. In time, she learned to love him and couldn't say she still didn't love him now. But she couldn't remember the point where she fell in love with him – it wasn't a specific moment in time.

Michael had used humour as his weapon of choice with her. She *liked* him almost immediately, and that warmth and fascination grew. The sex was the best she'd known, but she had few experiences to compare it with, apart from the awkward fumblings encountered at university. Emma could count her lovers on the fingers of one hand.

Their lovemaking had become what she could best describe as proficient. Michael knew exactly which buttons to press to give her satisfaction, and she believed she was able to return the compliment. It was definitely '*making love*' in a literal sense, but making babies was their only real agenda from the beginning of their marriage, and that had affected everything.

Simon had no prior agenda and wasn't trying to win her heart – that was the magical difference. Ironically, it was humour that had flicked the switch, but there was no ulterior motive in his actions. She had simply known Simon for a few moments and then she loved him.

Despite the turmoil of the last hour, she smiled as she remembered him calling her '*Ella*'. When they'd both laughed, and she saw that smile and those creases in the corners of his eyes, *that* was the moment she loved him. She loved him more than she'd ever loved anyone.

Emma would have sworn on a stack of Bibles that this sort of thing could never happen to her. But it *had* happened to her. It was both wonderful and catastrophic.

At this moment, she wanted to be curled up tight in bed, her head pressed against her knees, sobbing until the tears ended forever, and she fell asleep.

*

Michael hadn't heard from Penny. Of course he hadn't; he scolded himself for even dreaming that a woman like that would give him a second thought. He was fifteen years older than her, certainly didn't look any younger than his age and had been spectacularly drunk. Hardly the rich, good-looking and famous route to success.

Anyone could dream, though, and he still wished he'd asked for her number. Even if she hadn't given it to him, at least he could find some solace from having given it his best shot. But he'd forgotten because he was pissed ...

He wondered where Penny would be now. He remembered her saying she flew back to Heathrow last Wednesday. Perhaps she'd done a return trip to LA again by now and would be on his flight home tonight? Michael beamed with delight at the thought of it.

He could have been home for the weekend but saw no point. Tonight's flight would get him into London on Monday afternoon. After chilling out and a good night's sleep, he'd be ready for work bright and early on Tuesday morning.

It also meant he'd avoided driving up to their flat in Cambridge on the weekend. He'd decided not to call Emma as he wasn't prepared to apologise. It was *her* who ruined last weekend with some decidedly suspect behaviour – why the hell should *he* apologise? He also worried that if he were in London this weekend, he wouldn't be able to resist the temptation to go and see her.

But that wasn't going to happen. That would mean losing face and displaying a huge sign of weakness. That was a definite no-no. He'd keep his mind occupied with Penny, which seemed entirely justified and fair. And keep his fingers crossed too.

He did miss Emma, though. He really *did* miss her.

*

The flight back was uneventful but for one minor statistic. It was the first time Michael had managed to avoid drinking at the Upper-Class bar since first introduced to this exalted flying atmosphere. He was quite proud of the achievement, and this worried him a little – he'd never found it difficult in the past to go without alcohol from one week to the next unless clubbed into submission by Irish Jerry on a Friday night.

Penny hadn't been on the flight of course, but he'd spoken with a pretty colleague of hers called Kim and discovered Penny was based in London. This made not having her contact number even harder to bear. He'd asked Kim to send Penny his best wishes, and that he was still hoping to hear from her. Futile he presumed, but at least something.

The following morning, in the middle of a board meeting where he was presenting his latest progress report on the never-ending California saga, he felt a vibration in his pocket.

Back in the privacy of his office a while later, to his surprise and delight he saw a text message from Penny. She'd received the message from Kim and hoping that he was still in London, wondered if he wanted to meet up for coffee that afternoon. Sorry it was such short notice, but she was back on the LA flight again the next day.

The euphoria lasted until Michael had composed his reply and his finger was hovering over the send button.

Something began to dawn on him. He'd chased this girl knowing he'd never catch her, so the hunt was completely irrelevant and totally innocent. Now the ante had been cranked up several notches. He may be crossing a line from which there was no easy and innocuous route back.

Michael leant back in his chair and stared at the unsent reply. He brought his hands together as if in prayer and steepled his index fingers, tapping them lightly against his lips. He liked to think of this as his 'academic in contemplation' look, used to little or no effect as yet with the yank lawyers.

Were any sacred marriage vows being broken by having a coffee with someone?

Most certainly not.

Would this coffee escalate to anything potentially more volatile?

Almost certainly not. He was punching way above his weight, and who the hell did he think he was kidding.

Before he'd had time to rationalise why Penny might have sent the message, he'd pressed send. This afternoon at three o'clock would be perfect – he'd meet her next to the Statue of Eros in Piccadilly.

*

Coffee had escalated. Via the shops of Oxford Street and a ridiculously trendy wine bar in Carnaby Street, they eventually found themselves in a reasonable Italian restaurant in Shaftesbury Avenue. They shared a cheese platter in order to finish the remaining half bottle of Barolo, the second of the evening.

The waiter asked if they'd like any coffee. He looked at her and tentatively suggested they could always have it back at his flat, only a few minutes away by taxi. Penny had giggled in a way that reminded him of Emma – his heart lurched as he took a deep breath and a final sip of red velvet courage.

Michael sweated and grinned his way through the growing anxiety and requested the bill while Penny was powdering her nose – probably with cocaine. The waiter returned with a silver-plated tray and announced '*Il* Conto', but Michael was beyond insults at this stage.

12.5% discretionary gratuity on restaurant bills had been *de rigeur* in London for some time. Staff had become quite adept at making customers feel uncomfortable about asking for it to be deducted from the bill if they felt the service wasn't up to scratch. On any other night he'd have kept twenty pounds back and had a word with the management about foul-mouthed waiters, but with Penny heading back to the table, he dropped the cash on the tray and went to intercept her.

*

The coffees were sipped while sitting in a soft and expansive black leather sofa, with the dimmer switches wound down to darker than *Off*. Michael initially used the playlist on his phone for background music. Bluetooth linked to the expensive sound system; he thought the sound quality was superb. However, this quickly became either too inappropriate (Propellerheads, Eminem, The Very Best of Glenn Miller) or too painful (any slow track of which there were many, every single one of which reminded him of Emma). He moved to a radio station specialising in elevator hits of the 80s and 90s.

Like a sprinter taking his position to the command of '*Take your marks*', Michael wiggled his toes onto the invisible white line when asking Penny if she'd like to move to somewhere more comfortable. He quietly cursed the ability of the costly sofa to give the very real sensation of lying in a cumulus cloud, thus somewhat undermining his suggestion.

By accepting his offer to move to the bedroom, Penny had pushed the starter's instructions to '*Set*'.

If it were possible, Michael would have been disqualified no less than five times. He registered false starts at 12.14 a.m., 12.19, 12.46 (the extra delay caused by attempts to adjust his 'equipment' in the bathroom), 12.53 and 1.02.

Penny was an absolute angel and as understanding as any girl could possibly be. Unfortunately, to any male on the planet, the space between comprehension and patronisation is negligible at best.

They parted with a kiss on the cheek and a limp handshake by the open door of a black cab. Michael passed a £20 note and a knowing shrug to the driver, who returned the gesture with widened eyes and turned down lips, expertly simulating a sad clown. It was a perfect human emoji for '*desolation*'.

Walking forlornly back to his flat, his absorbent slippers scraping along the damp London street, Michael felt like he'd attempted to rob a bank but on a Sunday. He was still guilty and going to jail, but there was no cash. He was a country mile and five false starts from the money shot.

He made a mental note to download the British Airways app in the morning. He wasn't travelling Virgin to LA again. He couldn't – it was impossible. He pictured the cabin crew gathering tomorrow for their pre-flight meeting; 'So how were your days off, Penny? Did you have a great time?' 'Well you won't believe it, Kim, but you remember that guy who tried to pick me up …'

And whichever way he looked at it, Michael had let his wife down. He'd betrayed her and ruined everything.

He'd have to phone Emma and apologise for the letter. She'd done nothing, and he knew it. His fucking ego had let him down. He was sure he didn't have an ego when he managed a care home. All he was concerned with was the well-being of the residents.

And that's all his beloved wife was concerned with. How on earth could he have been jealous of a poor, sick guy who probably couldn't even string a coherent sentence together and had all the sex appeal of a jellied eel?

He shook his head in dismay as he approached the flat and attempted to open the front door.

It was locked. The keys were inside on the entrance hall table, just where he left them. He could see them as he opened the letterbox and peered in.

It started to rain heavily.

8

Thursday 08 June to Saturday 10 June 2017

Maddy was getting out of her car as a van she didn't recognise arrived at the main entrance. A woman opened the back doors and gathered two large bouquets from within.

'Good morning. Very nice – I bet neither is for me.'

'If you're Julie at reception or Emma Lowry, then one of them is.'

'Ah. Alas no, but I'll take them from you and pass them on – they'll both be here in the next half hour. They're beautiful.'

'And expensive. I've just driven up from London – the client insisted on hand delivery.'

Maddy took them and left one for Julie in the alcove behind reception and the other in Emma's office. Hanging her jacket up, she went off in search of the senior carers on each floor before their night shifts ended – always her first duty of the day.

*

'I'm truly sorry, Em. I don't know what came over me. I've sent some flowers. Oh, and can you say sorry to Julie for me? I'll apologise face-to-face when I see her next.'

'Yes okay. The bouquet arrived, too. There was no need for that – perhaps I over-reacted. You should save the flowers for when you're *really* in the doghouse.'

Emma chuckled, and Michael blushed profusely, silently thanking God he was on the end of a telephone line. He quickly broke the guilt-laden pause.

'Anyway, apart from calling to apologise, I've got a little treat lined up.'

Emma started to fidget in her chair.

'Right. Sounds good. And what might that be?' She hoped he couldn't detect the fear in her voice – she certainly could.

'Well, you know I'm meant to be in Dublin this weekend?'

Emma felt the tiniest bit sick. It was normally '*but*' that skewed a sentence and delivered the bad news. '*Meant*' seemed to be just as effective.

'Yeahhsss.'

'Well I've switched things around and don't need to be there until Monday. So, rather than doing one of my stupid surprise weekends without a minute's notice, I thought I'd tell you a good day in advance so there's no screw ups. We're going to do exactly what I planned a couple of weeks ago. It's even the same hotel in Oxford, dinner at Le Manoir and a really good hike in the Cotswolds. The forecast looks great too. What do you think – pick you up about four o'clock tomorrow?'

Emma created the awkward silence this time.

'Em? Emma??'

'Yup. Here. Here I am – sorry, bad line.'

'So what do you think? Great, eh?'

'Yeah, great. Ummm, just a little bit awkward, though.'

'Uhh? You're kidding? I mean we're still going, right?'

'Errr, yeah. Sure. I'm just going to have to re-schedule things. I'd ummm, swapped shifts and was going to work this weekend. I'll need to cancel things. I just need to make a couple of calls – I don't want to let someone down. Some people, I mean. Let some people down.'

'Are you alright, Em? You sound a bit weird. Anything happened at Orchard?'

Emma felt a rush of relief.

'Oh yes, actually. A real drama. Simon fell, I mean Mr Carter fell into the pool last week. We had to rescue him. It was a bit of a drama, but everything was fine. Just shaken everyone up a bit, you know?'

'Oh? I didn't see it on the weekly email report. Who was on duty by the pool? That sort of thing has to be reported immediately.'

Emma cursed her choice of fill-in subject.

'Oh, I'm just exaggerating. All a bit of a storm in a teacup actually. Just a slip and, well, nobody was hurt, and it was over in a minute. Anyway, I'll call you back within the hour, okay? Must dash now.'

'Sure, call my mobile – I'm off home early today. Feel a bit tired after last ni…' Michael tried to stop himself, but it was too late.

'Why? What happened?'

'Oh, you know. Keys. Rain and keys. Stupid. Anyway, speak with you soon. Bye.'

Emma's panic had been tinged with a bit of confusion, but she had more important things to worry about now. She didn't know what to do – this was a disaster. The fear and adrenalin had smothered the bitter disappointment.

She couldn't let Simon down, but she certainly couldn't let her husband down either.

*

'Thanks for popping in, Julie. I wondered if I could change your roster this weekend and add in some overtime. Does that work for you?'

'Sure. I don't have anything planned, and the overtime always comes in useful. Anything important?'

'Mr Carter, Simon, had a trip planned this weekend. Going tomorrow by train and coming back Sunday, with two nights at a hotel. I thought I'd have time to accompany him, but other things have cropped up. He won't need any nursing as you know but just look out for any signs of confusion. Would you be able to manage that?'

'All okay with me. Simon's a really nice guy, and it sounds like fun. Where are we going?'

To her dismay, Emma felt a tiny pang of jealousy wash over her.

'The Cotswolds. Simon's booked to go to the Cotswolds. It'll be a hiking weekend – are you okay with a fair bit of walking?'

'Yup, no probs, especially if the weather's like this – it'll be great.'

'Good. Oh, and those flowers in reception came from Michael, my husband. By way of an apology – he promises to deliver one to you in person, too.'

'Awww, sweet. He needn't have done that. Hey, shall I go and see Simon and find out when and where we meet tomorrow?'

'I've already organised that. We were going to leave ... Sorry, I meant you'll leave here at two. I'll organise a taxi to the station.'

This was tougher than Emma had imagined. With the disappointment of how her weekend had turned out, she wanted to talk with Simon as soon as possible to explain everything. She'd catch him when he came back from his morning run.

*

'Simon, can I have a quick chat?'

'Of course. You look worried – have I done something wrong?'

'No, not at all. It's me that's done something wrong. Can we talk in your room?'

Emma felt miserable. As they walked up the stairs and back to his room, she imagined hiking in the Cotswolds on a sunny afternoon. Perhaps they'd be walking to a pub for lunch or heading to the hotel for dinner.

'Simon, I'm so sorry, but I can't join you this weekend. Everything's gone wrong, and I just can't make it.' She felt like crying.

'What weekend? When?'

'Oh. I was talking about tomorrow. We'd arranged to go to ...'

'Yeah, I know, I know. I was just playing silly buggers and pretending I'd forgotten, so I didn't have to hear the bad news. Sorry, I promised I'd stop doing that sort of thing. What's happened?'

'I'm terribly sorry for letting you down. I feel dreadful about this.' They were sitting on his bed facing each other, and she put her hand on top of his.

'My husband called unexpectedly. He wants me to go with him somewhere this weekend. It put me in a really difficult position, and I didn't know what to do. I'm terribly sorry.'

She looked at his dejected face and wanted to hug him. There was no way she could tell him where Michael was taking her, but the chances of them bumping into each other were zero. The Cotswolds was a huge area.

'It's not a difficult situation at all. He's your husband – of course you need to go with him. We'll try again another time.'

He put his arm around her and smiled. Emma looked at him and wondered how she could freeze this moment to play back at will. Time would always be their most precious commodity, and she hated the thought of this lost weekend.

While they sat on the bed, she told him she'd organised for Julie to take her place. Simon couldn't hide his surprise.

'But it just won't be the same. If you hadn't already told her, I'd have cancelled it. Does she definitely want to go?'

'Yes, she's really looking forward to it. I'll sort out a taxi to collect you both from here tomorrow after lunch. Two o'clock will give you plenty of time to make the train.'

Emma had been aching to tell Simon how she felt about him, but their combined disappointment and talk of taxis and trains had robbed her of the moment again.

*

Julie had left the wrapping around the beautiful bouquet. She'd take it home tonight and spend time arranging the flowers as the temporary centrepiece of her small apartment. There was an attached card which she opened. Michael had been totally out of order, but it was a generous gesture, and the promise of a personal apology certainly counted for a lot.

I'm so sorry. I don't know what came over me, but I promise it will never happen again.

The next time we see each other, I'll be a different person.

You're a sexy gorgeous woman, and I've thought about nothing but you this past week.

I'm aching for you now and can't wait to see you again.

Special wet kisses – exactly where you want them …

Michael xxx

Julie stared at the card and read it again, then looked at the flowers. Then she read the card one more time and heard herself mumbling.

'Oh. My. *God.*'

Mavis and her Zimmer frame were walking past reception as Julie repeated herself for the third time.

'It's so refreshing to see a young girl like you embracing the church. There's not many like you left, dear. It's disgusting what goes on in the world nowadays. You're a good girl.' Mavis beamed at Julie and her wide open mouth, then continued the epic journey to the lounge.

Reality, horror, and excitement all kicked in together. Julie put the card back in its envelope and picked up the flowers, walking quickly out of the building to leave both in the safety of her car. Her heart was beating out of her chest, and she'd gone bright red.

She'd only been back at reception a moment when Emma walked up to the desk.

'Simon's delighted to be going on a trip with you. He told me to thank ... Julie? Are you alright? You look very hot.'

'Sorry? Oh, yes. I mean no, I'm fine.'

'You sure you're okay? Come and see me if you need to take a break.'

Julie's face went from red to white.

In her office, Emma looked at the flowers. It was a sweet gesture, and she smiled to herself. Maybe it was for the best that she wasn't spending a weekend with Simon. It made her sad to even think about it, but she knew the damage it could cause her marriage.

The horrible letter Michael had left at their flat was so out of character. When he left her notes, they were always sweet and thoughtful. He was often a little naughty as well which she secretly enjoyed, though would swiftly deny if he ever asked her.

She opened the envelope stuck to the cellophane wrapping;

Hi
Sorry about the other day, it won't happen again.
Michael

Emma was crestfallen. In its own way, this hurt her more than his letter last week. She ripped the note up and threw it in the bin. The flowers were about to follow, but then she thought of Doreen. Doreen used to work in a florist's shop and loved arranging flowers. She held a class every now and then which a few of her fellow residents attended. The arrangements normally ended up gracing the lounge for everyone to enjoy.

If she hadn't already organised for Julie to go with Simon this weekend, she'd have called Michael and told him not to bother coming up to Orchard. Then she and Simon would have a beautiful time in the Cotswolds where she could at last tell him of her true feelings. Emma sighed heavily.

*

She watched them drive off in the taxi and felt like weeping. When Emma went to call Simon from his room, he'd held her shoulders, kissed her cheek, and told her he hoped she'd have a lovely weekend with Michael. She *knew* he meant what he'd said, and that made it worse.

She was mortified Julie would detect something between them as she'd said goodbye to Simon, but the girl seemed preoccupied and in a world of her own. It was probably just the responsibility of looking after Simon. If only Julie knew what a lucky woman she was to be spending a weekend with a man like him.

Julie was thinking about Michael, remembering him driving out of Orchard in his flashy new sports car. She'd now decided it suited him to perfection, whereas before he looked a total prat. She thought of the last part of his note and attempted to swallow, but there wasn't enough saliva in her mouth. She wondered if Emma knew what a lucky woman she was to be spending a weekend with a man like him.

*

Michael turned up promptly at four o'clock, parking his little rented Toyota next to Emma's car. He'd thought about hiring the big Mercedes convertible again, but it seemed brash and flashy now. He wanted to be humble and gentle but obviously not too subservient. He hadn't, after all, technically broken his marriage vows. In his current mental state, that detail was becoming increasingly important to him.

'Hey Em, you look gorgeous. Come out from behind that desk and give me a big kiss.' He beamed with genuine delight and a little nervousness, holding both arms outstretched in her direction.

'Sorry Michael, but I'm right in the middle of replying to a potential new resident. Can we meet in the lounge in half an hour or so?'

'Oh. Errr, sure. Is everything okay? We're going to have a fantastic weekend, babes. Promise.'

'Right. Look, I just need to concentrate on this – I'll see you in the lounge.'

Michael was stunned. And nervous. She couldn't have found out about Penny? Surely that was impossible? He felt his heavily-deodorised armpits begin to let him down as he walked out of her office. He needed to think about something else – engage with the residents and see how they were keeping. He saw two ladies arranging a selection of flowers into a large vase and went to talk with them.

*

The drive to Oxford was notable only for the silence, which was palpable. Michael had put the radio on after half an hour, but Emma had turned it off almost instantly.

'As long as I haven't done anything wrong, then I'm happy with the silence. I haven't done anything wrong, have

96

I?' He hated the undertones of pleading which seemed to be dribbling out of his mouth.

'I don't know, Michael. *Have* you done anything wrong?'

Michael wished he'd chosen a car with air conditioning. Even with his window wide open at 70 mph, he was still sweating. Christ, how the hell had she found out? He tried bartering silently with his God. If He could somehow bail him out of this shit unscathed, Michael faithfully promised to never look at another woman again, let alone touch one. Apart from Emma, obviously.

'Why are you mumbling to yourself?'

'Was I? Is it swelteringly hot in here, or is it just me?'

'It's windy and coolish, but we can solve that problem by you putting your window up. Take the next exit in a mile – the phone's telling me we'll have arrived at the hotel in twenty-five minutes.'

He'd take that – the exit *and* the comment. Anything was better than the executioner's silence. The not-knowing was bubbling up his tummy – an urgent toilet break was only moments away, however close they were to the bloody hotel. He had to get some sort of clarity.

'Look Emma, I'm not sure what I've done, love. This was going to be such a special weekend. Off to Le Manoir tonight. A hike in the Cotswolds tomorrow. A lovely old pub somewhere for dinner. I've said I'm sorry, babes – I've tried to make it better. And the flowers. And the note in my own handwriting specially delivered.'

'Oh, perrr-leassse. Give it a break.'

'What?'

'How times have changed, Michael. You used to write such sweet things – really made me feel cherished and wanted. I don't know why the hell you bothered.'

97

Michael was baffled. He'd spent a while composing that note, and the bloody florists in Covent Garden had charged him an extra hundred and fifty quid to have the damn thing delivered. *Does sir realise the impact of a note to a special loved one written in one's own hand,* and all that malarkey?

Christ, he'd even selected the sodding flowers himself – a rainbow-coloured selection of orchids and roses. Similar to the ones in the lounge at Orchard, now he thought about it, but his were much nicer.

Surely she couldn't have been upset by his sexy comment at the end? He thought she liked that sort of thing? He sighed and slumped back in the seat. At least he didn't need the loo anymore – she definitely wasn't on the Penny warpath.

It was still this damn letter he'd left at the flat, and that kind of irritated him. Michael still wasn't convinced he was in the wrong. He was a bit heavy with the wording, true, but wasn't a little jealousy a kind of compliment?

Feeling slightly vindicated, he breathed deeply to calm himself and then broke wind skilfully and silently, grateful he hadn't shut his window. A very final attempt was in order before they got out of the car.

'Okay, we're nearly there. Just time for one last apology. I can't get on my knees while I'm driving, but I'll do that when we're in the room. Then you can go for that offer, or you can just ignore me. Whatever happens, it's over. No wait – I meant the argument is over, not the marriage is over. Obviously.'

Emma wondered if the constant flying back and forth across the Atlantic had caused this madness. She looked at him; his face was red, and he was sweating. And a bit smelly too if she was honest. Perhaps it was a bug going around? Julie had looked the same way a few hours ago.

*

The hotel was great, and the meal was superb. It should have been the perfect recipe for a night of love, but Emma's mind was elsewhere, and Michael didn't seem that disappointed. They bid each other goodnight in a strangely formal manner and turned away to face their respective walls.

There was a four foot void of bedding and mattress between them, but Emma felt it could just as well have been the Atlantic Ocean, which it invariably was nowadays. Sleep was a long way off for her. She couldn't stop thinking about Simon and what he may be doing now, at one o'clock in the morning. She imagined Julie sharing a twin room with him because there'd been another cock-up with the booking, and this thought made her teeth grind.

Yet what right had she to be jealous? Julie was younger and more attractive than her, and single as well. Who could blame Simon if he grabbed the opportunity? He wasn't with anyone, so why not?

She was thinking like a teenager yet again, winding herself up until she wanted to scream or sob with frustration. And beside her lay Michael who she should be making love to right now, grateful for the weekend and the attempts to apologise. He was probably just incredibly busy when he wrote the note. At least he'd taken the trouble to go into the florist and not just order online.

If she weren't sure he'd be in a deep sleep by now, she almost felt it her duty to roll over towards him and let things happen. But in the darkness of the night, who could say if her mind wouldn't transpose Michael with Simon. The thought of making love to Simon made her shudder with pleasure and guilt. Thank God her husband was asleep.

Michael couldn't keep his eyes closed. It was as if he'd brushed his teeth with a treble espresso. They'd had a stunning meal and some superb wine in a highly romantic atmosphere, but all he could think about was Penny.

Every time Emma started to talk, his buttocks had clenched as he waited for her to accuse him of adultery. During the long breaks in conversation, his mind wandered to Penny and her friends. He felt himself blush as he imagined them laughing at him. Why hadn't he been able to do the business? More importantly, why the fuck had he thought to do the business in the first place?

He wanted to make love to his wife now. It wasn't a physical desire as much as a marital one. He wanted his marriage to be perfect again. He wanted to erase the last week from his mind and his life. He'd have rolled over and kissed Emma on the back of the neck if he wasn't certain she was in a deep sleep and would bat him away with the back of her hand.

*

Simon had felt tired after dinner at the hotel. Julie was happy to go to her room and watch catch-up TV on her laptop, so they'd bid each other goodnight at 10.30. She was a very pleasant and conscientious girl. She'd stayed on sparkling water throughout the meal while he had a couple of glasses of wine, then seen him safely to his room a floor above hers.

During the meal, Julie had asked if he'd ever met Emma's husband. He hadn't, but when he asked why, she'd seemed a little flustered and brushed it off. There was nearly *always* a reason when someone said, '*Oh, no reason.*'

He had no idea what the man looked like, though he presumed Michael was of similar age to Emma. Simon imagined he was good-looking – he'd have to be unless he was punching way above his weight.

He didn't like to think about Michael. He didn't understand him either. However difficult it was on a practical level, how could the guy not want to be with Emma every moment of the day?

Although tired, sleep had eluded him. His gaze became unfocused as he stared at the dim red digits of the television clock. What would Emma be doing now? He hoped she was asleep – he really did. The alternative was not palatable in his mind, and he screwed his eyes tight shut, hoping sleep would suddenly rescue him.

Then he thought about his death sentence and misery washed over him, just as an anaesthetist's liquid coils into the body, tracing and chilling the veins into blackness.

*

Emma was at her happiest when walking briskly in the fresh air, surrounded by beautiful scenery. They'd driven from the hotel after breakfast and started their hike just outside a hamlet of pretty cottages. Michael estimated it would be about seven miles to the next village and a break for a light lunch. After that, it was another eleven miles before arriving at a country pub for dinner, famous throughout the region for its hearty stews and potent cider. They'd already booked a taxi back to the hotel later that evening and would collect their hire car the next morning.

The pint of real ale at lunch had mellowed Emma. Not long into the afternoon walk, she was holding Michael's hand, though she couldn't remember when that had happened. The Cotswolds weather had been kind, and they both had their jackets tied around their waists, down to T-shirts and shorts.

The couple had talked mainly of their work. It was a default setting that felt the most comfortable, though both were secretly wondering how long their marriage had left to run. Emma pondered whether Michael was having an affair. His lifestyle certainly afforded him all the opportunities to conduct one, and he was still an attractive man. To her surprise and dismay, playing with this idea in her head made her realise she didn't actually care.

Perhaps that was due to her own feelings for Simon; she honestly didn't know. But of one thing she was certain – Emma longed to see him again.

*

Julie had never walked so far in her life. Her thighs and calves were aching, and she knew she was in for a whole world of pain when she woke the next day. Simon had been the perfect host, repeatedly asking if he was walking too fast or if she wanted a rest. She refused both, naturally – she *was* his carer, after all – there to help him when he felt tired or needed a rest. Fat chance!

She'd tried to join in with all the topics of conversation one goes through on an endless hike in the wilderness, but a lot of the time her mind had been on Michael. She'd now read the note enough times that she knew it in her sleep. He was a good-looking man anyway, but her constant fantasising had gradually turned him into an Adonis.

She remembered having crushes as a schoolgirl, but this was very different. At school, she'd fantasised about boys that hadn't hit on her and probably didn't even know she existed. This time, the man had made it very clear that he desired and wanted her. Julie wondered when she'd see him again and hoped it would be soon, even if it involved the presence of Emma. She blushed at the thought of it.

'We've gone a heck of a distance for a novice walker. You've done incredibly well. By my reckoning, we'll be at the pub for dinner in the next half an hour, maybe less. I've already booked a taxi back to the hotel for nine o'clock. Is that alright with you?'

'Not so much of the *novice walking*, you. My mum tells me I've been at it since I was ten months old.' Julie was glad to be back in the present. 'I could definitely do with a bite to eat, though. I might even have a glass of wine. Just the one, mind.'

'Sounds good to me. I guess you're not meant to be drinking while on duty? Only joking – you've been great company, and I don't kid myself I'd have been completely safe on my own.'

Julie looked up at him, smiled genuinely, then put her arm through his for the last few minutes of the journey.

*

The beautiful old pub was heaving, both inside and out. Michael had reserved a table for two in the garden, and they were led to their seats by the waitress. He asked what Emma wanted, and she suggested a gin and tonic. An innocuous enough request, but it sent Michael reeling back to that fateful flight two weeks ago.

'One of those, and I'll have a pint of the local bitter, please. I know your cider's famous, but it's just too strong for me.'

'Certainly, sir. Our gin of the week is Pink Pepper, and we recommend that with Aromatic tonic – it's delicious. Would you like one of those, madam?'

Michael's left knee started to involuntarily jiggle up and down – he hoped he wouldn't faint. He closed his eyes and saw the older blonde woman and Penny laughing at him, then all the flight attendants joining in. The male crew members were holding up their little fingers and wiggling them at him.

'Michael? Hello? Anyone there?'

'Sorry? Oh, right. What?'

'The lady's asking if you want the wine list.'

'Oh, yeah. Yes, thanks.' Michael had lost track of the last few seconds of his life.

'I'll come back in a mo with your drinks and take your order if you're ready. No rush.'

'What was all that about? You looked like you were going to faint. Are your blood sugar levels all to cock after that walk?'

Emma looked genuinely concerned and though still feeling queasy, Michael took some pleasure from that. She obviously cared for him a lot, and that wasn't a million miles away from loving someone, was it? He looked into her eyes and smiled. Delightfully, she returned his smile. Then her eyes moved to somewhere just above his head and refocused.

Emma went very red, very swiftly. She lifted her hand up slowly as if to wave. Michael waved back at her, though it felt rather silly.

'Julie. Simon. Fancy seeing you two here.' Emma stood up on legs that were shaking, and not just from nineteen miles of hiking.

Michael stood and turned around. Christ, that woman he'd been shirty with at Orchard – what was her name? And an older, decent-looking partner. Oh shit, the guy looked very fit too. Had she pointed him out as the man who'd insulted her? Fuck it. Maybe not, though – the guy looked happy enough.

'Emma! How fantastic to see you. What a weird coincidence.'

'Errr, hi. Simon, Julie. Hi there. How strange to see you guys here.' Emma's face had never felt so hot, and her heart was forcing its way up her windpipe. An introduction was unavoidable unless this was just some sort of sick dream and she was already back at the hotel.

'Michael, this is Julie who I think you've met already? And this is Simon Carter, who's staying at Orchard. As a resident, that is, so to speak.'

Michael stood up and went into his feeling-socially-awkward default mode.

'AHA. Oops, sorry, didn't mean to sound like Alan Partridge,' he said, trying to sound like Alan Partridge.

Emma rolled her eyes. She'd heard this a hundred times over the years – Michael *never* sounded like Alan Partridge. His thick Scouse accent even permeated through the *'Aha'* bit.'

'Lovely to see you again, Julie. It's safe to shake hands with me – I don't bite.'

Emma put a hand to her face and rubbed a sheen of sweat away. Fair play to Michael, though – it certainly felt as awkward as an Alan Partridge sketch.

Julie shook Michael's hand, turned bright red, and put on the most moronic grin – Emma didn't recognise her for a second.

'And Simon. I've heard so much about you. How are you? Well, under the circumstances, as it were. I mean, you look fine, just fine. As you should, of course.'

Emma assumed the moronic-grin look must be contagious.

'Hello, Michael. Yes, fine thanks and not dead yet. In fact, on a good day I can still get dressed and go to the loo on my own, *as it were.*'

He shook hands with Simon while looking at Emma. 'Your wife's so beautiful, and yet you apparently spend so little time with her. Why is that?'

There was a slight pause before Emma joined in the moronic-grin club, then all of them stared at their own shoes.

Divine intervention came in the form of a young, slightly overweight waitress.

'Will you all be sitting together?'

Simon now appeared to be the spokesman. 'We will, my dear. My three friends are temporarily reeling from severe social embarrassment, though this will soon pass. For now, if you'd be so kind as to bring us your finest bottle of shampoo and four glasses, that would be splendid.'

Simon took the gin and tonic bottle from the girl's tray and passed it to Emma, then took the pint of bitter and proceeded to down the entire contents in one long slug. He smacked his lips and wiped his mouth with the arm of his T-shirt.

The waitress had stopped where she was, frozen in time, holding the empty tray. Simon turned to her.

'And while you're here, can we have a bottle of your finest shampoo, please?'

'You've already said that, sir.'

'True, but if I hadn't said it again, we wouldn't get two bottles, now would we? But still only four glasses, obviously.' Simon smiled graciously at the waitress who clearly found him rather appealing if her eyes and the colour

106

of her cheeks were anything to go by. The girl semi-curtsied as she backed away from the table.

Emma, one of three people in the group still intently examining their shoes, bit her tongue and squeezed her lips tightly together. The giggle came out as a fart sound.

Simon turned to Michael. 'Was that you?'

9

Saturday 10 June to Sunday 11 June 2017

Unsurprisingly, the meal had been a fairly quiet affair. To Emma's great relief, Simon had not pursued his intimate line of questioning any further – she suspected he might have forgotten what he'd asked Michael. It was the first time in her experience that a reasonable amount of Champagne had not encouraged people to talk more.

Michael had been staggered by Simon on many fronts. What was a guy like him doing in a residential home? Sure, eventually he'd obviously need one, but his social behaviour suggested that was a while down the road yet. And boy, was he right to be furious with Emma for gallivanting off to Manchester – that wouldn't be happening again anytime soon.

He'd watched Emma carefully throughout the meal to see if there was any exchange of glances with Simon that would suggest they were already up to something. The man was constantly staring at her, but she didn't seem to be looking his way. Then he thought about Penny and winced – taking the moral high ground was very much more difficult now than a couple of weeks ago.

He was also furious with Simon for drinking his pint. There was something despicable about that sort of behaviour. However pathetic it sounded, Michael felt he'd lost a little bit of his mojo during that incident. Men didn't drink other men's pints. They just *didn't*.

And as if the evening wasn't weird enough already, Michael had become aware of Julie making eyes at him. At first, he thought he must be mistaken, but twice he'd felt her foot rubbing his shin. If there were any doubts left, they were well and truly extinguished when he went to the gents.

Julie was there as he came out, faking surprise at bumping into him. She pushed up against him, her chin on his shoulder, whispering her gratitude for the flowers. It jogged his memory, and he was starting to apologise when she'd put a finger on his lips and told him to save it for another time, and preferably one night soon.

As he stared at her, utterly lost for words, she told him how nice he smelt and then sauntered off to the ladies. More tragic than anything, he'd found himself watching her bottom as she walked off.

Michael sighed, shook his head and seriously contemplated punching himself in the groin.

*

Simon was feeling a little tipsy. Drink had often caused him to forget things, and this was one of those occasions. He remembered the waitress, and of course he remembered Emma, but the other young girl and the guy who looked a little bit like him were puzzling. He was enjoying the warmth of the late sun and the ambience of the busy pub, but he couldn't remember how he'd got here.

Strangely, this didn't worry him. He'd decided not to say anything and just listen to the others, but they weren't saying much either. As he studied the faces, it occurred to him that the young girl must be with the other guy. She was looking at him, and unless he was mistaken, there was passion and desire written in her eyes and over her pretty face.

He looked at Emma a few times simply because it was a pleasure and a delight. If the other two were a couple, it would make sense that he and Emma were as well, but he knew this wasn't the case. She seemed to be staring into the horizon, and he was unable to make eye contact with her.

It gave him an opportunity to study her features – he found her stunningly beautiful. He desperately wanted to kiss her. Surely he'd done that before?

*

The waitress approached the table. 'Guys, there's a taxi for Mr Carter.'

'Oh, that's me, excellent. Are we all ready to go?'

'That's just for us, Simon.' Julie stood up and put a hand on his arm.

'Really? Are you sure? What about Emma?'

'Michael and Emma are going back a bit later.'

'Oh, that's a pity. Would you both like to come with us?'

Emma smiled and was about to accept the offer, but Michael got there before her.

'No, we'll stay on until our own taxi arrives, thank you very much. Is that a problem for you, Simon?'

'Yes, it is, really. I wanted to go back with Emma. Would you like to come back with us, Emma?'

Michael swiftly stood up with his fists pressed on the table. 'Well of all the …'

This time, Emma was able to interrupt her husband.

'That's very sweet of you, but Michael and I should wait for our taxi. I'll see you tomorrow back at Orchard, okay Simon?' She smiled at him, not attempting to hide her reddening face.

'Bye-bye, Julie, take good care of Simon. Michael, let's go inside, it's getting chilly now.'

Michael moved towards her, and she grabbed his arm, dragging him into the pub.

*

Michael had finally managed to buy and drink a pint of his own by the time Emma came back from the ladies. Some of his mojo had returned, along with a nice little buzz.

'I don't fucking believe that guy – I should have punched his lights out. And he orders two bottles of Dom, and *I* get to pay for that *and* the whole damn meal, the bloody con merchant. Is he one of these guys we're going to have trouble getting residential fees from? Have you done financial due diligence on him, Em?'

Emma could no longer contain herself, buoyed by the alcohol and her heartache.

'You fool. You stupid fool. Is it really that long since you were a carer that you've forgotten all the signs of Simon's illness? Can't you tell he didn't have a clue where he was or what he was doing?'

'Oh really? So what about when he grabs my drink off the tray, *knowing* it's mine and drinking it in front of me. Then he asks why I don't see you more often, the cheeky sod. I should have given him a slap. That Champagne came to two hundred and seventy quid, for fuck's sake! Perhaps you told him I'm wealthy so I can afford it, eh?'

Emma couldn't remember ever feeling so angry.

'You're so wrong on every level. No, he didn't know it was your drink. As he walked up to us his expression changed. I know him well enough to realise something snapped in his mind.'

'I bet you do.'

Emma stood up, and her chair clattered to the floor.

'How dare you, you bastard. Dream on about giving him a slap or punching his lights out – you'd have been on the floor before you'd raised an arm. And no, you're *not* wealthy, Michael – not compared to Simon. He's a multi-millionaire, you idiot. If you'd looked in his file, you'd see his financial situation and how open he is about it. You'll get your lousy money back. Couldn't you see how totally confused he was before he left? Damn you, Michael. Damn you to hell!'

The pub had gone eerily quiet as Emma stormed out of the door, slamming it shut behind her. Michael jumped up out of his seat and ran after her, but two rather large local men stood in front of door and politely asked him to calm down and return to his seat. They suggested he have another drink and leave the lady alone.

As Michael was arguing, one of the men's companions went outside to find Emma. She was leaning against a table, sobbing. The woman put an arm around her.

'It's alright love, it's okay. Are you far from here? Can we give you a lift?'

Between sniffles, Emma told her they had a taxi arriving soon. As they were talking, the cab pulled into the car park, and the woman helped Emma into it.

Back in the pub again, Michael was still arguing with the men – the woman spoke to one of them, and they all sat back down at their table.

Michael was just in time to see the taxi's tail lights disappear down the road.

*

Julie was now in full carer mode. Simon was a little agitated and having problems remembering the past day. He initially didn't know who Julie was.

She stayed with him in his room until well after midnight, by which time he'd been asleep for nearly an hour. She'd sent Emma texts to keep her posted and was prepared to stay on the sofa in Simon's room, but Emma was confident that now he'd been asleep for a while it would be okay. Even so, she was relieved and grateful that Julie would be setting her alarm at 3 a.m. and 6 a.m. to go and check on him.

Emma said she'd be at their hotel by 7.30, so the three of them could have breakfast together, then they'd all take the first train back to Cambridge. Julie wondered what would happen to Michael but didn't dare ask. She blushed at the thought of how provocative she'd been with him earlier that night, but he'd started it.

She could see a car crash coming in the distance, but her heart and other parts were secured with a six-point racing safety harness, or so she hoped.

*

Michael was fortunate their hotel had a vacant room. It came as no surprise to him when his room card didn't operate the lock, and his knocking went unanswered. His suitcase sitting in the corridor outside the room had been a big clue.

He'd never seen his wife so angry, and the entire contents of a florist's shop would not placate her this time. Women were very strange people, and he didn't think he'd ever understand them, especially the promiscuous but admittedly pretty Julie.

A massive cloak of self-loathing wrapped itself around him. How on earth could he be thinking about one of his wife's junior colleagues while his marriage was simultaneously falling apart?

The answer was probably because he couldn't remember the last time he'd had sex. Well, sex with someone other than himself. Penny didn't count for obvious and best-forgotten reasons. And as for Emma? Well, he couldn't really remember the last time.

He sat on the bed in his new room – considerably pokier than the one he'd been ejected from, yet irritatingly more expensive due to the lack of advance booking. The cost made him think about the Dom Perignon and the meal he'd been landed with, and that made him think about Simon bloody Carter. Fit and good-looking, multi-millionaire Simon.

He knocked back the miniature brandy from the room-bar, and his self-loathing increased. How the hell could he be jealous of a man with Alzheimer's?

In a fit of frustration and misery, he threw the little bottle hard against the wall with all his might. It bounced feebly off a framed print and fell to the carpet.

Michael turned into the pillow and wept.

*

Simon's fogginess was beginning to lift. He decided he was definitely at his happiest when Emma was with him. He found himself wanting to go for a run with her after breakfast, but he knew she wouldn't be able to keep up with him. He wanted to run faster than ever today – faster than he'd ever run in his life.

He had an inkling he'd messed up badly yesterday but had no idea what he'd said or done. It was so desperately frustrating.

'Why do I remember the things I don't want to remember, but the things I'm desperate to recall just evaporate?'

Julie stood up from the table. 'I'll just go and get my stuff. Be down at reception in fifteen minutes?'

Emma smiled at her. 'Sure, see you then – maybe half an hour. The taxi's not here until nine o'clock.'

She turned to Simon and put a hand over his. 'It's not going to be easy, but if we live each day one at a time, it'll work out. You know the rules – you tattooed them on your arm.'

'It would be so much easier if that were true.'

'I don't understand. You know it's always best if each day is just a new day, to be enjoyed to the fullest?'

'Oh, I know that, and you're absolutely right, but you said '*we*' – 'If *we* live every day one at a time.' That would be very different.'

She still had her hand on his and gripped it tighter. 'I *will* be there, Simon – we'll both be at Orchard together. I'm not going anywhere; I promise you.'

She looked at him, and it took all her willpower not to lean over the breakfast table and kiss him deeply. Had she known he was feeling the same way, her world would have changed forever at that very moment.

'Your husband was there last night, wasn't he? I remember four of us at the table. Shouldn't you be with him now? I'm sorry – I don't remember his name.'

Emma sighed. 'Yes, Michael was there, but no, I shouldn't be with him now, and I won't be. You, Julie, and I are heading back home in a few minutes. Does that sound okay?'

'It sounds good, but what's Michael going to do? I don't think he likes me, does he?'

'I think he's jealous of you. There was a time not so long ago when I thought you were both very similar men. I now know I was very wrong. I don't know what he's going to do, and I don't really care.'

Julie had walked up behind Emma's chair as she continued, 'The way I feel at the moment, Michael is history.'

10

Thursday 15 June to Friday 16 June 2017

The routine at Orchard had brought Simon back from his confusion at the weekend. He'd seen less of Emma as she focused her time on all of the residents, but enough to realise he hadn't felt this way about a woman before.

Admittedly, memory was no longer his strong suit, but even when engaged and first married to his ex-wife, he couldn't remember experiencing such powerful feelings. Women before and after her were less memorable, and he couldn't remember their names. There weren't that many – of that he was sure.

Crushes and dates while at school were ironically still crystal clear, but he knew that was the nature of his disease. Nowadays, he often wished he knew a lot less about his problem – it was impossible not to be consumed by it at times.

Running was his answer. There was something about the isolation which he was unable to replicate anywhere else. He was at his happiest when he felt his heart and lungs working hard and the endorphins flooding his system. It was his purest form of escapism.

The swimming had been invigorating, and he enjoyed it, but he wasn't good enough to get the workout he craved. Another problem was the necessity for a member of staff to be present whenever anyone used the pool. He could see the logic when elderly residents were in the water, but it seemed a wee bit excessive for a proficient swimmer like him who was never out of his depth. Still, the rules were the rules.

Simon wanted another weekend away soon but feared Emma would turn down the offer. He was sure she liked him and enjoyed his company, but she seemed pre-occupied and a little distant at the moment. Looking for an activity to keep him occupied, he studied the notice board to see what was on offer. Tomorrow morning there was a trip organised in the Orchard minibus to the Botanic Garden in Cambridge. He'd never been there, and it sounded interesting.

There were seven places available, and after checking that Emma was also going, he decided to tell the activities organiser to count him in. There was apparently a nice café there where the group would have lunch before enjoying the gardens. It was subject to good weather of course, but the forecast was in their favour.

Having decided on tomorrow's plans, he put his running clothes on and went downstairs for his first session of the day. On the edge of the car park at his regular starting point, he was about to press the timer on his watch when he heard his name called out.

'Simon. Darling, it's me.'

He turned and saw a blonde-haired woman wearing a tight-fitting white dress. It was as if she'd come straight off a tennis court, but the very high heels on her immaculately white shoes suggested otherwise. She was tanned, tall, and rather beautiful. The woman had that look about her which cost a lot of money and took an excessive amount of time.

He wondered if it may be another Simon who she was calling to, but then distant strands of recognition tugged at his memory. He didn't remember her name, but as she walked towards him, it came flooding back in all its technicolor gore.

It was the last girlfriend he'd had before leaving London. She'd started accusing him of being creepy and weird, and it had really hurt. When he discovered the worst from his doctor, it was her he thought of first. How was he going to break it to her, and how would she react.

He'd decided to put the news on the backburner and try and hold things together. She was the most attractive woman he'd ever dated, and he often wondered what she saw in him. The obvious answer was that he was reasonably well off, but he'd always thought she was in a similar position. It was always the impression she gave him. In the end, she'd unceremoniously dumped him via a text message.

She embraced him and kissed him hard on the lips. Her heavily intoxicating perfume took him back vividly to their times together, and he wondered obtusely if scent could help with memory. As these thoughts filtered through, her mouth moved from his lips, and he felt her breath on his ear.

'You're just as gorgeous as ever, Simon. I've missed you.'

Those first couple of weeks after the text message, he'd have given anything to hear those words. He wondered why they had no effect now. And why he wasn't holding her in his arms and kissing her back?

No matter how much of this scent he inhaled, he wasn't going to remember her name. She moved back and held his shoulders, her perfectly symmetrical face beaming at him.

'You have no idea what a difficult man you were to find. I've missed you so much. Are you going to invite me into your new home? I mean house. Place.' She flicked her fringe away from her eyes, and Simon remembered the mannerism perfectly.

'Well, I'm just going for a run, actually. I'll be about forty-one and a half minutes, or forty if I'm very lucky. Any less than that, and I'll be ecstatic.'

Her smiled melted a little, and she stepped back but regained her composure swiftly. Towards the end of their relationship, she'd had some experience of this sort of behaviour.

'Well, let's hope you come back ecstatic, sweetie. We used to have a lot of *ecstatic* moments together. Do you remember them? Oh, I didn't mean to suggest that you wouldn't remember them, obviously. I just meant ...'

Simon smiled and waved, then pressed a button on his watch and was gone.

*

'Could I speak to the manager, please? My name's Victoria Orpington-Wells.'

'Yes, that's me – how can I help you?'

'My partner, Simon Carter, is staying here with you, and I'd like to know how he is – how he's been keeping. It's come as a huge shock to me that he's staying in a ... a place like this.'

'I see. I'm a little confused, Vicky. May I call you Vicky?'

'No, you may not. My name's Victoria and *only* Victoria, but Ms. Orpington-Wells will suffice, thank you.'

Emma wondered if Vicky had a similar sense of humour to her so-called partner, and that this was just some kind of hilarious prank. In the second it took her to observe Ms. Orpington-Wells from coiffure to heels and make a judgement call, she decided this was probably not the case.

'I can put your mind at rest. Mr Carter is in very good hands. As for his well-being, I believe you saw him sprint off from the car park a moment ago? You mention you're his partner, so I guess you must be an accountant, too? I thought he'd given up his partnership of the firm?'

Victoria bristled – a constant state to those who had the dubious pleasure of knowing her. Emma wondered if the make-up might crack and leave a mess on the floor. This was a trifle harsh, so she attempted to retract her claws and smiled politely at the increasingly irate woman.

'Not business partner! We were only weeks away from being engaged. To be married.' She turned around and peered into the lounge. 'This place is full of old people – what the hell is my fiancé doing here?'

'COW.'

'I beg your pardon? How dare you!'

'I meant if you'd married and kept your surname, sorry, surnames. Carter-Orpington-Wells. COW.'

Victoria's lips formed a perfect bright red circle as her jaw dropped. Emma wondered if she was going for the lipstick, but surely there wasn't room for any more?

'I repeat, what is my Simon doing here?'

'Well a lot of the time he's running. He's a very good runner, you know.' Emma dialled up her most demure smile.

Victoria remained unmoved and definitely unimpressed. 'I suppose I'll have to wait until he gets back. He said he'll be forty minutes.'

'Probably forty-one and a half today. Maybe a few seconds less. He's normally a little quicker on his evening run.'

'What? Whatever. I'd sit in here and wait, but there's quite a strong smell.'

'I'd noticed that.'

'I think I'll go and wait in my car.'

'That should solve it.'

'Pardon?'

'Umm, solve the problem of where to sit while you're waiting for Mr Carter?' A stiff smile full of teeth this time.

As Ms. Orpington-Wells turned and minced out of the door, Emma's eyes focused precisely where nearly all men's attention would have been. It was a depressingly reasonable sight.

For her age.

Emma put an elbow on the reception desk and cupped her chin. She tapped the table rhythmically with the claws of her other hand.

*

'Simon. *Simon.*' Victoria leapt out of the car and wobbled on her heels. She changed tack and sauntered up to him. Just about to embrace him again, she abruptly froze.

'Oh. You're all sweaty. Perhaps you could have a shower and then maybe take me out to lunch? Somewhere away from here?'

Simon held his wrist up at Victoria's face.

'*Yes.* Look at that – forty minutes and fifty-eight seconds. I've cracked it.'

'It's a plastic watch. Where's your Patek Philippe Nautilus sports watch?'

Simon was confused. He wiped his forehead with his palm and flicked the perspiration on the ground, some of which splattered on Victoria's shins and stilettos. 'I don't remember that. Perhaps I gave it to that cat's home near where I used to live?'

122

'*What?* That was forty grand's worth of watch. Are you insane?'

'Not all the time. That sounds like a lot for a watch – are you sure? How do you know what it's worth?'

Victoria flushed slightly. 'Oh, well I looked it up on a website. I was worried you might be under-insuring it. Anyway, never mind about that. I tried to call you, but your phone was off. Then I went round to your place, and there was someone else living there. You sold the house – that must have gone for a lot of money, Simon.' Victoria tried to disguise a grimace as she put a hand on his wet face.

'Yes, I guess it did. I can't remember what it sold for. Emma would know – do you want me to ask her for you?'

She folded her arms in an attempt at indifference, Simon's sweat now smearing the side of her dress.

'Don't be silly – it's none of my business. Just curious, you know? Who's Emma?'

'Oh, she's the boss. I'm sure you'd get on well with her. Let's go in, and I'll ask her for you – she's bound to know that sort of thing.'

Simon jogged to the main door and opened it.

'*No*. No *wait*. Simon. Siiimon.' The heels were now a significant hindrance.

'Emma, how much did my house sell for? My friend wants to know. I feel terrible, but I can't remember her name.'

'Really? Are you sure you want to give out that information? Her name's Victoria, by the way, but she likes to be called … Ah, Ms Orpington-Wells – hello again. Mr Carter was just telling me you wanted details on the sale of his London property?'

'No, of course not. Simon, please, I was just saying how surprised I was that you'd sold your beautiful home and simply vanished off the face of the earth. And leaving your company, too – it was such a shock. As I said, it took me ages to find you.'

Emma's eyes narrowed. 'I imagine it might have been a lot easier to simply hire a private detective?'

Victoria looked rather startled at this trumped-up manager's telepathic skills. 'Don't be absurd. Someone at your firm told me where you were, Simon. Your partner.'

Emma was unable to resist. 'Another partner? I'm getting confused now.'

Simon looked at the two women bickering. They were both lovely to look at – it was like watching a tennis match, but with words instead of balls. He thought Victoria looked lovely and very professional, but Emma was in a different league. She seemed to be winning too, whatever game it was they were playing.

'I'm going to have a shower. Will you still be here for lunch, Vicky? It's great food – they have an award-winning chef.'

'It's Victoria – you *know* you've only ever called me Victoria. *Everyone* calls me Victoria, sweetie.'

'But Emma just said you like to be called Ms. Orpington-Wells?'

Simon couldn't be absolutely sure, given the intricacies of women and the time bomb in his brain, but he thought he might just be joining in their game.

*

'The food's fine, but it's hardly what we used to eat at restaurants in the city. Are you sure you wouldn't like to have a coffee and perhaps a Calvados at a wine bar somewhere? You always used to have a Calvados at the end of your meal.'

'You're probably right, but I don't think I do that anymore. Besides, it's Thursday today – look at the huge sign on that wall – *Thursday 15th June 2017*. On Thursday afternoons I play in a crib league. There's only six of us in it, but I'm in second place at the moment, and this month's prize is a hairdressing voucher. I think I could win it with a bit of luck. If I do, I'm going to give it to Emma.'

Victoria involuntarily rolled her eyes. 'Simon, I went online and had a look at the cost of this place. You realise you're paying seventy-eight thousand pounds a year for a room? To spend your days with people old enough to be your parents? Or your grandparents, for fuck's sake.'

'I think I'm actually paying ninety-eight thousand – I've got one of the rooms for couples. Emma said I could have it for the single occupancy rate, but I didn't think that was fair.'

'Oh my God, are you insa … I mean … I mean that's just ridiculous – ninety-eight thousand pounds a year? Think what lovely holidays we could go on with that, sweetie. Don't you remember when you took me to Paris? It was so romantic, darling. Do you remember when we went to that jewellery shop on the Place Vendome. When we looked at those incredible diamond rings? Surely you remember, sweetheart?'

She leaned in close until their faces were touching. Simon noticed some of the residents watching and felt a little embarrassed. He also saw Emma in the entrance to the dining room. She seemed to have a slight smile on her face and winked at him. He winked back and grinned, then leaned away from Victoria.

'I can't remember going to Paris. Are you sure it was with me?'

She looked shocked and tried to move closer, but he put his hands in the air. 'My fellow residents are looking at us. Do you think you could sit back in your seat? Sorry, but I don't want to upset them. Sometimes they get upset very easily.'

Victoria looked at the room and immediately saw Emma in the doorway, smiling at her and waving with the fingers of one hand. She scowled and turned back to Simon.

'Of course they get upset easily, darling, they're all loopy. And you're *not*. Please sweetie, why don't you think about getting a place somewhere, and I'll come and live with you? It'll be perfect, just like the old days.'

'These are my friends, and I like living here. Why would I want to move?' Simon was having a joyous moment of complete clarity. How could someone so outwardly attractive be so inwardly ugly? He knew he was being naughty but couldn't help it.

'I'm still confused, though – do I call you *Vicky* or *Ms Orpington-Wells*? You told Emma it was the latter, but I'm sure I used to call you *Vicky*, didn't I?'

Victoria was trying very hard to maintain her composure whilst still attempting to look impossibly alluring. 'It's *Victoria*, darling – *Victoria*.'

'Oh. And I definitely can't call you *Vicky*?'

Emma had moved across the dining room and was walking up behind the woman in white, now within earshot of the conversation.

'You've *never* called me that, Simon. How would you like it if I started calling you *Sime*? Would you like that?'

'Hmmm. Well, if you didn't like *Simon*, you could always call me *Mr Carter*, perhaps? And I could call you *Ms Orpington-Wells*?'

'Oh Simon, what's the matter with you? What's going on in your head, babes? Whatever it is you think's wrong, we can beat it. We can beat it together. You're going to be alright, darling, trust me.'

Simon was never going to be alright but boy, did he feel clear-headed at the moment.

'I think I remember that jewellery shop in Paris.'

'There, you see? I knew you would.' Victoria's matching white teeth were on full display as she put her hand over his. It seemed a shame to ruin the expression, but Simon felt compelled to continue.

'I'm confused, though. I don't wear rings. Why would you be buying me a diamond ring?'

The perfect, shiny red lips moved over the dazzling teeth. Simon noticed Emma put a hand over her own lips and screw her eyes up.

'It wasn't quite like that. I thought we were going there so we could look at engagement rings.'

'Who for?'

She took her hand away and looked at Simon in utter frustration. The lamb casserole remained untouched on her plate, the salad having been rearranged with a leaf or two now missing.

Simon looked up at Emma and smiled. 'Hello. Are the crib tables set up, or shall I go and sort it out?'

Victoria swivelled around and stared at her with undisguised hostility.

'All sorted, thanks. Brian's not playing today, so Julie's going to take his place. Hello Ms Orpington-Wells. Did you enjoy lunch?' Emma looked down at the barely touched plate. 'Oh, was there something wrong with the casserole?'

Victoria stood up and dropped her napkin over the plate. 'I'll be going now, Simon. Would you see me out, please?'

'Yes, of course. Hold tight, Emma, I'll be back in a jiffy. Just saying goodbye to Vicky.'

In reception, Simon immediately recognised Michael, even though he looked very different in a dark navy suit and tie. He was standing at the desk talking to Julie.

'Hello, Michael, how's it going?'

'Oh. Hello, Simon, I'm fine thank you.' Michael had no interest in how Simon was, so didn't see the point in asking. He did, however, *really* want to know how the woman was; the one with her arm linked in Simon's.

'Hello, I'm Michael. I don't believe I've had the pleasure?'

Simon's manners automatically cut in. 'Oh, I'm sorry, this is Vic ...'

Victoria didn't let him finish. She'd already taken in the Versace suit, heavy gold Rolex and expensive Italian loafers. She quickly removed her arm from Simon and extended her manicured hand.

'I'm Victoria. It's lovely to meet you, Michael. Are you visiting someone?'

'No, no. Not at all. I'm a director of the company that owns the care home group. Lovely to meet you, too.'

'*Kerching,*' thought Victoria.

'*Perfect,*' thought Simon.

'*Bollocks,*' thought Julie.

'I was just saying goodbye to Simon, an old friend of mine. He's rushing off for a game of cards, aren't you dear?'

'I most certainly am. Oh, Michael, do you want me to tell Emma you're here?'

'No, that's fine; don't trouble yourself. So are you a tennis fan, Victoria? You look as if you are. I went to the final last year – Murray just blew Raonic out of the park.

Fantastic game. Great seat, too. Right next to the Royal Box.'

Simon heard Julie huff loudly as he headed for the games room.

*

It was a perfect midsummer day for visiting the Botanic Garden. Seven residents and three carers enjoyed a lunch on the tables outside the café, Simon having managed to sit next to Emma, or possibly the other way around.

After lunch, the two men in wheelchairs decided to stay at the table and have another glass of wine. They had a never-ending supply of war stories to share with each other. Both were in their mid-90s and had fought throughout the Second World War. However, one was in the army whilst the other served in the RAF. They could never agree on which service played the key role in winning the war.

Hayley, one of the newest members of the Orchard team, was entrusted with looking after the war heroes, just to make sure it was a clean fight. Maddy, who was beginning to develop a sixth sense, led the four ladies away to some of the extraordinary and exotic conservatory plants nearby. This left Emma to take Simon for a stroll around the extensive and stunning grounds.

They walked away from the café, and Simon linked his arm in Emma's. It was a strange role-reversal of tradition, and one which he found rather odd for a moment. Not that memory could serve him well ever again, but he didn't recall putting his arm through a woman's at any time in his life. It felt passive as if the woman was somehow caring for the man.

The thought pierced his heart and took his breath away. He was vaguely aware of Emma asking him something.

'They make a handsome couple, don't they – Michael and Ms Orpington-Wells?'

'Well, they're both attractive, but I don't know about the *couple* bit. I imagine his wife might have something to say about the matter.'

'Oh, she kept well out of the way; I can assure you. I knew exactly why Michael had bothered to come up from London, and it made my blood boil. I was thinking of how I could make his stay as unpleasant as possible and then bingo, along came your fiancée – perfect.'

'I couldn't swear to it, but I'm ninety nine per cent certain I wasn't engaged to Victoria. So why did Michael come to Orchard?'

'Possibly two reasons. One I'm certain about and the other is with the jury at the moment. He primarily came to check your financial records. Slightly ironic, given what your non-fiancée seemed keen to find out.'

They looked at each other and grinned. Simon took his arm out of Emma's and put it lightly around her shoulders.

'Is he allowed to do that? Look at my private files?'

'When you gave me all that information, it went straight into your file. Michael has legal access to any of the residents' files. Because he got lumbered with the bill for Champagne and dinner when we were in the Cotswolds, he thinks you might have financial problems. His reason for looking will be that he's concerned about your ability to fund your future residential care.'

'Oh. I see.' Simon's smile had dropped as a frown spread across his face. 'But surely everything's fine on that front? My house sale and my savings?'

'Simon, you could *buy* Orchard Care Home, live there for free and still have enough left over to pay the staff for years. The sale of your house brought in a huge amount, but not as much as the sale of your business. To use a very blasphemous expression, you have more money than God.'

Simon's face brightened, and he laughed, then his arm held Emma tighter as he kissed her on the head. She looked down at the grass and pledged a week's salary for the lack of a blush. It wasn't enough.

'Hey, hold on. That means I didn't pay for the meal. And … Oh, shit, I ordered two bottles of shampoo as well. Oh, hell. Can you take funds out and pay Michael please, and tell him I'm really sorry. I can't believe I did that,' Simon muttered to himself – he was genuinely shocked. This had definitely never happened before.

'Forget it. His ego wouldn't allow him to accept the money, anyway. You should probably sack me as your bank manager. Michael and I were in a heated argument about your financial status. To shut him up I inadvertently mentioned you were a multi-millionaire. It somewhat deflated him, and I suspect he's actually come here to discover just how rich you are.'

Simon stopped walking and looked at Emma. 'Oops.'

Emma looked up and saw his eyes sparkling in a mischievous way. She put an arm around his back, and they carried on strolling, seemingly with not a care in the world. In a dim and distant past, she could remember walking like this. It felt like such a long time ago. It thrilled her to think that people would assume they were a couple.

'What was the other reason you thought Michael came up for?'

'Let's call it intuition, and I think Victoria may already have thrown a spanner in the works, but I think my husband and Julie might be having an affair.'

'Are you kidding? Where did you get that idea? And how come you're not mad with rage?'

'Well, I'm not sure I'm right for starters, but I'm also not sure I even care anymore.'

They both stopped and looked at each other again. As Simon searched her eyes, she felt the tingle of imminent tears. He wrapped his arms around her, and she let her head rest on his chest.

It was painful and beautiful, and quite the saddest and happiest moment of her life.

As they moved on, hand in hand, Emma told him of a feature in the garden she thought he'd like. The area appeared to be overgrown, but then they came upon some stone steps which led to a narrow path. She led the way, still holding Simon's hand.

They passed rare foliage in the soil between the stones of an ancient rockery, little signs proudly announcing their identities in English and Latin. Further around the pathway, they came across a semi-circular wooden bench. It nestled between the overhanging tree and bushes, a few feet below ground level.

They sat down close together, and Simon put his arm around her again. It was almost a magical place and offered them more than a degree of privacy from above.

'I wish I could know when I'm going to have forgetful moments, and how long they were going to last. Then I'd make sure I was on my own, or at least not near you.'

'Don't be silly. I love ... I mean I really like being with you as much as possible, however you're feeling. It doesn't matter to …' But Simon had put a hand gently on her lips. He needed her to hear what he had to say.

'Let me finish. When I'm my normal self, like now, I'd try and make sure I was with you all the time. Well, all the time you could manage while still looking after everyone else. I want to make plans to go away with you again. Not just a weekend in the distant future, but lots of times. Lots and lots of times until I can no longer behave the way I do now.'

The lump in Emma's throat was growing.

'Please Simon, stop talking like this. Everything's going to …'

'I'm nearly finished. Everything's *not* going to be alright, Emma. That's why I wanted to say something while it's crystal clear to me.' Simon put his hands on her face, and his eyes began to tell her.

'But before that, I want to do this one little thing first.'

Emma closed her eyes as she leaned towards his lips.

'Sorry, Emma, is that you down there? The Major's having a coughing fit. Maddy's with him now. She told me to come and fetch you.'

*

Hayley was a little shaken and left Maddy to drive the mini-bus back. Emma was holding an oxygen mask to the Major's face, but his colour had returned, and he was going to be fine. The ladies were taking it in turns to tell Simon the adventure, while Raymond, the RAF aerial photographer, had taken it all in his stride and was sound asleep.

Back at Orchard, everyone was settled down in the lounge until dinner was served, though there was more to talk of than usual. Simon ran upstairs and was in the car park a few moments later in his shorts, attempting to break the 41-minute barrier again.

Emma and Maddy stayed in the lounge while Julie sat behind the reception desk. Emma could see her as she sat with the Major and Raymond, who'd reverted back to who Winston Churchill was more grateful to in 1945, the Army or the RAF.

Emma could spot a scowl from a hundred paces, and Julie was less than half that distance. She wondered if it might be her or Victoria that was the cause of this angst, but she knew it was far more likely to be Michael. Things were getting very complicated.

She saw Simon flash across the window on his circuit, and her mouth went dry as she thought how near they'd been to something very special. She balled her hands tightly, closed her eyes, and sighed, loudly enough for the Major to ask if she was alright.

Yes, she was fine. Never better, thank you. Her life was falling apart, and the man she loved was going to slowly disappear in front of her eyes, but she was okay. She had to be, and she would be.

After making sure everyone was comfortable, she went to reception to ask Julie how everything was going.

'Everything's alright – nothing to report, really. Who was that woman yesterday? The one in the tennis dress?

'That'll be Victoria – an ex-partner of Simon's.'

'Oh. Is she going to be a regular visitor? Just curious, as nobody's come to see him since that young girl a while back.'

'No, I somehow don't think she'll be coming here again.'

Julie seemed satisfied with the answer.

Emma turned and walked to her office. 'Or Michael,' she said under her breath.

11

Thursday 15 June to Sunday 18 June 2017

It was lust at first sight. She'd given him her phone number in the car park by calling his mobile – he was terrified Emma would see the exchange of a piece of paper, put two and two together, and come up with precisely four.

He could see Julie craning her neck behind the reception desk too, with a nigh on full view of this delicate manoeuvre. Quite why he was concerned about what she might think was a little confusing for him, but then he remembered his second reason for coming up to Orchard that day ...

The first reason had produced a very disappointing result. He was so hoping that Emma had been exaggerating, well downright lying actually, about Simon Carter's finances.

On the train up to Cambridge he was playing out a routine in his head involving breaking the difficult news to Emma – so sad and all that jazz. It looks like we'll regrettably have to ask the local authorities to find dear Simon another place to stay, obviously commensurate with his unfortunate financial circumstances.

In less than ten minutes of delving into Mr Carter's files, he'd discovered more than twenty million reasons why the man was going nowhere. Armed with this depressing news, he'd sought out the company of young Julie as consolation, to see if she was just as keen on him as she'd been the previous week.

He'd seen the logistic pitfalls of this idea, the closeness of Emma's office, and the reception desk being the main one. He'd hoped one of them would be somewhere else, and his luck was in. When Julie enthusiastically confirmed his wife was currently in the dining room, the day looked as if it wasn't going to be a complete disaster.

He had little time to beat about the bush so used her initial invitation last weekend as an opening gambit, suggesting they meet at the bar next to Cambridge station the following evening. The noise of the dining room door opening had made him jump – he feared it was Emma.

How wrong he had been.

The relief that Carter wasn't with the delicious vision had made him weak at the knees. Whether it was wishful thinking or not, this blonde bombshell seemed to be flirting with him. He couldn't take his eyes off her. Even Julie seemed a little transfixed.

Michael had no time to cancel the date with Julie. As he jumped into his car after seeing Victoria drive off, he thought to go back and sort things out but convinced himself she'd know he wasn't really serious about tomorrow night.

He could see that Emma had now come into the reception area, so another reason not to go back. If Emma wanted to see him, she could come out to the car now. He had no reason to speak with her after the disappointment of Simon's bank accounts.

*

Following a plethora of texts and calls, Victoria had come to see him in London the following weekend. They'd met at a bar in Piccadilly, and he couldn't help but notice the size of her bag – it definitely looked big enough to be an overnight one. A splendid meal in opulent surroundings was followed by a nightcap at his apartment, and the bag did indeed turn out to be an overnighter.

The woman was insatiable – he'd never known anything like it. Three long weekends with Victoria had left him not knowing if he was coming or going. Trips to the States were cancelled as he spent from early Fridays to late Mondays in his flat, barely venturing outdoors. It was the first time in years that he'd put pleasure before business.

During that time, he sent Emma just one text, enquiring how she was. A pang of guilt had hit him when Victoria chose to wear a perfume that he was sure Emma had worn at one time.

There was no reply.

To all intents and purposes, his marriage was over, yet mulling it over one day in the office, it cracked him up. Worst of all, he couldn't deal with the thought of Simon Carter with his wife. Although he knew their time together was severely limited, it didn't seem to help.

The irony hit him hard. Most of his working life had been dedicated to caring for sick and elderly people, yet now he longed for someone to succumb to their own dreadful illness.

He hated himself to the core.

*

Julie had waited for over an hour at the Station Tavern. On the short train ride down to Cambridge, she'd wondered if this would be a wasted journey, but she had to find out for herself.

Everything had been going just as she'd hoped. Michael had smelt gorgeous as he leaned over the desk and kissed her face, and he looked so good in a suit. Then that cow had appeared on Simon's arm, and Michael's tongue had fallen out of his mouth. It was suddenly as if Julie didn't exist anymore.

She watched them talking in the car park for a few minutes – the woman had called his mobile, so now he had her number. Michael had looked around nervously to see if anyone had noticed, presumably terrified of Emma catching them. It was so pathetically obvious what they were doing that she'd actually snorted out loud.

Then they'd leaned towards each other for a polite goodbye kiss, but the slut had put her hand around the back of his neck and their faces touched for far longer than necessary. Emma had come out of the dining room as the whore drove away. A shame it hadn't been a minute or so previously, just to cement the end of their marriage.

Having arrived a few minutes early, Julie had waited at the bar before eventually taking her drink, the second large white wine, to a table close to the main door. When he was half an hour late, she gave him a final fifteen minutes, and when that came, she did the same again. She didn't even have his number to call him, unlike that damn woman he was probably with now.

The short train journey home seemed to take much longer than normal. If a guy had hit on her at that point, she'd have seriously considered going along with it. Why did that sort of thing never happen when it was really needed?

Life was just like Victoria Orpington-Wells – life was a bitch.

*

As much as Emma had tried to recreate the atmosphere of their magical moments together at the Botanic Garden, it was impossible. She was always so busy with all the residents, and the time she could spend on her own with Simon was limited. Quite often that time tended to clash with his runs, and when she did manage to speak with him for more than a couple of minutes, he seemed more distant. She knew only too well that his emotions would be more and more affected as time wore on.

Simon had mentioned wanting to go on a weekend trip to the beach four weeks ago and was going to have a look at various locations online. Emma had offered to drive instead of getting the train – the thought of that weekend thrilled her. But as the days and weeks went past, nothing more was said. She was tempted to try and jog his memory about the idea but felt awkward about it.

Patience was normally a virtue, and that state of mind came to her naturally, but she knew it didn't apply for Simon and her. He'd become more and more obsessed recently with his running and was reading much more often. Where he'd often help out and join in on the regular morning and afternoon activities, he was becoming less social.

Their closest moment together was when he'd knocked on the door and came into her office with something behind his back. She couldn't imagine what it was but guessed it might be flowers, perhaps picked from the gardens during one of his runs. It was a voucher to have her hair cut at their in-house hairdresser.

The emotions flooded her so suddenly and intensely that she wanted to hold him as tightly as she could and never let go.

She wasn't sleeping well at the moment. It was partly to do with Michael and the way their world had fallen apart, but more to do with Simon. Much more.

Every day that went past, she loved him that much more. She wondered if it was the limited time they had left which was driving this feeling, or the fact that her professional situation prevented her from directly approaching him.

But did her job really make that much difference? If he took her in his arms this very minute and asked her to go away with him today, then she'd just go. She'd leave everything she'd built her life on and just go. Simon meant *that* much to her.

In the hours she lay awake at night, she went through all the practical scenarios. She convinced herself that Maddy could step into the breach with no notice and would do just as good a job of running Orchard. When she woke up still tired in the morning, it shocked her that she was capable of these thoughts.

Emma couldn't continue like this. She'd have to approach Simon and say something, but what does a woman say to a man she can't live without? A damaged man who may have no recollection of their brief times together. Who may not remember how he felt for her a month ago.

And this was where she felt horribly presumptuous – just how *did* Simon feel for her last month? The moment before Hayley had broken that spell in the Botanic Garden, she was certain Simon was going to tell her that he loved her. But before that, he was going to kiss her, and that kiss would have changed their world.

Emma reddened in the confines of her office as she contemplated being completely wrong. Maybe he was just going to admit to her how scared he felt about his disease? And perhaps it wasn't going to be preceded by a kiss? There was no way of knowing. She could do nothing but wait until Simon made another move.

The day's paperwork in front of her made no sense. Her eyes were tired, and she couldn't focus on the print. She needed to get her act together before everything came tumbling down around her.

*

It was a great feeling when a personal best could be followed back-to-back with another personal best. In the last month, Simon rarely ran his circuit in over 41 minutes, and as he nudged ever nearer to 40 minutes 30 seconds, he began to wonder if he could break the magical 40-minute barrier.

He'd spent some time trying to figure out how he could be getting faster at his age. He knew his illness didn't come into play at the moment, though inevitably it would one day. Then he wondered if it may be because the path he trampled around twelve times a day was getting more compact and quicker to run over.

Whatever the reason, it thrilled him. The spreadsheet showing every run at Orchard glowed from his laptop. Recently he'd had to put all the figures into bold script, as they weren't as clear as they used to be. He felt rather devastated that one day soon he may have to go to the optician and be prescribed glasses. He wouldn't look the same in glasses.

Then it occurred to him what he was fretting about, and he burst out laughing.

Books were now arriving in the post on an almost daily basis, yet there was rarely a time when there was one sitting idle, waiting to be read. One of the carers had suggested he download them onto an electronic book, but he loathed that method of reading. He'd had enough staring at screens when working to last him a lifetime. Besides, he liked the feel and the smell of books and lining them up on the shelves he'd had fitted in his spacious room after reading them.

He'd borrowed a tape measure from the maintenance man and calculated that the two rows of bookshelves running all the way around his room, from doorframe to doorframe, would take him three years and five weeks to fill. He'd had to make a judgement call on the average width of a book to arrive at this calculation.

He was pondering whether a third bookshelf would go above or below the other two when the hopelessness of his idea dawned on him.

He'd walked into the shower in his running gear, turned the hot water on to as hot as he could bear without yelping, then sat on the floor with his hands in his face.

His tears were invisible.

As the water pounded his head, he imagined unscrewing his skull without any pain or difficulty. He'd let the steaming hotness pour over his fucked-up brain until it started to cleanse all the poison running through his mind. Then he'd screw his head back on, turn the shower off, get dressed, and walk out of this place.

And everything would be fine again.

Except for one thing – there was a woman he'd met here, and he couldn't leave without her. When he thought about her, he couldn't remember if he'd known her a short time or a long time – perhaps all his life. Sometimes it felt like that.

He wondered how well he knew her. It was difficult to judge. He wanted to ask her that exact question, but he imagined he'd die of embarrassment, not that that was a bad way to go, given what fate had in store for him. Then he berated himself – despised the pathetic self-pity he wallowed in.

She didn't notice him as much as he noticed her. She was always so busy. Perhaps he'd said something that had really upset her? But why and how could he upset someone that he loved so much? Was his mind already so damaged that he'd hurt the person that meant more to him than anything?

What could he do or say to make her feel the same way about him? She was the only reason he had to carry on with this life he'd been dealt. Without her, he might as well drown in this never-ending deluge of heat.

He looked at his right forearm, blurred by the cascade. Dark blue script - *Carpe Diem*. He hated the stupid tattoo. Hated how it looked and hated what it meant. Why the hell had he done that to himself? Never mind *this* moment – what about the fucking future?

Next to the shower gel and shampoo, a safety razor sat on the floor of the shower. He picked it up in his left hand and stared again at the little tattooed words, then drew the razor across it. His hair came off first, and he watched it swill and spiral down the drain. He kept pulling the razor across the writing, again and again. The skin started to go red, but he could feel nothing. He just wanted the tattoo gone and forgotten forever.

After a while, it started to sting as little pinpricks of red appeared, instantly sluiced, but he was sure the blue ink was disappearing. When it was all gone, he could start focussing on the future. The future he so desperately wanted with Emma.

*

The square red alarm light flashed in Emma's office. She looked up from her confusion of paperwork and saw the number 30 blinking inside the display. She ran out of her office, taking the stairs two at a time up to Simon's room. There she found Jamie, one of her four male carers, and Simon, sitting on the bathroom floor. Both of them were soaked, and Simon's right arm was bleeding badly, already being stemmed by a towel Jamie was holding against it.

'I'm sorry, I'm sorry. I was just trying to do something. Really, I'm sorry, there's no need to fuss.' Simon was looking pale and confused.

'It's okay, Simon, take it easy. Calm down.' Emma knelt on the floor and used another towel to dry his face. 'What happened? Jamie? Any other injuries?'

'I just found him sitting in the shower. A lot of blood, but I can't see any other problems apart from this arm.'

Emma lifted the towel and could see a deep graze, but stitches wouldn't work. She held the arm up in the air, and they lifted him onto the bed.

'Get him out of his wet clothes and into pyjamas and a dressing gown. I'll get some bandaging.'

*

It took all of Emma's efforts to dissuade Simon from going on his evening run. As she'd noticed on many an occasion over the years, severe bouts of confusion in those suffering from Alzheimer's was often followed by a reasonable period of lucidity.

They were both sitting on his bed. 'When we take the bandage off in a couple of days, I fear you'll be tattooless. Can you remember what happened?'

'I remember wanting a shower but not much else. I think I must have wanted to get rid of the tattoo, but I don't know why.'

'It could be a number of things, but I think you have to try and take on board that every day is your future. This evening, tonight, tomorrow morning? That's the future. If you look ahead all the time, you miss the now.'

'Well I like the now now – the sitting with you now. I'm really sorry for all the hassle I've caused.'

'It's what I'm here for. It's not a problem.' They smiled so easily at each other that she felt she'd known him forever, and she so wished she had.

'Is it really why you're sitting here now? I know you're here to look after all of us at Orchard, but are you happy to be with me too? In my room? I'm asking because I'm sure that's what I was thinking about in the shower. I was thinking how happy I was when you were around, but when you didn't want to see me, it made me incredibly sad.'

Emma was baffled. 'Since I first met you there has *never* been a time when I didn't want to see you. To be honest, I've missed you a lot this past month but understand when you want your own space.'

Simon was also baffled. 'But I thought you didn't want to see me? That's why I read so much. I know you have lots to do, but when we briefly talked or bumped into each other, I thought I'd said or done something to upset you? I couldn't work out what it was, so I just assumed it was my memory letting me down.'

They broke eye contact, and Simon stared at his books on the shelf. Emma put a hand on his leg.

'Do you remember when we went to the Botanic Garden?'

'Yes, it was a lovely day. We spent quite a bit of time together, but then the Major took a turn for the worse, and we all went home early. Was that when I upset you? If I did, I don't know what to say except sorry. I'd honestly never consciously do anything to upset you.'

'Do you remember when we went to that little rockery with the wooden bench?'

'I do. It was lovely being on our own and away from the others. I wish it could have lasted longer.'

'So did I. You were about to speak to me, but you wanted to do something first.'

Simon was still staring at his books. 'I'm so sorry, but I can't remember the details. I do remember sitting there with you, though. It was lovely – perfect.'

Emma was getting so frustrated that she found it hard to remain calm. The time for shyness was over. She put a hand on his face and turned him towards her.

'Remember what I'm going to tell you now. Write it down when I go and keep it somewhere. It's really important to me that you do that. Can you do that for me, Simon?'

He looked into her eyes and smiled. 'Scout's honour.'

'You mean more to me than you realise. But before I tell you how much you mean to me, I have to do something.'

She leaned towards him, and her lips touched his as their eyes closed. Then she kissed him, and her life changed, just as she knew it would.

They looked at each other, and she spoke very softly. 'I've wanted to do that since I first saw you dripping on the reception floor. Do you remember that day?'

'I remember wishing I hadn't run here. When I first saw you, I wished I'd got a taxi so I looked more presentable.'

She smiled at the memory. 'Now this is the bit I want you to write down when I go. I have to get back to my office, but I'll come and see you later. Ready?'

'Absolutely. Consider it written.'

Emma stood up and leaned down so her mouth was close to his ear.

'I love you.'

She walked out of the room and quietly closed the door.

12

Sunday 18 June to Friday 23 June 2017

Simon was absolutely sure he wouldn't forget those words, but he wrote them down anyway. He looked at the piece of paper and the three words then added the number '2', folded the page, and put it in an envelope. He went downstairs to reception – Emma's office door was closed, but Julie was behind the desk.

'Hello, Julie, can you give this to Emma for me, please?'

'Sure, but I can ask her to come out and see you if you like? How's your arm, by the way?'

'Looks like I might need a new tattoo, but apart from that all good. Don't disturb her. I'll leave it with you to pass on. Thanks.'

With instructions not to run for a couple of days, Simon decided to make plans for the coming weekend. He didn't care where they went or what they did; he just wanted to be on his own with Emma. He felt so happy and elated that he yearned to tell someone, but that wasn't possible. He instinctively knew that both the residents and the carers were the last people who should know about this.

He didn't know if she'd be able to have time off this weekend, so he'd think of something local, where she could get back to Orchard at short notice if necessary. Maybe a meal somewhere special in Cambridge on Friday evening, then a movie the following night. He spent some time online looking for good restaurants and checked the cinemas for suitable films.

Life was very strange. He hadn't loved a woman since he was married, but now he was in love with a married woman.

At dinner, he decided to sit at a small table on his own for a change. He brought a book down with him so the residents he normally ate with wouldn't think anything was wrong. He wasn't as hungry as normal and made do with a bowl of soup and some smoked salmon sandwiches.

Whilst having coffee, Emma walked into the dining room. She went to the six other tables first and chatted with everyone. He did his best not to make it obvious, but he couldn't take his eyes off her.

'Good evening, Simon. Mind if I join you for a coffee?'

The dining room on his floor was much smaller than the main one where most of the residents had lunch. It didn't afford as much privacy, and there was much less background noise, but they kept their voices down, and no one paid them any attention.

'Thank you for your note; it made me cry. With happiness, I should add. Are you able to tell me how long you've felt this way?'

Their hands were resting on the table a few inches apart, but neither dared move closer in case one of the residents noticed. Simon picked up a dessert spoon and placed the tip of the handle against Emma's middle finger, then put his finger on the other end. 'Contact. Of a sort.'

They stared into each other's eyes, and anyone observing would have assumed they were deeply in love. That they were lovers already, aching for more privacy.

'I was thinking about that. I feared I wouldn't remember, but it came back to me in a flash. Will you remind me if I forget?'

'I'll write it down and keep it at home. Girl Guide's honour.'

'I can't be sure what love is. I don't know if there's a point where you like someone hugely, then the scale tips and that defines official love, or whether love has a huge scale that starts with quite liking someone? I've sometimes thought that loving someone wasn't quite as big a deal as being *in love* with someone. Is that possible?'

'Anything is possible where love's involved.' Emma moved the spoon and slid her hand further across the table until just the tips of their fingers were touching. 'Contact. For real.'

Residents were getting up from their tables, and members of staff were helping them back to their rooms, though some would wander down to the main lounge to chat and watch television.

Simon looked down at their hands. 'If we work on my second theory, and I'm sorry to sound like an accountant on such a special subject ...' He looked up at Emma and winked, '... Then I'd say I started to love you before you met me.'

'What? How's that possible? You're teasing me.'

'It's true. You weren't here when I came and saw Maddy, but after our meeting, I wandered around and looked at the display with all the staff photos and names. I looked at yours for much longer than the others, and I was really excited about meeting you one day. It was your eyes and your smile – I knew the type of person you'd be. I think I may have started to love you then.

Emma's fingers had crept over Simon's without her realising. She couldn't put into words how much she desired this man.

'And then very soon after we met, I found myself lonely whenever you weren't around. I just wanted to be with you all the time, even though I knew that was impossible. I guess it was then that I realised I was in love with you.'

She was lost for words. The times she'd been so close to saying something or throwing her arms around him were skating across her mind. It would have been easier to get up, move over to his chair, and kiss him deeply. It would also have been impossible – they still weren't on their own.

'I see.'

'I was thinking of things that we could do this weekend. Would you be able to get a weekend off, or even one day? I thought we could go to Cambridge and see a movie, then go and have a really nice dinner. Or the other way around if you prefer? Then I worried that it wouldn't really feel like going out to you. But at least you're near to home, and I could get a taxi back here?'

Emma pondered for a second. 'I was really hoping you'd ask if we could do something together this weekend. As I said before, I'm owed months of time off if I care to count, which I don't. I love your idea, but let's double up on it? How about going out for a meal and a film on Friday *and* Saturday. I'll pay for one, and you pay for the other – deal?'

'Oh. Well, I love the idea of the whole weekend, but there's a fundamental problem.'

Emma looked a little crestfallen.

'You see I'd never be able to let a lady pay for the meal. I can't start that sort of thing now. That wouldn't work at all.'

She frowned. There had to be a solution.

And there was.

'Okay then – how about you pay for the meals and the cinema, but I look after the accommodation?'

Simon was puzzled now.

'But there aren't any hotels involved. Oh. Hold on. So we could make a whole weekend of it? I'd love that. Oh, but there's still a problem; you're not paying for two rooms at a hotel. No way, Emma.'

'I wasn't talking about a hotel. I thought, if you like …' She'd begun to blush and looked away, cursing her cheeks. Angry with herself she looked back at him defiantly.

'I thought you might like to stay at my flat for the weekend.'

They held eye contact as the information processed in Simon's mind, then Emma looked away again. She'd gone too far and too fast. Why had she ruined everything?

She didn't see the beaming smile start to spread across his face.

'That sounds like the most perfect weekend I could ever imagine.' He was holding her hand tightly. 'I'll be on my best behaviour, of course. I must ask you this because it's been worrying me for weeks. When we went up to Manchester and had that twin room together, did you think I'd booked it on purpose?'

'No, not for one second. I actually felt terribly embarrassed for you – I could imagine how awkward you felt. But the strange thing is that I was more worried about you cancelling the booking and finding another hotel where we'd have two separate rooms. I really enjoyed sleeping in the same room.'

'That's such a relief. I liked it too but was worried that if I showed my pleasure, you'd be bound to think I'd orchestrated the whole thing.'

Though still smiling, Emma closed her eyes and shook her head. She sighed as she thought what might have been. What should have been.

She looked at him again with a serious expression. 'Simon, please don't.'

His smile disappeared too. He was confused by what he could have done.

'I'm sorry, I don't understand. What don't you want me to do?'

'Please don't be on your best behaviour this weekend.'

There was no longer anyone in the dining room. They were still holding hands as they stood up and left.

*

Sometimes people received emails bearing news that was so wonderful (or so awful) that they read them twice. Immediately. Just to make sure that what they'd read had actually been written.

Michael read the email three times. He stood up from his desk at home and slowly paced from the office to the kitchen and back. Walking past the bedroom door, he was spotted.

'Darling, come back to bed. It's sooo early; I need some more of you. Then let's go to breakfast. I'm starving.'

This was so irritatingly wrong on so many levels that he wanted to hurl abuse through the open door.

No, it wasn't '*sooo early*'. Well, not unless you lived in New York, when it would be. Or even earlier in California where he should have been now, damn it. And should have been last week and the week before that and the week before that, damn it to hell.

And no, they wouldn't be going for '*breakfast*' because it was half past twelve, '*Darling.*'

And surprise, surprise, she wouldn't be getting '*some more*' of him because she'd had every sodding atom he had to give for the past month or was ever likely to give again for that matter.

Michael limped tenderly back to his laptop. He was living proof that one really *could* have too much of a good thing. He imagined Penny and Victoria exchanging intimate details about him on a Virgin Atlantic flight, only to come to the conclusion that they clearly weren't talking about the same man.

As he gingerly sat down and stared at the screensaver on his laptop, he wondered if the email had magically evolved from awful to brilliant, or even just awful to very bad.

It hadn't.

Caring for Life Inc. regretted to inform that they had decided to sell their business to another California-based residential care home group. They wanted to thank Michael for his time these past few months, and it had been a close-run thing. Up until a month ago, the American owners were leaning towards selling to Collins Knight Young, and that was solely down to Michael's dedication and enthusiasm, and going that extra mile – or 5,318 bloody miles in his case …

Unfortunately, the lack of contact with Michael in the last month, together with the accelerated enthusiasm of the local opposition group had swung the decision.

They trusted he wouldn't be too disappointed, hoped he'd have a nice day, and were missing him already. The email was copied to Head Office as well as Messrs. Collins, Knight, and Young.

Michael joined his hands together, made a steeple out of his index fingers and tapped his lips. He could hear his mum's voice – '*Now Mikey, let's not see any more tantrums from you, do you hear? You count to five like a good boy. You know what you're like when you get all hot and bothered in that little head of yours ...*'

'One.' He was probably going to be dismissed.

'Two.' That wasn't right – he was *definitely* going to be dismissed.

'Three.' That wasn't right either – by now he'd *already* have been dismissed. The decision would have been made. The email had been sent at 9 a.m. yesterday Californian time, so 5 p.m. London. He hadn't read it until now because he was busy giving his all. He looked down at his slippers, then his pyjama trousers and T-shirt.

'Four.' He put his hands on the back of the screen and slammed the laptop shut.

'Five.' 'FUUUUUUUCCCCCCKKKKKKKK!'

'Oooo, yes perleeease. But then can you take me out for brekkie, darling? And then Harrods?'

*

The scab had healed nicely on Simon's arm, and he was back running on Wednesday. His times were a little slower that day and Thursday, but he put it down to a break in the routine. His mind was elsewhere as well; he could think of little else but the weekend.

He'd noticed that one of the carers now tended to be with him in the morning when he had his shave. Not offering to help but just tidying up the room, fluffing the bed, or bringing him another cup of tea which he hadn't requested. He understood completely, and it didn't upset him. He was in a great place where he enjoyed everyone's company, and they looked after him perfectly.

He was nervous about Friday evening but so excited he couldn't escape into his book. He found himself reading the same page twice, then completely forgetting the thread of the story. He prayed to a God he'd never believed in, that his mind would stay focused until at least Sunday. He wasn't shy or embarrassed of being forgetful in front of Emma, but he just wanted to feel as he did now.

He knew her apartment had two bedrooms, but he'd only seen the kitchen and living room. He wondered if they'd share a bathroom again, then smiled at the memory. If he could remain this happy for a little longer and be fully aware of that happiness, that's all he could ask for. That was enough. And next week, he'd get a tattoo on his left arm. If he remembered …

Emma was having exactly the same thoughts about sleeping arrangements for the weekend. She'd already had her weekly housekeeper make up both beds with freshly ironed bedding and would go back after work tonight to tidy the place before tomorrow. She was very nervous.

It had been a long time for her and she guessed the same for Simon. She decided to assume that he would go in his own bedroom, but she would do all she could to eventually end up in bed with him. From preference, she would like to have been in his room, on a bed she'd never before made love on. But either room was okay – she shivered with anticipation at the prospect.

*

The story she'd given Maddy was that she was accompanying Michael to an athletics meeting in London. They had a couple of rooms booked in a hotel and would be back on Sunday evening. There was some truth. There *were* two rooms available to them, and they *would* be back on Sunday evening. However, Emma was living on borrowed time, and this weekend would confirm her future direction. She had to assume her position at Orchard would soon be untenable. Incredibly, that now meant so little to her. She loved this man enough to dedicate herself to the rest of his life.

They arrived at her apartment with plenty of time for Simon to settle into his room and unpack his small suitcase. It was tempting to have a glass of wine, but they resisted and took showers before getting into smarter clothes for the evening. Simon was both relieved and disappointed that they had their own bathrooms.

The meal was at a place Emma had never been to before. One of two Michelin-starred restaurants in Cambridge – very special and very expensive. It had been Simon's idea, and she was secretly delighted that she'd never been there with Michael before.

They had a glass of Champagne to start the evening off – Michael toasted '*To a perfect weekend – the first of many,*' and it was all she could do not to break down and cry.

They shared a superb bottle of red wine with their meal, the last of it accompanying a wonderful selection of French cheese which they feasted on together. It left them in a perfect state of mind for what lay ahead. The restaurant was near enough to her apartment that they decided to walk, Emma thankful that she hadn't worn excessive heels. She smiled to herself at the thought of Victoria attempting to run after Simon in the car park in her pristine white stilettos.

It was nearly midnight when they made coffee at the apartment and sat on the sofa together. Simon had his arm around Emma, and their voices were whispers. He kissed her, and this time it was for real. Nothing had ever felt so natural and right, and Emma wondered what the weeks and months of tension and anxiety had all been about. She didn't want anything to ever come between them again.

She parted from his lips with reluctance and looked into his blue eyes. 'Shall we continue this meeting in the bedroom? We have lots to discuss.'

'I think that's an excellent idea. Should we go to your place or would you like to come back to mine?'

It was just the answer Emma wanted. 'Why don't you go to your place, and I'll have a quick shower and change at mine, then come over and see you.'

'That's an even better idea. This really is going to happen, isn't it? I've dreamt of this moment but never dared think it would happen.'

'So have I, Simon. We're on our own at last. It's going to happen.'

They kissed once more and parted. In his room, he took his clothes off and ran the shower. He was about to step into it when he heard Emma scream. He turned and ran, throwing his door open and sprinting towards her room.

He heard her before he got there. 'What the fuck do you think you're doing?!'

It had to be a burglar. He burst into the room, naked as the day he was born, his hands balled into fists. There was a dishevelled man in her bed, squinting and holding his hands up against the glare of the ceiling spotlights. Emma was still screaming at him from the doorway.

It was Michael.

13

Saturday 24 June 2017

Something, somewhere, perhaps not of this world, was conspiring to keep them apart.

Michael was unceremoniously bundled out of the house, and his key taken from him. Yes, he paid half the mortgage, but as from now, he wouldn't need to because he wasn't living here any longer. If and when Emma sold the flat, he would be given his half, valued at today's date. Three estate agents would be asked to value the property next week, and an average figure would be taken.

The latter idea came from Simon. Emma had asked him to join the discussion around the kitchen table once he'd put some clothes on. Michael found it very difficult to disguise his loathing of the man so didn't really try.

Simon made things worse by appearing entirely calm and placid, though he was quite prepared to lay Michael flat-out on the deck if required. The certainty of this outcome in Simon's mind had somehow transferred itself to Michael, and it was this which seemed to restrain him from hurling abuse at what was now very clearly his ex-wife.

He was left to wander around the city at 1.30 a.m. in search of a room, which at this late stage would cost him at least double the normal rate. He was painfully aware of this from the last time he'd been with Emma. That, in turn, jogged his memory about the two bottles of Dom Perignon he'd had to pay for, and he wished he'd thought to ask Simon for reimbursement. Then he decided that under the circumstances, that might not have been the cleverest move.

If there were no rooms at any of the various inns in town, then he was scuppered. There were no trains to London, and even if he'd used a taxi, he had nowhere to stay. The company apartment had ceased to be available to him at the same time his job ceased to be available to him. As he'd predicted, this occurred very swiftly after the yank email had landed in the inboxes of his bosses.

Victoria had initially tried to placate Michael, but as soon as she realised he'd lost his lucrative job, he became almost instantly unattractive. There was no trace of her when he came back from a liquid lunch at the nearest pub, save for the heavy scent of the latest perfume he'd bought. In case he ever thought to contact her again, he immediately deleted her number. It then occurred to his sozzled mind that he had no idea of her address or even which county she lived in.

He made a mental note to book an appointment with his doctor on Monday. For now, he'd head to the only place he had left – his apartment in Cambridge.

*

Emma wasn't a violent woman; far from it. But when she walked into her bedroom, turned on the lights and saw Michael in her bed, she could have been. Her dreamlike state had been shattered like a champagne flute hitting a marble floor.

She hadn't meant to scream. With her thinking cap on, she could have woken him and demanded he get out of the flat immediately and quietly. Then she could have taken her shower, slipped a robe on and walked to Simon's room as if nothing had happened.

She'd spent plenty of time thinking about how Simon would first lay eyes on her, and the white robe felt the most appropriate and comfortable. True, it had the Maldives hotel motif where Michael had bought them both three years ago on their second honeymoon, but needs must. Simon had the other one in his bathroom, so perhaps he'd be thinking along the same lines?

Emma didn't consider herself to be unattractive, but she was no spring chicken either. The thought of wearing some sort of sexy lingerie had put the fear of God into her. She'd taken Simon's naked image in, of course. As had Michael. She had to chuckle – served him bloody well right.

Mr Carter was even sexier with his clothes off than with them on. He had a very toned and athletic body, which seemed only fair with the amount of running he did. Emma hoped he'd appreciate her body even half as much as she yearned for his.

Naturally, Michael had ruined the entire evening before he was unceremoniously kicked out. All the magic she and Simon had built up was gone. After hugging in the kitchen and with the promise of tomorrow night to come, they'd gone to their separate bedrooms.

She'd decided to cook Simon a meal tomorrow evening, and they were going to the market in the morning to collect all the ingredients. She drifted into sleep as tomorrow evening played out in her mind. She imagined reaching his room and knocking on the door, but Emma was in another world before anything else had happened.

*

Simon Carter had never been involved in a fight in his life, but there was no question he'd have leapt on Emma's bed in a heartbeat. Had her husband (or ex-husband as she was keen to emphasise) uttered a word in anger, Simon would have given him the thrashing he deserved.

It was only when Michael had hurriedly pulled his clothes on, that Simon looked down at himself and realised he wasn't wearing any. Emma had passed him a dressing gown which he put on before following the man to the kitchen for a brief discussion on the new ownership details of the flat. Simon had then seen him to the door and locked him out.

She'd kissed and hugged him when they were on their own again, but it just wasn't the same. He was so hoping tomorrow night would be different. The whole episode had made him anxious, and he knew that could trigger his mind into letting him down. So far he'd been okay, but sleep was avoiding him now.

He couldn't believe that a woman like Emma could have ended up with someone like Michael, but he only had to think of Victoria to realise how unpredictable life was. Tomorrow *had* to be a much better day.

*

There was a strange phenomenon with regard to being shat on. Michael cast his mind back to when he was fourteen. He'd just been caught smoking behind the bike shed at school (why did kids *always* choose to go there when it was the first place the teachers looked?). The very next day, a group of his friends had found a carton of old eggs and thrown them at houses. He wasn't one of them, but his father didn't believe him and gave him six-of-the-best with a slipper.

Later that same week, his mum and dad had decided his school wasn't suitable and sent him to a horrible place where he was bullied. Even worse, he never saw Jan Sheppard again, and he rather thought he'd marry her when they left school.

This week hadn't been so dissimilar. After losing a contract he'd been chasing for over a year, he'd been fired. The woman he was living with had then disappeared, her parting gift probably something he needed a course of antibiotics to clear up. And then he was kicked out of his own apartment by his wife and a naked nutcase, who she'd chosen instead of him.

There was very little sleep to be had at the one hotel he'd finally managed to find with a vacant room. The accommodation had cost £360 and had plumbing problems, making maniacal burbling noises throughout the night. As he sat in a noisy coffee shop, he prayed to a God he fervently believed in, but his faith was currently being stretched to the limit.

He had savings, but they wouldn't last forever. He needed a job sooner rather than later, and he knew he had to go back to caring. It was the only thing he'd ever done, and the only thing he was good at. Apart from fucking his life up, obviously. He'd excelled at that, and a First Class Honours Degree was in the post.

He watched the youngsters; the dregs of the summer term still in their digs and enjoying the freedom from study. The nearest was gabbling away about some quantum tunnelling problem. Others behind him were contemplating the importance of fluid mechanics and buoyancy to the

Ancient Greeks. He felt profoundly stupid and decrepit – he was old enough to be all these kids' father. Except, of course, he couldn't be anyone's father.

His life would never be complete, and he felt an overwhelming shame that he'd concealed his infertility to the most important person of all. If nothing else, he owed it to Emma to tell her that, and one day he would. For now, he'd head back to Liverpool and go and stay with his parents; his life had come full circle.

*

Simon had insisted on cooking breakfast. It was the least he could do with Emma cooking tonight. He admitted he was certainly no chef but could manage a cooked breakfast and just one or two simple dishes. He'd scoured the kitchen for ingredients and had come up with something Emma had never seen before. It was so simple but so good; runny boiled eggs with lightly boiled asparagus acting as the soldiers. It was different, and she loved it.

He'd also cleared the kitchen up afterwards and put everything away. Admittedly, Emma had limited experience of men in domestic situations, but this was a new one on her.

They roamed around Cambridge for the day, hand in hand and sometimes with his arm around her. They bought all the ingredients for supper and then took in a film at the cinema. In the middle of the afternoon, they went back to Emma's apartment to drop the shopping off and then revisited the Botanic Garden. It was another perfect summer day, and the Garden was much busier than during the week. Simon and Emma had to wait for another couple to leave but were determined to have just a few minutes in the little area where they'd previously sat.

164

This time they kissed as they'd both wanted to weeks ago and felt like teenagers when another couple politely coughed while standing on the path – it was their turn …

And near the main gates they found a little space on the lawn and held each other close.

'I won't be presumptuous and tempt fate, but whatever might or might not happen tonight, I want you to know what a beautiful woman you are. I want you to know that I love you. I can't tell you how happy you make me.'

Emma wanted this moment to remain in her memory forever.

'I feel just as happy as you. I love you too.' They kissed again, then Emma pulled a phone out of her pocket. She held it at arm's length, and they looked into the camera lens.

'So we never forget this moment in time.'

*

The meal had deserved the best wine he could find. He managed to conceal the cost from Emma because he feared she might think him mad. Simon smiled at the thought.

He bought two bottles – a six-year-old Puligny Montrachet Grand Cru for the scallop starter and the monkfish that followed it. Then a 1976 Chateau d'Yquem he'd had to nearly wrestle from the owner of the wine store. From experience, he knew it was a very different but perfect accompaniment to the cheese they'd also bought.

Simon realised they'd get nowhere near the second half of the dessert wine while at the table, but he secretly hoped they could have another glass while in bed. It was a special wine that would complement their first night together.

The atmosphere was altogether different than the previous evening. The tension had evaporated, and Emma wondered if in some strange way she had Michael to thank for that. After that incident, it was difficult to imagine how anything else could go wrong.

There was an almost intoxicating and delightful inevitability about how their night would pan out, and she felt beautifully relaxed once her cooking duties were over.

Simon was either the best actor in the world, or he thoroughly enjoyed the meal. And as for the wine, she wasn't sure if she'd ever tasted anything more delicious.

She felt very naughty when she made a mental note to check the price of the two bottles online but knew she wouldn't be able to resist. Just like tonight when there would be absolutely no resistance.

*

Simon sat on his bed in a seemingly unworn white gown. The logo was an outline of a sailing boat in gold with a red sun setting behind it. Underneath were the words *Maldives Paradise*. He imagined it would be, but he was more than happy where he was right now.

He was also wearing a pair of boxers. He'd taken them off and looked at himself in the mirror, then put them back on and had another look. He preferred them on, especially after last night when he'd tried the other way. He should have felt embarrassed, but it just made him grin instead.

He experienced a similar dilemma with the lights. Fortunately, the dazzling spotlights in the ceiling were on a dimmer switch. He played with the dial like a photographer focusing on his subject – a little brighter, a little darker, and perfect. Then he dimmed it down just a little more.

Life was continual until it stopped, but it wasn't a linear journey. It was full of moments. He guessed he'd forgotten an awful lot of past moments, but he still had enough to keep his mind occupied.

But that was the past.

He hoped he'd have plenty of moments still to come. There'd be the high moments, nearly all of which would involve Emma. They'd be up there in the clouds. And maybe his running, when he looked at his watch and the first two numbers were 39. Inevitably, there'd be the low moments. Some would be very low. And some would be so low that...

But that was the future.

The *now* was all that counted and all that mattered. Seizing the moment for all it was worth. Like the man who clung desperately to the branch of a cherry tree, looking down at the hungry tiger below. The branch snapped and as the man plummeted with the broken branch in his hand, he picked a cherry.

And it was sweet.

There was a light knock on his bedroom door.

14

Monday 07 August 2017

Life had been confusing but wonderful for the past six weeks. Orchard had run on an even keel as it always did, even though Emma wasn't pulling as many hours as normal. She now took weekends off, ostensibly to look after Simon (who was now going to 'regular athletics meetings'), but it certainly wasn't fooling Maddy.

Last Friday before the lovers left the home, Maddy had approached Emma in the privacy of her office. She'd asked her to stand up and come around her desk, at which point Maddy had opened her arms and hugged Emma warmly and fiercely. No words were needed; the two women had known each other for years.

'Do you know what you're doing? Whatever it is, I'm with you one hundred per cent of the way. You know you can always rely on that. But the gossip is going around the staff. Julie found out that Michael's no longer at head office, and everyone's finding it strange that you're not here at weekends. That you're busy looking after Simon.'

Emma sighed; she was getting exhausted of the façade. 'I know, Maddy. And thanks, by the way – I know I can trust you, and it means so much to me. I just love him so much.

This can't continue as it is for much longer, I realise that. I'm close to contacting London and suggesting you take over.'

'What? You've got to be joking?'

Emma held her hands up. 'I know, I know; I should have discussed this with you before. And I would have done before making the phone call, of course I would. I can't remain working here and be with Simon. It's impossible, and we both know that.'

'I can't believe I'm hearing you say this, Emma. Orchard is your life. It'll never be the same without you. Surely you can't ...'

'Simon is my life now. I'm begrudging every minute I'm not with him, and that's no way to conduct myself with the other residents. I can't give them the attention they need and deserve because my mind is constantly elsewhere. As much as anything, it's not fair on them.'

'Please, you have to stop and think. However powerful your feelings, Simon's not going to be with us forever. A long way short of forever, sweetie.'

'And that's why I hate every moment I'm not with him now. Can't you see that? I don't want to be here anymore. Not in this capacity, at any rate. I'll still be here all the time but as a visitor, not the manager. He's all I want now, Maddy.'

'I don't know what to say. What if head office doesn't want me running the place?'

'Don't be ridiculous. There's no one more qualified to run Orchard than you. You know the place like the back of your hand, and you're assistant manager. It's a no-brainer.'

Emma had started to go pale and put her hand on the desk to steady herself. 'I'm sorry; I have to rush to the loo. I'll catch up with you later.'

'Sure, okay, I'll see you later.' Maddy put her hand on Emma's shoulder and squeezed, then pecked her on the cheek and left.

In the privacy of the bathroom in her own room, Emma was violently sick. She washed her face with cold water but still felt clammy. It was another hot day, but that wasn't the problem. She stared at the little box she'd bought from the chemist's that morning. How many times had she bought these damn things, and always, *always* the same result?

And now, the one time in her life when she hoped for a different outcome, she feared the worst.

*

She was still staring at the little white plastic spatula, though the image was blurred now through her tears.

It was impossible. It *had* to be impossible. Yet when she missed her period a couple of weeks ago, something told her this was no innocent anomaly. Though she put it to the back of her mind, she knew her life was about to change in an even greater way than she'd anticipated.

She'd go and see her doctor tomorrow, as much for the advice as the confirmation of what she already knew to be reality. She was going to have a baby. She was going to bear Simon a child.

Emma lay on her bed in a foetal position. Tears were still running, but she made no noise. She put a little piece of the cotton sheet in her mouth and gently bit up and down on it with her teeth. It was something she hadn't done since a little girl.

There was a small list of people she'd have to tell, but she couldn't put them in any order in her mind. There was Maddy; she could imagine how the poor woman just wouldn't know how to react. And there was her mum and dad, who she hadn't seen for weeks. She imagined they'd initially be over the moon, and mum would break down on the spot, but the news about Michael would be devastating.

Then there was Simon.

How would the most important person in her world react to being a father for the first time? Would he be overjoyed, then right in the middle of his elation, realise the child would probably never really get to know their father? Even if they did, would he still be able to know who *they* were?

Now the floodgates truly opened, and she cried her heart out. Great wracking sobs. It was an agony so pure that she could barely take the next ragged breath.

She awoke may hours later to darkness – it was after ten o'clock. There was nothing for it; she'd get her act together and help the night shift. It was while having a shower that she remembered what she'd been thinking about earlier. There was one other person to add to that list, though she could have been forgiven for temporarily forgetting. Michael would need to be informed too.

Then something dawned on her. It began as an idle thought and gradually gained momentum. By the time she reached her conclusion, Emma was clenching her fists in a rage.

She couldn't prove it, and he'd almost certainly deny it, but she was sure it was true. Michael already knew that *he* was the reason they'd never had children. They'd never openly discussed the matter, but he'd somehow always made her feel that every failure to conceive was down to her.

Emma had *always* thought it was her problem, her fault. But during all that time, Michael just *had* to find out that it wasn't him. He was that type of person; he'd just have to know. And when he'd found out, he kept it from her. The bastard had never told her.

She made a pact with herself then. She would never speak to Michael again.

*

Emma was shattered by the time the morning shift started at 6 a.m. It was too bad, and she'd have to muddle through somehow. Perhaps she could take a power-nap instead of lunch and then an early night. She called her doctor and made an appointment for that afternoon, promising herself she'd have dinner with Simon in his room and tell him that evening.

She phoned her mother at lunchtime and said she'd pop over to see them that weekend. Yes, she was fine. Yes, she had some news. No, she wouldn't be bringing Michael.

Maddy started at two o'clock, and Emma asked her to come into the office whenever she could after 4.30. She'd be back from the doctor by then, and the news would be official.

Her doctor was a woman she counted as a true friend. They'd often been out together with their husbands for dinner and had once been on holiday together. It was going to be awkward and embarrassing, but life was sometimes like that. As much as anything, she wanted something to sort out the constant nausea.

Liz had initially been delighted for Emma and was close to hugging when the bombshell was dropped. She hid her surprise well, but it was clear Michael hadn't been to their doctor to discover his infertility. Liz made every effort to remain straight-faced when Emma divulged the father, but it was a tall order.

Emma was already aware of this, but on learning of Simon's illness, it was Liz's responsibility to point out the increased risk of the child contracting Early Onset Alzheimer's. She also wrote out a prescription which would help with the morning sickness and asked how she was feeling in general.

Emma was stumped. How did she describe elation, tiredness, sorrow, uncertainty and fear? She came up with the only obvious answer; she was fine. They made an appointment to meet again in a month, and Emma drove back to Orchard, nervously wondering how Simon would take the news.

*

They tried not to meet in Simon's room for obvious reasons. Apart from what the staff may think, it was also agony to be in a bedroom and not in each other's arms. This time, however, she didn't care. Emma came back from the doctor and went straight to his room, not knowing what she'd say.

She didn't want to beat about the bush, but she couldn't avoid it, and Simon was confused.

'I don't understand. How can the news be either wonderful or terrible? I can't think of anything you could tell me where it was possible to react so differently. Maybe I'm being stupid? I've had a long enough good period that a bad one can't be far away now.'

'That's a good introduction to the news, actually.' Emma could have done with a glass or two of wine, but this was no longer an option open to her. There would no longer be any alcohol until the baby was born.

'You've lost me. Not difficult, I know.' He kissed her tenderly, and it gave her the courage to continue.

'It's about periods. Or in this case, the lack of one.'

She'd seen this expression on Simon many times when he was doing a crossword or Sudoku puzzle. Then enlightenment would dawn as he gradually solved the problem, just as he was doing now.

'You're not saying … I mean, you're not trying to tell me that … Oh, my God, Emma! Oh, Good Lord, are you pregnant?'

She looked away from him and down at the floor. The discovery but not the verdict. She felt sick with the tension.

'Oh, Emma. Oh, my word. That's just the most beautiful thing in the world.' He knelt down on the floor and put his arms around her hips as she sat on his bed. Then he gently pressed his ear against her stomach.

Emma put both hands in his hair and tried to stifle the tears. 'I didn't know what you'd think or how you'd react. Hey, I don't think you'll hear the baby yet.' She wiped her eyes and sniffed.

They hugged each other tightly for a long while, Simon still on his knees and Emma sitting on the edge of the bed. No more words were spoken. It gave them both time to think about the enormity of their situation and what life would be like for this little boy or girl they'd created.

Simon held her tight because he feared if he didn't, she'd feel him shaking. Emma was right; the news was wonderful and terrible. She was going to bring his child into the world, knowing that he couldn't hope to help her. He'd be either dead, dying, or wouldn't have a clue who the baby was. Even worse, he'd given his genes to that baby, increasing the likelihood of the same fate as him.

It was a disaster, and it was beautiful, and he was lost for words.

*

It was much easier to tell Maddy, and this time Emma came straight to the point. Her reaction was similar to that of Liz and Simon – barely disguised shock followed by guarded delight and concern.

'You realise I can't remain at Orchard any longer, Maddy? It's impossible now. I should phone up tomorrow morning and hand in my resignation with immediate effect. Are you ready to take over the helm?'

'Oh, sweetheart, you can't just give up like that. Nobody else needs to know for a long while yet. Sure, there are rumours amongst the staff, but I can sort that out. Why don't you give it another three months and see how everything works out? As long as you feel fit enough, of course. If you'll agree to that, then I'm prepared to offer my services from then, but only if you really feel you have to resign. I wish you wouldn't, though. The place will never be the same without you.'

Emma hadn't thought of this possibility. It certainly bought her some time, but if anyone were to find out, she'd be instantly dismissed. That was far worse than handing in her notice and would certainly mean she'd never be employable as a carer again after Simon had … She bit her lower lip hard.

'Let me think about it. I'd like to hope all the staff were on my side if it did get out. At least long enough for me to resign instead of being reported. I'm not sure about Julie, though. Things are very different between us now; very icy.'

'I can't say I haven't noticed. What's going on there? She always used to look up to you like a big sister. She'd have done anything for you.'

'I know, and it's something to do with Michael, but I'm not exactly sure why. When Julie took Simon to the Cotswolds, and Michael and I were there, we bumped into each other at a pub and had dinner together. She was all over him with her eyes. It would have bothered me under normal circumstances, but with how I was feeling for Simon by then, I was hardly in a position to complain. She's been a little off with me since then, and when Michael was sacked, it's been worse. I feel like she's blaming me for something, but I don't have a clue what it is.'

'I'll have a word with her. I normally seem to be in her good books. Similar to how it was with you really, but I think she looks up to me as her mum instead of her big sister.' Maddy grinned in a self-deprecating way.

Emma smiled, moved closer, and gave her a hug. Maddy was probably the only genuinely true friend she had.

'I don't know what I'd do without you – I truly don't.'

15

Thursday 12 October 2017

'It's always more difficult to tell if it's a girl. I've made errors before with girls, but rarely if ever with a boy. Let me ask you both once more; do you definitely want to know the sex if it's possible?'

Emma looked at Simon, but the grins already gave the woman her answer. 'Yes please; we'd love to know.'

Less than a minute later, the black and white image on the screen had been frozen and captured. The legs were wide apart which made identification positively easy.

'Well, Mrs Lowry, I can confirm with more than a small degree of confidence that you are going to have a baby boy. As you can see here, it's really not a difficult diagnosis on this occasion.'

*

They sat in her car in the hospital car park. Both were in a daze.

'Will you always be Mrs Lowry? I'd marry you this minute, but from experience I know it takes a few months to get a divorce, and that's if both parties agree. What do you think Michael would have to say about that?'

She turned to Simon and prodded his shoulder with a finger. 'If I didn't know you better, Mr Carter, I'd say that was some convoluted way of saving your trousers from getting dirty on the knees.'

'Eh?' Simon was genuinely puzzled.

'I'm teasing you, silly.' She kissed his lips. 'Only a couple of weeks ago, I was thinking of officially changing my name back to Thornton. I don't really want to contact Michael, but I'm going to have to, I guess.'

'If he agreed to a divorce and signed papers this month, it would still be a while. I don't think that's good enough for us, do you?'

Emma turned back and stared out of the windscreen. 'Please Simon, don't talk that way. I'd love to think we could get married next year. In fact, I'll make it happen. I'll call Michael today.'

'If you do that and he agrees, I'll phone my solicitor today.'

Emma didn't understand. 'Why? Why would you need your solicitor?'

'By then, I could be in a state of mind that prevents me from taking marriage vows. If I give instructions whilst still in this state, maybe it won't be a problem?'

She gripped the steering wheel until her knuckles and fingers throbbed. How could God allow an illness like this? How dare He?

She decided she never wanted to see the inside of a church again, but even that thought cut her to the quick. She thought of being in a church at Simon's funeral and wanted to scream with the unfairness of it all, but then in the midst of despair, the blackness lifted.

'Can we have him christened in a church? And what will we call him?' Even as she spoke the words, she knew the answer. There could never be any other name for him.

'Of course we can, darling. Do you have any names you really like?'

'Yes I do, actually. Is it okay if I decide? Will you promise to agree if I tell you now?'

'Absolutely.'

'I'd like to call him Simon.' She took his hand and put it on her stomach.

He smiled, then turned away as his eyes moistened.

*

'Hey Em, it's good to hear your voice. How've you been keeping?'

'From what I've heard, a little better than you. Where are you?'

'Oh, up in Liverpool with Mum and Dad. They're both good. I'm sure they'd want to send their love when I tell them I've been on the phone to you. How's Orchard, by the way? All good? I guess with you running the place, it's like clockwork as usual?'

'Thanks, and please send my love back to them. Look Michael, I'm very sorry about what happened to you, but I need to get a couple of things off my chest. I'll start with the easy one.'

'No probs, fire away.'

'I want a divorce. I want to sign papers this month that allow us to be separated in the minimum possible time, by mutual consent. It'll take a few months, but that's how the law works. Please, Michael, will you do that?'

'Christ.' She could hear Michael sigh and take a deep breath. 'I'd prepared myself for this. At least I thought I had. Is there nothing I could ...'

'There's nothing, Michael; our marriage is over. If you still have any feelings for me, you'll go along with this. I don't want to beg you, but I actually *will* if I have to. Is that what you want?'

'No. No, of course that's not what I want, Em. It's just that ... It's just a shock, that's all.'

'It's not a shock, and you've already admitted you were prepared for it. You knew it was over when you went off with that woman. I'll have my solicitor send paperwork up to your parents' place next week. All I want now is to just move on with my life. I'll get him to confirm the flat is fifty-fifty at the point you stopped paying. When I sell, that money is yours. If you insist on wanting it before then, I'm not sure what I'll do. Maybe I could get a bigger mortgage; I don't know.'

'Don't be like that, Em. You know I'd never ask for that. When you sell is fine. There'll be no pressure from me, I promise you.'

'Thank you. That's a big relief to me, especially with the position I'm going to find myself in by the autumn.'

'Why? What's happening then?'

'That's when I hand my notice in.'

'You've *got* to be joking?! Why the hell would you do that?'

'Because I won't be able to disguise my pregnancy anymore.'

There was a long enough silence that both parties wondered if they'd lost the phone connection. Emma expanded.

'I'm pregnant, Michael. I'm having a son. I'm guessing that sounds less of a miracle to you than it did to me?'

Michael could only stutter, so Emma saw no reason to stop.

'You *knew* it was your problem all this time, didn't you? You *knew* it. How long had you known for, hmmm?'

'You're being ridiculous. I had no idea. Of course I didn't, Em. Be reasonable.'

'One of your few virtues – you're a hopeless liar. You've known for years, but your male ego prevented you from admitting it. All the things we could have done to have a child, but oh no, if you can't father it, then we're not having one. It's pitiful, Michael, it truly is. I'm going now, goodbye.'

Emma cut the connection and began to shake. She leaned back from her chair and stared at the pile of paperwork on her desk. It didn't use to be this untidy, she was sure of it. She picked up an account, but it didn't make sense. Nothing made sense.

There was a knock at the door; it was Julie.

'Chef wants to know if you've finalised numbers for the Hawaiian evening.'

Emma was perplexed. 'Sorry? I'm not sure what you mean.'

'The dinner dance on Saturday? You said you'd know roughly how many guests of the residents would be coming by today. Chef is ordering this afternoon for delivery tomorrow.'

'Oh hell, it totally slipped my mind. Let me check my notes – please tell Mr Patel I'll go and see him in half an hour.'

'Sure, okay.'

Julie was shutting the door when Emma called out. 'Have I done something wrong, Julie? If I've upset you in any way, you only have to talk to me.'

'Errr, no, you haven't. I don't know what you mean.' Julie's face had flushed, and she couldn't look her boss in the eye.

'Is it something to do with my husband? Has Michael upset you again?'

'No, of course not. I don't know what you're talking about.' Julie was holding on to the door and clearly wanted to shut it with her on the other side.

Emma was struggling to think of anything that Julie and Michael may have in common, but an inability to lie could definitely be a starting point.

'Fair enough, but please, if there's anything I can do, you know you only have to ask. He's going through a tough time at the moment, so please accept my apology on his behalf if he's upset you again.'

Emma was sure she heard Julie sigh '*Whatever*' as she closed the door.

*

As Simon pounded his circuit before dinner, he felt as if he was almost floating. He looked down on himself, and his breathing was as calm as if he were drifting into sleep. The laps felt faster too; much faster. When he went back into his own body and looked through his eyes, the vision was blurred, so he went back up in the air again. From there he could see with crystal clarity.

He felt embarrassed to admit that he actually looked like a professional athlete. Like an Olympian in the marathon, chasing the gold medal. There was no one ahead of him, and the rest of the field were far behind. Sometime soon he'd see the stadium ahead and hear the buzz of the vast crowd. When he entered the stadium, they'd erupt into a crescendo of noise, eighty thousand fans cheering his every pace.

He'd never felt this good in his life. The light was brighter now, as if he was surrounded by powerful floodlights; following him, above him, in front of him. He felt movement behind him. He didn't see or hear it; he just felt it. He looked back, and a Paralympian in a wheelchair was just on his shoulder, about to overtake.

It made no sense. He looked down at his body – the body of a man with no impairments. As he increased his pace, the athlete in the wheelchair drew level with him and then gradually eased ahead. As he watched the distance between them grow, another man drew level with him. This one had blades on both his lower legs, attached below the knees.

Simon's breathing grew harder as he forced himself to run faster. It wasn't so easy now, as he watched the two athletes disappear. He'd have the bronze whatever happened. At least he'd win a medal.

The voice behind was familiar. When he turned, he should have been astounded, but it was of no surprise. The woman looked at his face but not his eyes. Her focus was on something within another world. She wore a pink dressing gown with the belt flapping behind, running effortlessly beside him. Her voice was as familiar as his own: 'Who are you? What do you want with me? Leave me alone and don't come back. Stop thinking about me and missing me.'

He watched his mother go past him, her mumbled words becoming incoherent.

His lungs were beginning to hurt now, and not in a way he was used to. A pain deep inside the tissue that threatened

183

to tear the organ from the inside out – to cause his breath to turn into liquid and make him choke on his own frothing blood.

As his mother evaporated in front of his eyes, he heard panting and wheezing behind him. At first, he thought it was his own body beginning to shut down and wither, but the noise was coming from behind his shoulder again. The crackly breathes were accompanied by an incessant squeaking noise. Tiny wheels scudding along the ground, but not revolving smoothly with the forward motion.

He knew the noise. He had no idea why, but he knew the sound well. He had to get away.

Simon dug his fingernails into palms and began to grind his teeth. He couldn't see very well anymore; it had to be the acrid sweat dripping into both eyes. He couldn't run any faster, and his lungs were going to explode. Breathing was pure agony.

An oxygen cylinder drew level with him, the wheels on the base wobbling maniacally next to his feet. There was a clear plastic tube running from the top of the bottle to a mask. It rested on an elderly man's face, held there with a thin band of tatty green elastic behind his head.

Simon's eyes traced the contours of the old face; a jaundiced yellowish-grey with sunken eyes. A cigarette would be dangling from the lips. Simon already knew this. Most of it had already been smoked, but the ash still extended the full length, precariously drooping. The wind seemed to have no effect on the fragile little tube of ash, though it would eventually fall on the man's shirt. Again Simon knew this – he'd seen it happen so many times before.

'I'm going to join your mum, son – no need to follow just yet. Don't be too long, though. Don't be too long, son.'

*

Emma had lost track of time while trying to finalise numbers for Saturday's party. It was one of the annual highlights at Orchard, and in past years there'd been more than 150 people attending the evening function; a mixture of residents, staff, and residents' friends and relatives. She'd ordered 200 colourful paper garlands just in case – this year's theme was Hawaii by popular vote.

She was going to join Simon for dinner on the first-floor dining room today, but she was over half an hour late. With luck, she'd still join him for the main course and dessert.

Not able to find him eating, she'd checked with a carer who'd told her he'd gone out for his run around four o'clock so should have been there for the start of dinner. Emma guessed he'd be in his room, logging down the latest time on his computer. Not finding him there, she went back downstairs and looked in the lounge.

'Julie, have you seen Simon? He's not in the first-floor dining room or his bedroom.'

'I saw him go out for a run just after four but not seen him since. Want me to put a call out?'

'Hold fire for a few. I'll go outside and have a wander, though he can't still be running by now.'

Emma went to the edge of the car park where Simon always started and finished his runs and headed down the path he took in the grounds. The days were rapidly drawing in, and it was a little chilly now. She spotted him about a third of the way along his route. He was sitting on the ground in a small pile of leaves, leaning up against a mature oak tree. His head was bowed, and his hands were resting on his thighs with the palms facing up. It was almost a position of meditation, but she knew better.

Running up to him, she knelt down, touching his arms.

'What's the matter? Simon, are you okay?'

He lifted his head and looked at her face. He was void of any expression and said nothing, his eyes open but not blinking.

'Simon, what's happened? What are you doing here like this? It's time to come in, darling, it's getting cold.' Emma was beginning to get very worried though showing no sign of it. She needed Simon indoors straight away and tried to get him to stand.

'I came last, didn't I? Even Mum and Dad beat me. I'm hopeless; don't want to run again. Never again.'

She couldn't leave him here while she ran back to get help, but he didn't seem to want to get up. The sky had darkened, and spots of rain were filtering through the curled red and brown leaves.

'Simon, listen to me. We need to go back inside. We need to go back home. You're very tired, and we're going to get soaked if we don't hurry. Please darling, stand up for me. Did you fall – are you hurt?'

'Won't run again. I hate it.' He looked at the bright blue digital watch on his wrist – the stopwatch mode was still running – *2h. 17m. 28s* ... He raised his arm and smashed the back of his wrist against the rough bark. Emma flinched. He did it once more before she could grab his arm and hold him tight, her face now pressed against his.

'Simon, *please*. Come home with me now. Please darling. It's me, Emma. I love you. Please get up now.' She tried to lift him, but he still wouldn't budge. He was staring at his watch again. The plastic face was missing, and the grey screen was blank.

'I came last. Did you hear that? I came *LAST*.' The final word was almost screamed, and Emma was now a little frightened. That couldn't be an option now, though, so she forced herself not to be. This was the man she loved, and she'd love him in whatever state he was in.

'Take my hands, Simon, I'm going to pull you up. Try and get up for me. Come on darling, try.' She leaned back with all her strength and tried to drag him up. His torso leaned towards her, and his bottom briefly came off the ground but then dropped back again. He was staring at her, but there was no recognition. She still hadn't seen him blink, and his face was expressionless.

Emma dug her feet more firmly into the ground. The rain was coming down hard now, and they would soon be soaked through.

'Come on darling, help me. I'm going to count to three, and you're going to get up, okay?' She was shouting so he'd hear her above the rain, but the thunderclap still made her jump.

'One ... Two ... *Three.*' Emma leaned back and pulled with all her might, and Simon started to come off the ground, but then she screamed in agony as pains tore through her stomach.

She let go of his wet hands and fell onto the leaves, painfully jarring her lower back. Emma thought she was going to pass out with the pain. She staggered back up, holding her stomach and back.

'I'm going to get some help, Simon. It's going to be okay, baby – I'll be back in two minutes. I love you.'

It wasn't possible to run or even jog, but she limped as fast as she could back to the home. Another jagged crack of thunder exploded in the gloom of the impending dusk. On the edge of the car park, she saw one of the gardeners about to get into his car.

'Daniel, I need some help. It's Simon Carter – he's collapsed a few hundred metres up the track. Can you go and help him now and bring him inside? I'll see you in reception.'

The man ran past her, and she slowly shuffled to the front door, still holding her stomach. The breathtaking pain had passed, but there was a painful dull throbbing which made her sick with worry.

*

Maddy was insisting on taking her to hospital immediately, but Emma refused until she'd seen Simon come through the door. Luckily, she didn't have long to wait, as Daniel and Simon walked into reception moments later.

Julie grabbed Simon's hand. 'Thanks very much, Daniel. We'll take it from here.'

She turned to Maddy. 'Up for a shower, then a meal in his room?'

'Yes, but call the doctor first. Get him over straight away. Ask Janet to cover at reception while I take Emma for a quick check up. She's had a nasty bump on her back; we should get it x-rayed just in case.'

Emma couldn't express just how grateful she was to Maddy. She looked at Simon as he walked past her, but it was as if she wasn't there.

'Simon, I'll see you later. I'll pop in and make sure you're alright.' It killed her that she couldn't embrace him and kiss him, but it was impossible. Perhaps it would be even more painful if she could have done, only to realise he wasn't aware who she was.

'Let's go, Emma. Stick close to me under this umbrella.' The two women walked out into the torrential rain, heading for Addenbrooke's Hospital.

*

'I'm pleased to say everything seems fine with your baby, Mrs Lowry. There's a small bruise on your back but nothing broken. Take some ibuprofen for the discomfort, and you should be back to normal shortly. Other than that you're free to go, but I'd suggest no more strenuous exercise.'

'Of course not, and thanks very much, Doctor.'

It was a mightily relieved Emma that sat down gingerly in Maddy's car for the drive back to Orchard.

'Thanks again, Maddy. That frightened the hell out of me.'

'You're going to have to take it easy from now on. Do you want me to drop you back to the flat? Get an early night and see how you feel tomorrow?'

'Let's go back to Orchard – I have to see how Simon is. I'm dreading it, actually. I know I'll have to get used to this, but it's just such a shock. It's so different when it's on a personal level.'

'It hurts to see you like this, Emma. Is this really what you …'

'Don't Maddy, please don't. I know you're only thinking of me, and that means so much, but no more questions. Please? I've never been so sure of anything in my whole life.'

*

Emma went to Simon's room and knocked on the door before walking in. Julie was sitting in a chair next to his bed.

'Jamie gave him a long bath and put him to bed. We sat him on the bed in his dressing gown first, but he didn't want to talk – just stared at the wall. He's been asleep about an hour and hasn't stirred.'

'Thanks, Julie, I really appreciate it. You get back downstairs, and I'll take over now.'

She pulled a chair up to the bed and stared at his face. Simon was completely peaceful, and his breathing was slow and regular. It was as if nothing had happened. Emma found herself pretending that he'd wake up later and no longer have the disease. She tried to imagine what was going on in his brain at this moment; thousands of little plaques and tangles attacking the nerve cells, gradually ridding him of his existence.

Emma so wanted to touch his face or hold his hand, but she didn't want to wake him. Worse than that, she didn't want him to look at her again and not know who she was. She couldn't take that at this moment. Instead, she looked down at her stomach and whispered to the boy within.

'I'm so sorry I startled you today. You're the most important little person in my life, along with your daddy. I hope you look like him, Simon. I hope that with all my heart. But more than anything, I hope you get to love him. To know who he used to be and what a wonderful man he was. And when he's gone, I want you to continue his life, live in his footsteps, and do what he'd have done.

Emma turned the bedside lamp off and quietly shut the door.

16

Tuesday 24 October 2017

It was a significant day in Emma's diary. Baby Simon had been conceived four months ago today. The doctor had told her his due date was the 26th of March, and it was the first entry she'd written in her 2018 diary.

There was one other entry for today next to '4M' and equally as cryptic – 'HIN'. Emma's diary was always left open on her desk, and anyone in the room could easily take a cursory glance. If discovered, the meaning of HIN would have spread around the staff of Orchard Residential Care Home within minutes; it stood for '*hand in notice*'.

Her tummy was getting harder to hide by the week, and by the end of next month, it may no longer be possible. She'd already composed the email she was going to send, which would be immediately followed by a phone call. If the company was agreeable, she intended for her last day to be the end of the year. Maddy had already begrudgingly agreed to be put forward as her successor, to start on the 1st of January.

Emma had spoken with Simon at great length about her decision. He understood but wished it could be different. He'd even said he wanted to speak with her bosses and explain the situation – maybe they'd agree to let her keep her position? It was a sweet and loving thought but completely impossible.

Since his episode last month, he'd stopped running regularly and never looked at his spreadsheet of times again. He occasionally went for a jog in the grounds, but it wasn't even the same route anymore. When Emma asked him, Simon claimed he'd lost interest. He now spent a lot of his spare time reading.

He'd also been to an electrical store with Emma and bought a digital cam for his room. When she enquired what he was going to use it for, he said he wanted to record the episodes when he *'went bonkers'*, so he could watch himself when he was back to normal. Emma had no idea how to handle this or what to say.

Simon had pushed her for details on his collapse in the grounds. She'd told him with as much detail as possible but kept back her trip to the hospital. Emma knew he'd be mortified if he knew what had really happened.

He'd suffered two other bouts where he was unable to communicate properly and was unaware of his surroundings or who anyone was. Fortunately, there was no venting of anger or self-harming on these occasions. He was much like many of the other residents on his floor – just so much younger than any of them.

The only other difference in the past couple of weeks had been regular visits from his solicitor. They always met in the main lounge and were busy studying documents for most of the time. Emma didn't enquire what the business was about but was certainly curious.

Simon had told her a few times how he wanted to settle all his financial affairs while he still had full capacity to consent. She'd thought it was a heartless legal expression, but it was vital in Simon's case, particularly when dealing with the large amount of money in his accounts. Emma assumed this must be the reason for these meetings.

She planned to have lunch with Simon and then send the email offering her resignation immediately afterwards. She'd then phone head office half an hour later. Emma had told Maddy of her plans first thing this morning and would meet up to speak with her later in the afternoon. Any doubts she had about what she was going to do today were dispelled when she felt two little kicks in the side of her tummy. She put her hand there, looked down, and smiled.

'I'm glad you're in total agreement, Simon. I need your support at the moment, so thank you. Give me another kick if I start to have second thoughts.' She tapped her tummy and walked to the main dining room.

*

Simon stood up as Emma walked to the table. A simple enough gesture but she'd never experienced it with any other man; manners were embedded in his soul. Another reason she could never tell him how he'd behaved last month – it would destroy him. She so hoped he'd forget about the webcam he'd set up in his room but feared the worst.

'How's your day been, darling? And how's baby, behaving himself?'

Questions like that were music to Emma's ears. She wanted these simple moments to carry on forever but always scolded herself for thinking that way. Enjoy the moment, woman, enjoy the now.

'Everything's been fine. We have a new resident moving in tomorrow. She'll only be a few doors down from you. Her name's Mrs Beryl Park. I'll be looking to you to make her feel at home; it means so much to have a friendly face close by. She's just lost her husband and needs all the love anyone and everyone can show her. She's a dear old lady.

Simon had folded his arms and now leaned back in his chair. He was looking at Emma with affection all over his face.

'Were you born an angel or did you have to work at it? It wouldn't have taken much work, that's for sure.'

Emma blushed and laughed the comment off – she didn't really know how to reply.

'That's definitely a biased view, Mr Carter. You could get me into trouble; you know that?' She grinned at him, blew a kiss, and then continued on a more sombre note.

'It's a big day for me today, actually. Do you remember?'

'As a matter of fact, I do. I'm rather hoping you haven't made any calls or sent any emails yet?'

'No, I haven't, but I'm going to do both after lunch. I know you think it's the wrong decision, but it's the only option. Trust me, if I don't do it now and my bosses find out our situation, I'll be instantly dismissed. I'd never be able to work as a carer again.'

She so wanted to hold his hand. It drove her up the wall sometimes, but she just couldn't risk it. On New Year's Day, it would be a whole different ballgame – Emma the visitor coming to see her loved one.

'It's best if you don't make that call. You really don't need to; everything's going to be fine. It's a case of *you* needing to trust *me* on this occasion.'

Emma wondered if Simon was thinking properly. She was normally able to read his behaviour and liked to think she could anticipate an escalating loss of concentration. Yet he seemed absolutely fine – he just wasn't making a lot of sense.

She looked around the room, but it just wasn't possible to hold his hand – there were too many residents, not to mention staff floating about.

'Simon, I love you for feeling so strongly about this. I know you're only thinking of me, but there's just no way around this. Our boy comes before everything, and he has to on this occasion too.'

'The two of you come before anything; you're the focus of my life. So with that in mind, I've kind of sorted things out.'

She looked at him, and though he was smiling at her, she was utterly confused.

'Sweetheart, you're talking in riddles. But whatever you're saying, I *must* hand my notice in. There's no other way.' The physical restriction was now unbearable – she leaned forward and put a hand gently on his face.

And still he continued to smile. 'You're wrong. There *is* another way.'

He took her hand, put a finger in his mouth, and gently bit it. 'You don't have to quit, and you won't.'

He thrust both arms in the air with fists balled, beamed at her, and shouted, 'YAAYY!'

The residents nearest their table turned around to look, and two of the kitchen staff stared at Simon. Emma was fearful he'd have an outburst in public and wondered if she should help him to his room as soon as possible. But there was something different about this – there was no anxiety or confusion. If anything, there was an unerring clarity about his behaviour.

'What's going on, sweetie? Please? This is going to cause a problem.'

Simon stood up and moved to Emma, bent down, and kissed her on the lips for a couple of seconds. She was so shocked, she did nothing to stop him. The two members of staff turned away and busied themselves with other tables. Some of the residents were still staring openly, a couple of the ladies now smiling.

'If you carry on like this, I won't have to give in my notice; I'll be sacked before the end of the day.'

'No you won't – I'd wouldn't give you the sack.'

She'd never seen Simon so elated. Emma also realised she'd probably worked her last ever day as the manager of a care home. The lid was well and truly about to be blown off her career.

Simon leaned down again and put his face against hers. Two other members of staff and Mr Patel had popped their heads out of the kitchen door. She closed her eyes and resigned herself to fate – it was all over.

He was whispering in her ear now. Emma understood the words, but they didn't make any sense. Things were getting a little crazy.

'I own Orchard, Emma. I guess you could say you work for me, though of course, you don't. Actually, it's really *you* that now owns Orchard.'

'I don't understand what you're talking about, darling. What on earth do you mean?'

'I just bought Orchard. It's in my name, but it goes to you in my Will, as does everything. So you could say you own it, really, as I'll be having nothing to do with it other than living here. If that's alright with you, of course? Oh, and I did hope you'd keep all the staff on as well, though that's down to you, boss.'

Emma's mouth was hanging open as she tried to process the words. She'd heard everything he'd said but understood next to nothing.

'How has this happened? How have you done this? Orchard wasn't for sale – it's one of the most successful homes in the group according to Michael.'

'It wasn't that difficult. My solicitor was about the biggest hurdle, actually. James wasn't happy at all about the price. About fifty per cent more than the business was worth, he reckoned. I guess your care home group thought that too.' It was a beaming smile worthy of any television quiz show host.

'You're mad. Simon, you are totally bonkers. Why in God's name did ...'

'Because I love you, and I love our boy. Doesn't this solve your problem? *Our* problem? I guess it's a bit of a shock for you, but still good news, right? You're happy, aren't you?' A trace of doubt crept over him, and his smile started to slip. Nearly all the residents were now looking at the couple; this was an unusual occurrence in the routine of life at Orchard.

Emma could think of nothing to say. Not a single sentence and not even a word. She stood up, brought both her arms around Simon and held him tight. Staring into his eyes, she shook her head very slowly as the enormity of his action soaked in.

'And you ask me if *I'm* an angel? *You* ask *me*?'

There was a full house now – *every* pair of eyes was fixed on the manager of their home. Carers on the ground floor had appeared at the main entrance to the dining room, including Julie and Maddy.

Emma's eyes narrowed as she stared into the iridescent blue of Simon's pupils.

Mr Carter, you seem to know just how to make a girl happy. Care to jump in the deep end with me?'

She leaned towards him and closed her eyes.

197

It started as two or three individual claps in various parts of the room, then grew. Emma assumed the hollering and whistles were coming from the staff and not the residents, but she couldn't be sure – her mind was elsewhere.

Amidst the noise, Julie smiled and turned to Maddy. 'Hah, I knew it.'

She didn't hear the reply as Maddy spoke under her breath.

'You don't know the half of it, girl.'

*

It was the first time Simon hadn't slept in room 30. The new owner was invited to the manager's quarters – a place he would get to know well.

Emma had sent an email to all the members of staff, asking them to meet with her in the empty main dining room just before their shifts ended at 8 o'clock. That way, with the next shift about to start, she could at least get two-thirds of the staff in one place to break the news.

Ultimately, there really wasn't anything that was new. Everything would remain exactly as it was, except ownership of the home had now changed. She was keen to point that out; it was a change for the good. She hoped everyone felt the same way.

Her residents couldn't have been kinder or sweeter about the whole thing. Nobody had a bad word to say about Simon, and they weren't holding back on how they felt for Emma either, much to her embarrassment. What she'd feared would be a stumbling block with some of them had proved unfounded. There was no point in hiding her pregnancy any longer because she no longer had to.

To anyone that asked, she told them she fully intended to marry Simon but was still waiting for her divorce from Michael. To that end, Michael had been true to his word. Her solicitor had received the divorce papers swiftly, and the process had begun. She knew not to look to the future, but it was far easier said than done. Emma couldn't help but wonder what state Simon would be in by the time of their wedding. In her darkest moments, she knew there was a chance she'd never marry him; that he'd be gone.

*

Simon read his Will again with a huge amount of satisfaction. James was the best solicitor he'd experienced, not that he could remember the others with any clarity. The man had shown signs of great integrity and genuine friendship. James had done everything he could to stop his client paying what he described as 'four bloody million pounds over the odds.'

Simon smiled at the memory. James was convinced the care group would drop their price, even though they held all the aces. After all, it was Simon who'd approached them.

To obtain a quick valuation of Orchard, James had deployed a firm of accountants who specialised in the acquisition of residential care homes. The freehold property and business together had been valued at eight million. When that offer was made, the owners had countered that Orchard was not for sale. However, if it was, the figure would be double that.

James was convinced Collins Knight Young would jump at an offer of ten million, but Simon wasn't convinced and was in a hurry. He knew when Emma planned to hand in her notice and wanted to act before then. His offer of twelve million pounds had been accepted within 48 hours.

It was a very strange thing – as an accountant, he was trained to be as reasonably frugal as possible, looking for ways to save money and certainly not overspend. Yet here he was without a care in the world. Perhaps he had something to thank his disease for after all. According to James, Simon still had an eight-figure bank account after the purchase. When he was no longer around, that was more than enough for Emma and baby Simon to be comfortable for life.

However much he'd like to, he couldn't trust himself to help Emma with the finances of Orchard. Someone would have to be brought in, and preferably with experience of nursing homes. Time and time again, he found himself coming around to the same conclusion. There was one big stumbling block to this conclusion, though – Emma wouldn't be happy.

It was probably more accurate to say she'd be very *unhappy* about the idea – she probably wouldn't even consider it. However, whilst he still had the capacity to put together a balanced and logical argument, that was what he needed to do. The more he thought about his solution, the more he knew it was the right decision.

Absolutely the right decision.

*

'Absolutely not. Not even over my dead body. Just *no*, Simon – no on so many levels that I don't know where to start, darling.'

'What about over my dead body? Would you agree to it then? I have no experience of running the finances of a nursing home. Even if I did, I can't be trusted any longer. What I'm proposing makes so much sense, Emma. Will you at least think about it for a few days?'

'Won't it upset you? God knows, it'll upset me, but won't it hurt you every time you see him?'

'Not at all. The more I think about it, the more I *know* he's the right man for the job. Would you ever consider anyone but Maddy as your assistant?'

'No, of course not. Nobody could take Maddy's place.'

'Well, that's just how I feel. Yes, we'll get an accountancy firm in every quarter to check through everything, but there's only one person to my mind that can control Orchard financially on a day-to-day basis. One that allows you the freedom to go about your business as you've always done. Tell you what, how about you let me make just one single request about running Orchard, and I'll promise never to make another one again. Scout's honour.'

'But that's not fair. I know what the request will be.'

'True. How about I phone him now and give him the news? It'll be my one interference into the running of the home. *Your* home, darling. Yours and our baby's. Please believe in my judgement; for the sake of Orchard, let me phone Michael?'

17

Monday 15 January to Wednesday 17 January 2018

Much to Julie's delight, Michael had started working again at Orchard. Staff accommodation had hastily been created for him before he travelled down from Liverpool, and he was now based at the home full-time. Emma's fears when he'd arrived a few weeks ago had been substantially allayed – it was a very different Michael to the one she'd last seen nearly seven months ago.

The self-assured and confident Michael, the only one she'd ever known, was now gone. In its place was an introvert of a man. His native wit and humour had disappeared, and if he outwardly displayed anything, it was shyness. She'd assumed that part of his day would be interacting with the residents as he'd always done when at Orchard, but most of his hours were spent in an office attached to his living quarters.

He was certainly earning his wages, though. He seemed to work longer hours than anyone, his ideas for changing and improving systems already proving beneficial. If his projected figures were accurate, the already profitable Orchard would be even more successful, yet with no additional cost to the residents or loss of staff.

Simon's bouts of confusion were increasing a little, but when he was in the right frame of mind to look at Michael's ideas, he'd been very impressed and told him so. The two men got on better than Emma could have ever dared hope. It was always her main concern, and she was left a little dumbfounded by the whole turn of events.

Julie was less enamoured by this new version of the man she desired. In an awkward conversation instigated by Emma just before he'd arrived, she was informed that Michael was very much a single man now, and if Julie wished to approach him along those lines, it was with her blessing. Julie had suffered a large dose of blushing which wasn't alleviated when Emma gave her a long hug and offered to help if she could.

During the few times Michael was in reception and had a moment to spare, Julie's attempts at striking up any meaningful type of conversation were met with a very different reaction than last summer. It was as if he no longer found her attractive; as if he couldn't remember the sexy words he'd written to her.

Well, Julie most certainly *could* remember those words, not that she needed to – the note still sat in a drawer next to her bed. If he could feel that way about her a few months ago, he could feel that way again. She obviously wasn't going about things the right way. She probably needed to be less demure and more assertive. Maybe get him in the same environment as before, where he could relax and have a few drinks.

Julie decided to invite him out to dinner. Perhaps not the traditional approach, but she knew what she wanted, and this time it wouldn't be breaking up her boss's marriage. Maybe she could even pluck up the courage and take up Emma's offer of help.

*

Simon was delighted with Michael's continuing progression at Orchard. Far more importantly, it wasn't the nightmare which Emma had feared.

It was great that he'd made a beneficial contribution, but what Simon hadn't told Emma was that it wasn't the most vital part of the equation. Michael's successful work was just a bonus.

The idea had come to him after he'd learned of the baby's existence. With luck, little Simon would still be too young to remember his father as he grew up. The best that could happen was for Simon to have died before the boy was two or three when the first lifetime memories could form.

What put the fear of God into him was the possibility that his son would remember him as the father that didn't know who his child was. He pictured the boy's eyes staring into his, only to have that unconditional love rejected by a madman, no longer able to function as a normal human being.

It was his greatest fear, even bigger than how he'd eventually behave in front of Emma – at least she had the benefit of knowing what was happening to him. He couldn't let this happen to little Simon under any circumstances, and when he looked at the problem in that light, it was easier to come to a logical and inevitable conclusion.

Despite further requests, he'd not received any assistance from the carers with regard to filming him during what he described as his 'bad times'. Simon reserved the right to change the first letter from a 'b' to an 'm' when things became worse, which they surely would.

He understood the staffs' reluctance but didn't agree with the decision, so he set about ordering a dedicated CCTV system. He had someone come in to install two discreet little cameras in his bed-sitting room and another one in his bathroom. Between them, the lenses now covered every inch of his accommodation.

With 24 hour surveillance, it was only a matter of time before he studied himself on the laptop for the first time. The immediate sensation was that he wasn't himself. He was prepared to feel overwhelmed with emotion and even devastated, but the feeling was less powerful; it was more one of hopelessness.

He watched a sad, pathetic man that in some ways bore little resemblance to who he looked at in the mirror on his ever-decreasing 'good times'. The posture seemed particularly different, and the speech was sometimes incomprehensible. He'd yet to look directly into his own eyes, for the man captured on the screen was completely unaware of his surroundings, let alone the cameras which lay him bare.

All the recordings were set to delete themselves within 48 hours. If his bad times were stretching for longer periods than that, he hoped his remaining lucid moments would allow his mind to give him the ability to extend that period. Ultimately, he never wanted to extend them past seven days. If his mad times were longer than a week with no respite, it was time to give up and check out, though that would obviously be easier said than done.

*

Michael had been stunned to hear Simon's voice on the phone. At first, he thought it was going to be more fireworks, but his surprise at the caller was nothing compared to the shock at what the man had to say. He had a lot of trouble believing that his old firm had sold Orchard to Simon, and even more trouble taking on board that the offer of employment was Simon's own idea.

The package was more than generous. He was so desperate at where his life had led him that he'd have worked for half that – even less. He found it difficult to believe Emma would have approved, but Simon assured him that he wouldn't be able to make this call without her approval. That was the first thing that actually made sense.

Simon had given him a couple of days to think the proposal over, but Michael had called back within half an hour. No, he wasn't doing anything else – he'd been in a low place for a while now, and wondered where and when it would end. Yes, the offer was more than acceptable, and he'd be happy to drive down to Cambridge as soon as he was required.

Two days later, he was settling into his new apartment in the grounds. A reasonably-sized brick structure that used to house all of the gardener's machinery, now kept in a new timber building. The place smelt of fresh paint, new carpets, and some brand new furniture. Double glazing was being installed the following week.

It choked him up and nearly broke his heart every time he saw Emma. There was a glow and aura about her that only pregnant women seemed to carry. The pain it caused forced him to stay in his apartment for as much of the day as he could. There were times when he inevitably had to come to Emma's office to discuss work-related issues, and that added further awkwardness when Julie was on duty.

He still felt dreadful about the way he'd treated Julie and initially expected her to be either cold or even hostile towards him. He certainly deserved it and would almost have welcomed it. Instead, the girl was still friendly and seemed genuinely interested in him, but a relationship was the last thing he wanted or needed now.

He'd liked to have been more involved with the residents as he used to be but hated the thought of the staff talking behind his back. There were still carers here from many years ago, and they knew of Emma's and his growing desperation to have a child. That meant every member of the current staff would know the problem lay with him, and this environment was too much for him to handle. Michael had become positively reclusive and tried to bury himself in his job instead.

Ironically, the only person he felt comfortable with was Simon. Perhaps it was the remorse he felt for what he'd once thought of the man, and what he'd secretly wished upon him. It may even be gratitude; despite himself, he was grateful to Simon for making Emma so happy. This was something he could never have conceived in the past, but he still loved the woman so much that if he couldn't give her happiness, he was grateful that at least someone could.

Simon had given him carte blanche in his role at Orchard, and it was this freedom that allowed him to implement some new ideas. Although Michael was answerable to Emma, it was with Simon that he'd chew over potential new strategies. At Simon's request, these meetings had always been conducted in the privacy of his room; he was worried that Emma would feel undermined if she saw or heard the two men talking about Orchard business.

This seemed an unlikely reason to Michael, and as time progressed, his suspicions were not unfounded. They began to talk less about the business of the home and more about personal matters. Simon admitted he now hardly ever left the home as his memory loss had increased. He'd asked Michael if he could care for him if his lucidness faded during their meetings, and not call for assistance. Being a carer by profession this was not a problem, but although he readily agreed, it felt a somewhat strange request.

There had been three occasions so far. Two of them had been mild, but the last time had involved Michael staying there for most of the day, calling for lunch and dinner in the room. Emma had come to see Simon late that afternoon and was surprised to see Michael tending to him. The three of them had stayed there until Simon had been put to bed that evening.

It was the first occasion Michael had spent a few hours with Emma in a very long time. He hoped she'd realise his focus was purely on her partner. He did everything in his power not to look directly into her eyes or pay her any personal attention, but it was extraordinarily difficult.

That night in his apartment the sadness had engulfed Michael, both for his own loss and her future loss. It led him to take solace in a half bottle of whisky. It was the first alcohol he'd consumed since July.

*

It had been a long time since she'd seen the old Michael. At one point that evening in Simon's room, Emma's mind had drifted back to when she used to work here for Michael as a junior carer. She'd watched him helping Simon and knew that was his true vocation, however good he was in his present role. He was a master of sympathy, practicality, and affection with his patient, for that's what Simon was tonight.

Michael barely even acknowledged her – it was as if she wasn't there. That evening, he was the best carer she'd ever seen. It was the person she'd aspired to be all those years ago. Emma sat in a chair and watched the interaction between the two men intently. Had she not thought to pop in on Simon, she'd have been oblivious to this scenario. She wondered how many times it must have occurred before, and how often it would happen in the future.

Once Michael had put him to bed, he'd moved out of the way so Emma could be with Simon. She just wanted to stroke his hair as he slept, whisper some words, and kiss him goodnight. When she turned around, Michael had already left the room.

*

Simon had not been his old self for two days. It was only now that he'd felt confident enough to go on his own to the main dining room for lunch. That afternoon, he went back to the room with just one thing on his mind.

There were over ten hours of footage to watch, and even fast-forwarding through periods of inactivity, he'd still had to call for supper in his room that evening. The note on his bedside table told him that Emma would be meeting him here at 9 p.m., and from there they'd go to her quarters for the night. Under no circumstances could she know what he'd been doing all day.

The first seven hours were much as he expected. He'd viewed two earlier occasions when Michael had looked after him. The man was devoted to the job he no longer had – it could have been a superb training video for carers. His understanding and anticipation of what was best to calm and pacify a very confused and unhelpful person were inspiring.

It was Tuesday's recording, however, which had him enthralled. It pained Simon to view himself in this advanced state of dementia, but he was aware of how strange his behaviour was becoming from previous recordings. The last three hours before Michael had tucked him up in bed were nothing short of a revelation. He had no recollection of anything he was viewing, and certainly not of Emma being in the room.

He paused the recording many times during the last part of the footage, closely studying the frozen screen. It told him more than he should ever have been allowed to know. It should have hurt him deeply, but it didn't.

Ultimately, his prying behaviour would be justified by the eventual outcome.

18

Monday 05 March 2018

J ulie was being driven to distraction. She was now seeing Michael more and more regularly in the reception area, as he came to and from Simon's room on a near daily basis. He was also coming out of his shell a little more, so two positive developments to cheer her up. But despite her very best efforts (and these included new clothes, new jewellery, new make-up and new perfume) she still hadn't clinched a date as yet.

She was getting on much better with her boss now. However awkward that discussion with Emma had been a while back, it certainly cleared the air. Julie had come so close to asking Emma for advice on a rare occasion when they'd had a working lunch together in her office, but she'd lost her nerve at the last minute.

She'd played that lunch over and over in her head. There were so many opportunities to raise the subject, but she'd chickened out every time. Now it was less than a month before Emma's baby was due, and then the opportunity would be gone for ages.

She needed to act now. The next time Emma was on her own in the office, Julie would take her a cup of tea, sit down, and bare her soul. What was the worst that could happen, for God's sake? She'd feel a bit embarrassed but finally know where the key was to unlock Michael's heart. And if Emma thought she was being a little delusional – well, Julie had proof that this wasn't the case.

*

Emma looked in her diary and couldn't believe it was still three weeks to go. How much bigger was she going to get? Even some of the residents were telling her to sit down and rest, asking if they could help. It was all very sweet; she had to admit that for all the backache and the loss of her figure, it was the happiest time of her life.

The baby had often managed to trigger Simon out of difficult and confusing moments. Even with the higher doses of Aricept and Exelon he was now receiving, it was often when Emma took hold of his head and pressed his ear against her stomach, that the rhythm of his son's heartbeat seemed to get through to him in a way that nothing else could. It was a very moving experience which Emma had videoed on her phone but forced herself to not question why she'd done this.

She'd watched Michael from a distance in the past month. His visits to Simon's room were now occurring nearly every day of the week. It was as if he were now Simon's personal carer. Emma had enjoyed a couple of meals together with the two men, where she'd said little but observed plenty.

There was a bond growing between Simon and Michael which was extraordinary to witness. Although the talk was mostly about Orchard when she was around, Emma was certain they'd developed a close friendship. She'd love to have become more involved at this level, but it felt wrong in a way she couldn't quite grasp.

Simon and Michael would sometimes go for walks around the grounds. She observed them from her office window and was sure they were using the same route which Simon had run all summer. Sometimes they came back to the home after a lap, and other times, when the weather was reasonable, they'd walk the circuit again and again.

She'd witnessed other episodes when Michael cared for Simon on his low points and shamefully had to admit she'd felt pangs of jealousy. Perhaps it was the care she could and should be giving Simon during those difficult situations, or the limited time he had left being spent with someone else. It was almost certainly both.

These thoughts had kept her awake at night when she slept with the man she loved, but Emma would rather die than divulge to Simon what was on her mind.

As always, Maddy had been the one person she could turn to. Emma wasn't going to discuss these feelings of jealousy, but her closest friend was always on hand to listen to the anxieties that were gradually building.

'Michael's changed so much these past few months. I wish I knew what happened to him – he's like a different person. Do you think it's the divorce papers or losing his job? Maybe it was Victoria?'

'It could be all three things, sweetie, and maybe more that you don't know about? How would *you* describe him now?'

'It's so difficult. For sure, it's a vast improvement on the way he was. I feel bad saying this, but I literally hated him when we were in the Cotswolds with Julie and Simon. It was a Michael I'd never seen before. Strangely, he was as alien to me then as he is now.'

'You mean you hate him now?'

'No. No, not at all. It's just that I could never imagine the way he was in Oxford, but I'm finding it hard to see him as he is now. He's just as hard-working as he always was, and he looks the same. Watching him care again is wonderful, I have to admit. You know as well as I do that he was a very special carer. I'm loathe to admit it, but he cares for Simon better than I can, Maddy, he really does. I've watched them both when Simon loses his grip, and it's well … Well, it's actually very special. There's a deep respect and a lot of care, but there's something extra. A sort of special connection between them both.'

Maddy was a little confused but very curious. 'Do you mean Michael's like he used to be when you first met him?'

'I guess a little, but he's much more reserved now. It was shyness at first, which just baffled me; I'd have thought anything but shyness with Michael. But now it's manifested itself into a sort of seriousness. I can't work it out; it's like a maturity I'd never noticed before.'

Maddy was tempted to ask another question but wasn't sure how to word it. She certainly didn't want Emma to know where her thoughts were going at this moment.

'How's the baby today? Just give me the word when you want to slow down.'

'Thanks so much, but I want to carry on as normal right up until zero hour. He's fine at the moment but kicks a lot at night like he's running. I wonder where he got that from?'

The two women smiled and went their separate ways.

In her office, Emma sat down and stared again at the paperwork in front of her. On the top of the pile was a letter from the audiology department at Addenbrooke's giving details of someone coming next week to carry out hearing tests. The hospital must be using a smaller font than normal, as she had to squint to read the writing. At least she hoped it was that. She knew eyesight started to deteriorate in the 40s; perhaps it was time for a test.

Emma held the letter further away from her, and that helped a little. As she was making a mental note of who to put on the list to see the audiologist, Julie knocked on the open door.

'Hi Emma. Can I make you a cup of tea? If you have five minutes, I'd like a quick word if that's okay?'

'Sure, sounds good to me. Is there a pair of non-prescription reading glasses lying around? I'm having a senior moment. I thought babies were meant to arrive before things like that happened.'

'I'll have a look in the drawer – I think there is. Back in a moment.'

*

The glasses didn't really help. The words were still a little blurred.

'Sorry to bother you, but I wanted to take up your offer from a while ago. The one where you mentioned to come and see you if I needed any help.'

'Of course, anytime. Help with what?'

Julie coloured a little – enough for Emma to be able to make a pretty good guess at what the subject might be. The poor girl must be a ball of nerves sitting there.

'Don't worry; I'll answer my own question. It's Michael, right?'

Julie looked down at her lap. 'Yes. Yes, it is, actually. How did you know?'

'Just a good guess. I was talking to Maddy only a little while ago about him. Maybe you're wondering why he's changed too?'

'Yes. I didn't know if it was because of me or something entirely different. I really like him. This is okay to talk about with you, isn't it?'

'Of course it is. I know you've had a soft spot for him for a while. The first time I really noticed was in the Cotswolds. Was that when you started to notice him?'

Julie started to fidget in her seat. This was a lot harder than she'd hoped, but it was still a relief to be getting it out into the open at long last.

'Yes, and I promise you nothing happened before that; you have my word. Well, nothing's really happened anyway, and I guess that's the problem. I want you to know that it was him chasing me and not the other way. I really need you to believe that.'

'It's okay, really. I believe you. There's nothing between Michael and me any longer. We've already filed for a divorce so I can marry Simon. I don't know why he's the way he is at the moment, but if you can end up making him happier, then that would make me happy too. He's doing marvellous things with Simon at the moment. The relationship they have and the way he cares for him. It's something very special to witness.'

Emma was trying as hard as she could to help Julie relax. The girl still looked so anxious and wouldn't make eye contact. She had to get her talking in order to help.

'When did Michael first make a pass at you? I'm guessing that's what he did?'

Emma took a deep breath and exhaled slowly. Apart from the embarrassment, she was also beginning to feel a little foolish. She'd rehearsed this speech in her head a few times, but now it felt a bit ridiculous to come out with it.

'Can I just get something clear in my head before I start? When the four of us met at that bar in the Cotswolds, you were already finished or finishing with Michael, weren't you?'

Emma cast her mind back. It was many months ago but felt so much longer. She took a sip of tea while she thought back carefully; the memory was patchy.

'We'd been seeing less and less of each other, and I was already in love with Simon by then. I'm sure Michael and I had a really big row around the time he was very rude to you at Orchard. I seem to remember he'd made a big effort to make up with me before we went on that weekend to Oxford and the Cotswolds. That would make sense, or I'd have never agreed to go with him. Anyhow, something happened, and it was a disaster. I can't remember what it was, but yes, to answer your question, when the four of us had that eventful evening together, Michael and I were already on a one-way ticket to separation.'

Julie exhaled deeply and looked at Emma for the first time. She'd always thought that was the case but if was such a relief to hear it in Emma's own words.

'Michael didn't exactly make a pass at me. Well, not in the traditional way, at least. Initially, it was the opposite, as you know. The first time I met him, he really upset me – probably more than I let on to you. He was really jealous of Simon being with you up in Manchester. I guess it turned out he had every right to be, but at the time I thought he was being ridiculous. Why would a guy like Michael who had a great life, great job, jetting off to America all the time and everything going for him, be jealous of a guy like Simon who has Alzheim… Oh, my God.' Julie put her hands to her face and covered her eyes momentarily.

'Oh my God, Emma, I didn't mean to say that. Please, I'm so sorry. I don't know what to say.'

Emma put on a brave smile – much braver than she felt.

'It's okay, don't worry. I understand. Go on.'

Julie took a gulp from her tepid mug of tea and tried to compose herself again. It was yet another of those moments where she wished she was anywhere but in Emma's office.

'I feel dreadful. I just meant to say that I didn't understand Michael's reaction, and I obviously said the wrong things. So he gets angry with me and storms out, but I'm guessing you had a word with him? Maybe you didn't, but he came to his own conclusion? I'm not sure. Anyhow, the next thing I know, I'm looking at that bouquet he sent to me.'

Emma thought she might have missed part of the story. Anything that reminded her of Simon's condition still blew her away, and the nearer the baby was to being born, the harder it seemed to hit her.

'So the flowers were when you realised he fancied you? When he wanted to start a relationship with you?' Emma had been momentarily taken aback and tried to disguise the incredulity in her voice.

'No, not exactly.' This was the moment Julie had been really dreading. She'd hoped her explanation could have negated the need for this, but she'd been woefully short of the right words. She pulled a piece of folded paper from her pocket and handed it to Emma.

'I think he makes his intentions pretty clear in this note. I'm sorry if it's … you know? I'm not trying to upset you; far from it.'

Emma read the contents. The handwriting was just as familiar as her own, as were the contents. She'd read notes similar to this many times.

'I'm so sorry. I don't know what came over me, but I promise it will never happen again.

The next time we see each other, I'll be a different person.

You're a sexy gorgeous woman, and I've thought about nothing but you this past week.

I'm aching for you now and can't wait to see you again.

Special wet kisses — exactly where you want them ...

Michael xxx'

Emma folded the letter back up and closed her eyes. The memory was still vague, but she remembered getting a note from Michael that had really upset her. It was short, impersonal, and void of any affection. It had been pivotal in what transpired that weekend.

Before that note, she'd been looking forward to seeing him and to their weekend together. She was making one last effort at reconciliation. To save their marriage before her feelings for Simon spiralled out of control.

And then the note. That was it. The contents of the note had infuriated her so much that it swung her mood. Their journey to Oxford was conducted in an icy silence, and it had gone from bad to worse, and from worse to irretrievable.

It had changed *everything*.

The pause in conversation had made Julie's mouth go dry. She couldn't bear the tension this silence was creating.

'I'm sorry, Emma. I *knew* I shouldn't have shown that to you. I never meant to upset you, but I just couldn't think of a way of explaining to you how I know Michael wants me. Why I need to be with him. Please forgive me? Let's just forget the whole thing, and I'll work it out another way.'

Emma had opened her eyes but was looking into an invisible distance.

'It's fine, honestly. Now I completely understand everything. I think the best thing you can do for now is not show Michael his note. Definitely don't do that, Julie, that's my advice. It'll probably embarrass him, and you don't want to do that.'

'Actually, that was my final idea. I thought if he saw the note again, it might remind him of what he used to feel for me. Don't you think it's worth a try?'

Emma felt so terrible for the girl that she wanted to cry. Instead, she said the only words she could think of to buy some time.

'Keep it to yourself for now, love. I don't think it'll have the effect you're hoping for. Leave it with me, and I'll speak to him soon. Just keep letting him know that you're there. Everything will work out in the end.'

19

Wednesday 28 March to Friday 30 March 2018

Baby Simon was late. Currently two days late and still no imminent signs. Emma was trying to carry out her duties as normal, but physical and mental challenges were making it very tough. She was desperately hoping that Simon would be in a lucid zone when the time came to leave for the hospital, though Michael had assured her he would get Simon to the hospital whatever the situation.

They'd agreed that if Michael had to care for Simon when Emma's waters broke, then Maddy would take her to Addenbrooke's. Michael would then get one of the staff to drive him to the hospital while he looked after Simon. Whatever happened, the father would be there for the birth.

Emma hated to admit it, but she was scared. Not for herself, but for little Simon. She'd had genetic counselling and knew the risks involved in having a baby at the age of 43. The odds of him having Down syndrome had increased dramatically by her age – they were now around one in sixty.

She tried hard not to think about the possibility that her baby could inherit his father's disease, though she knew the chances were drastically increased. Months ago, her genetic counsellor had informed Emma that early onset Alzheimer's was more inheritable than later onset, and the odds could be as little as one in two babies.

Emma was sitting at her desk with her head in her hands, trying to rid herself of all these thoughts. Suddenly and with no warning, her waters broke. It felt like a pop or a kick from the baby, and very soon her clothes and chair were soaked. Julie was at reception and rushed to get Maddy, who'd had every eventuality planned and covered. Within ten minutes, they were in Maddy's car and on the way to hospital.

Julie knocked at Simon's door, and Michael let her in. Simon was in a mildly confused state, but there had been far worse occasions. To be on the safe side, Michael accepted Julie's offer of a lift to the hospital and sat in the back of her little Volkswagen with Simon.

They were all reunited in a birthing room where Emma lay on the bed in a hospital gown, grimacing as the pain washed over her during contractions. Maddy was the first to speak.

'I'd love to stay Emma, but I think Julie and I should be getting back. Michael, will you be staying with Simon?'

'Yes, of course, and thanks for getting Emma here. You too, Julie – thanks for giving us a lift.'

Julie went to the door as Maddy hugged Emma. 'You'll be fine, sweetie – you'll both be fine. God bless.'

*

Simon was eternally grateful for the lucid period he was now enjoying. It gave him the opportunity to look after Emma as best he could, though holding her hand and letting her nails dig hard into his wrists seemed to be his main role.

Michael had literally taken a back seat, moving his chair to a wall by the door. When the drama of contractions had temporarily subsided, he'd asked more than once if he should go and wait in the hospital café. Each time, Simon had insisted he stay. When Michael went to the vending machine to get some coffee, it was Simon who raised the question with Emma.

'Is it okay if Michael stays for the birth? Just in case I need any help? I don't want to be anywhere but by your side.'

'I can't answer that. I only want you there, but I realise we both may need some help.' Emma smiled bravely – she didn't want Michael there but could feel the pain starting to build again. Unaware of this, Simon continued.

'I haven't mentioned this before, but do you have any thoughts on godparents?'

'I had, but completely forgot to talk about it with you. I was going to suggest that Maddy would be a wonderful godmother, don't you think? She really is the closest friend I have. Is that alright with you?'

'A perfect choice – I'd have chosen her myself. And I have a suggestion for a godfather.'

Emma closed her eyes, both with the onset of the contraction and the realisation of who Simon was referring to.

'Three months ago, I'd have fainted if you'd suggested Michael, but I know how close he is to you now. I wonder how often a man's been the husband and the godfather, but not the father?' Emma attempted a grin, but it turned into a grimace as another wave of pain left her gasping.

Michael walked back into the room and Simon turned to him.

'Can you hold Emma's hand for a minute? I need to nip to the loo.'

The men changed places. Michael wasn't sure what to do, but Emma was well beyond self-consciousness. As Simon disappeared into the en-suite bathroom, she grabbed Michael's hand and dug her nails into him. They stared into each other's eyes for the first time in an age, her thoughts enveloped in rage and pain, and his in love and sorrow.

Emma could bear it no longer.

'Call a nurse now. Hurry, for God's sake!'

He pulled a red cord above the bed, and within a minute a nurse had arrived. Michael hadn't seen this one before. She took a cursory glance, uttered some comforting words then disappeared to find a colleague. Emma still had a vice-like grip on Michael's hand as he turned his head towards the bathroom.

'Simon, are you coming out? It's time.'

'Yes, sorry – I'll just be a little while longer. Can you cope without me for a few minutes?'

'We'll have to. Quick as you like, and shout if there's a problem.'

The same nurse came back with a midwife. Michael had always envisioned this role being taken by a woman of a certain age, stature, and manner, but this was not the case. The girl beside Emma was gently spoken to the point of demure, in her mid to late 20s and skinnier than a catwalk model. While she engaged quietly with her patient, the other nurse spoke to Michael.

'Are you the father? I'm Jade, and that's my colleague, Emily.'

'Err, no. I'm the, errr, husband.'

'Hey, that's cool. I've heard every possible permutation in this job, and that's absolutely cool.'

'Ummm, the father's in the toilet.'

'Now that's a new one, but it works for me if it works for you guys.'

Emma was coming out of her latest bout of torture. 'Michael is Simon's carer and friend. *Our* friend, I mean.' She was still holding Michael's hand but now let go of it. 'But my husband as well, though Simon's going to be my husband. And a father soon.'

Emily wasn't the slightest bit confused. 'Michael, since you're Simon's carer, why don't you make sure he's okay in the loo, and I'll take your place. Is that alright with you, Emma? I don't think we're too far away from the main event of the night. Everything's looking great; textbook. Are we ready for a little push, Emma?'

*

In the eventual calmness, Michael had taken photos of the parents and baby on Emma's and his own phone but was very hesitant about being in the picture himself. He'd eventually been persuaded, and a nurse had taken a few of the four of them. Now Simon was insisting he take one.

'Come on, Michael, put your arm around Emma. I want to get a close one, but you won't fit in the frame.'

The baby was wrapped in a blue shawl and had been as good as gold but was clearly getting hungry. A photo was taken, and Michael hastily moved off the bed.

The very first thing Emma had done after giving birth was examine her son from head to toe, hardly daring to breathe. He seemed absolutely perfect, though. He *was* perfect.

She couldn't believe she was a mother. She'd known all the risks she was taking and chose to bury them. It was

225

selfish and shameful, she knew that, but she'd been lucky so far. From her research online, it seemed the risk of hereditary Early Onset Alzheimer's was greater if the child's mother carried the genes than the father. At least that was something.

Mother and baby would be under observation overnight and be ready to leave after midday. It was one o'clock in the morning when Michael and Simon took a cab back to Orchard.

'Thank you for everything, Michael. If I ever forget to say that, and we both know I will, please remember that I'm more grateful than you'll ever know.'

'It was a privilege to be there. I didn't think I'd ever witness something like that. Well, I wouldn't have under normal circumstances, of course.' Michael was grateful for the darkness in the taxi as he felt the pain and humiliation spread across his face.

'What does it feel like? To be a father? Do you feel different now?'

'I don't really know. I don't think so. Do you feel any different?'

Michael felt like he now lived in a completely different world, but he said nothing.

The taxi arrived at Orchard, and they went up to Simon's room. Michael waited until he'd brushed his teeth and got into bed. He passed him his pills and watched as Simon took them.

'You've had a hell of a day. Maybe not quite as big a day as Emma, but not far short. I'll leave you to sleep in and pop by about nine. We can have breakfast and a walk, then go and pick Emma and your son up. How does that sound?'

Simon could barely keep his eyes open. 'He has a middle name.'

226

'Who does, the baby?'

'Yes, the baby. Our baby.'

'What is it?

'It's Mi...'

But Simon was asleep before he could finish the sentence.

*

By the time every resident and member of staff had cooed and ahhhed over baby Simon and the proud parents, the three of them were exhausted.

It would have been wonderful to be able to live at her apartment during the three months maternity leave she planned to take, but impossible to look after both Simons when that became necessary. They'd have to live in her quarters at Orchard for now. It was a bit cramped, but they'd get by, and at least there was always a carer on hand to look after Simon when he needed assistance. Emma also had plans to help out in the home when she could, though avoided mentioning this to Maddy who would have had plenty to say about that idea.

Michael had been around to see if there was anything he could do to help out. Simon had gone for a late afternoon walk with him but seemed unusually tired – they headed back after only one circuit of his old running track. The four of them had a meal in Emma's quarters, and Michael left them soon after nine o'clock.

But sleep that night was at a premium – baby Simon was demanding attention at regular intervals. Simon had done his best to help, but Emma could see his behaviour start to deteriorate with the constant waking up. Late in the night, she'd suggested he get a few hours' sleep in his own room upstairs and taken him up there while the baby was finally asleep in his cot.

Simon had started repeating himself as they walked up the stairs. It was a sign Emma knew only too well.

'Our baby. Please don't let me forget. I'm going to forget, aren't I?' A pause, then the same words again. And again. Emma kissed him as he mumbled the words while drifting off to sleep.

*

It was Jamie's responsibility to look after Simon the next morning. An email sent by Emma in the early hours had reported that her partner was back in his own room and would need a lie in due to a disturbed night.

Jamie had called Michael a few minutes after visiting Simon at 9.30. Michael was there soon after, finding Jamie sitting on Simon's bed. The new father had both hands in front of his face and was shaking his head slowly.

Jamie stood up and beckoned Michael to a corner of the spacious room.

'I was told to leave Simon to sleep, but when I popped my head in the room, he was like this. I've offered him a drink and food but no reaction.'

'Okay, thanks; I'll take over from here. I'll catch up with you later.'

Michael took Jamie's place on the bed and put his arm around Simon's shoulders.

'Hey Simon, it's Michael. Tell me how you feel, buddy? Everything's going to be fine.'

Michael put his head against Simon's and spoke softly.

'Listen to me, Simon. I'm going to tell you what happened yesterday. Emma, your partner and your future

228

wife, had a baby. You're a father, Simon. You have a son, and he's called Simon as well. Do you remember that?'

Simon started to rock his body backwards and forwards. The headboard bumped against the wall rhythmically, his face still buried in his hands.

'No. No. No.'

Michael gently put his hands over Simon's.

'Can you put your hands down and look at me, Simon? I want you to look at my face.'

There was no acknowledgement, but Simon had stopped repeating himself.

'Why don't we have some breakfast; I'm starving, aren't you? Then we'll go for a walk outside – it's a lovely day. Can we do that, Simon? Will you put your hands in mine? Is that alright with you?'

Simon stopped rocking but wouldn't uncover his face.

'There's no rush. Anything you want to do is good for me. I'm going to get off the bed and move a chair next to it. Then I'll sit there until you want to say something or do something. I'm not going anywhere – I'm here with you, Simon. I'm Michael, your friend, and I'm here with you for as long as you want. Give me a nod if that's okay with you.'

'Michael?' It was a whisper spoken through his hands. 'Why can't I remember anything?'

'I can't hear you clearly, Simon. Can you take your hands down?'

The hands slid slowly down his face and came to rest on the bed. Simon was staring straight ahead, so Michael stood and moved to the foot of the bed to be in front of him. He watched as the eyes altered focus to take his face in.

'Hello, old buddy, are you hungry yet?' Michael smiled and with a warmth he could never have produced artificially.

'I know you. You help me, don't you?'

If he wasn't very careful, Michael was going to break down in front of Simon. He'd cared for many hundreds of people during his career, some of them over many years. Bonds of friendship formed which sometimes left him devastated when the resident passed away. But one learned to get used to it; to compartmentalise it.

When he'd looked after Early Onset patients, it was even tougher – of course it was. The tragedy was magnified by the cruelness of it all. But this, now, was on a level he had never experienced before.

It was easy to presume the strength of these feelings were down to Emma's involvement and how deeply it affected him, but it was more than that. There was something about Simon that transcended Michael's understanding of people.

The speed with which Emma had fallen under Simon's spell had been a mystery to him from the start. It had infuriated him and made his blood boil. He'd never been so angry and jealous in his life. It made no sense and defied logic.

But now, though he couldn't explain it to himself, he understood. He understood completely.

'Yes, I help you. I'm Michael, and I help you. I'll always be here to help you, Simon, you can count on that. Will you get dressed and join me for breakfast? You can go in your dressing gown if you like?'

Simon was still staring at Michael. A silence developed which he knew not to interrupt. A billion processes were occurring, the outcome of which would be apparent soon enough.

'I'd like that. I'll get dressed now. Where do we go for breakfast?'

'I'll show you. I'll wait here while you get ready, and we'll go there together.'

'That's very kind. I'm really sorry, but I can't remember your name. I'm Simon.' He got out of bed and walked to the bathroom.

'I'm Michael – your best friend,' he said to Simon's back.

Simon closed the bathroom door. 'So you are.'

20

Saturday 31 March to Monday 01 October 2018

The past six months had been much worse than Emma feared. She'd mentally prepared herself for Simon's gradual decline, but the speed with which the disease had taken hold was still shocking.

His lucid moments were less frequent now. Worse than that, when she did temporarily have her Simon back, much of the time he wasn't the man she'd first met. His speech was a little less clear which wasn't a problem, but his wit, humour, and love were less apparent. His emotions were fading.

Simon was gradually disappearing in front of her eyes. In front of his son's eyes.

Her plan to have three months maternity leave had failed. She'd tried to go back to work full time in July, but with the baby so close to hand, she invariably fell short of her duties. Maddy had insisted she have more time off, and at first she'd refused, but it was clear that Emma's ability to work at her old pace was not possible for the moment.

Her vision had deteriorated, and she now wore bi-focal glasses. Often these would give her headaches so she'd take them off, but then her poor sight made it difficult to read or write. A lot of the tasks she used to carry out without a thought were now proving more taxing. She hated to admit it but knew that family pressures were a major part of the problem.

In her darkest moments, she'd think about how different life was now. Would she have changed things if she could? If it were possible to wind back seventeen months to the day she first met Simon, would she have chosen a different path?

Emma hated herself for these thoughts.

She'd attempted some time at her apartment with the baby and Simon, but it was impossible without help, so Michael had joined them and slept in the second bedroom. Simon stayed in the bedroom reading for most of the day, which left the three of them in the living room. She watched Michael playing with the baby. The boy appeared more animated when with him than his father, and it made her want to cry.

But however much she instigated for her Simons to be together, neither of them would go along with her plans. They both seemed disinterested in each other and would sit there in silence until the baby needed something. It was very clear to her that Simon had lost the ability to comprehend his relationship with their son.

Back at the home, the doctor had increased Simon's medication to the maximum dose, and Michael was now spending much more time with him. They no longer had lunch or dinners in the dining rooms, and breakfast was also taken in his room.

The only time Simon ventured out of his room now was to walk around the grounds with Michael or to see Emma in her quarters. Even then, he didn't remain with her for long. He never stayed overnight any longer, and she couldn't remember the last time they'd made love.

She filmed the occasions when he was with their baby, but watching this when on her own was often too painful for her. It was here that she could most clearly witness her partner's deterioration, and it broke her heart. She went through the thousands of old photos on her camera and found one, a selfie of her and Simon, taken on a lawn in the Botanic Garden.

If ever there was something that could produce pure joy and utter heartache in equal measures, here it was. She went to town the following day and ordered a large canvas print of the photo, which she asked to have framed. She'd hang it on a wall in Simon's room when the right time presented itself. When they weren't together in her rooms, at least Simon would have a reminder of them both in his.

On the days Simon didn't come to see her, she would always go and visit him. During one of his good moments, he'd asked if she could leave the baby with someone when she visited. It devastated her, but she honoured his request. His room was now void of all personal possessions after he'd asked Michael to get rid of everything.

There were few things to remove, but he wanted the room returned to how it had been before he moved in. His laptop, phone, CCTV equipment and books had all gone, and even the shelves the books had sat on. All his clothes bar a few T-shirts, underwear, two jumpers, two pairs of pyjamas and a tracksuit were given to a charity shop. Even the dressing gown he now wore a lot of the time belonged to Orchard.

In his bedside drawer, he kept a small black and white print. It was from the hospital when he and Emma had chosen to know the sex of their baby. Other than that, his room was now exactly as he'd requested.

*

Maddy now shared Emma's office – something she was keen to assure Emma was a temporary situation until things were back to normal. Emma wondered if that could ever happen again.

It was mid-morning, and the baby was asleep in his cot in a corner of the office. It was a time when Emma always tried to be doing something to help with the running of the home. Baby Simon had taken to having a regular nap at this time after his ten o'clock feed, and Michael would be with Simon, either in his room or walking in the grounds.

Julie had put the post on the desk, and Emma was sorting through it. Amongst the normal Orchard mail was a personal one for her. She opened it, read for a few moments, and went pale.

Maddy looked up from her desk. 'What's up, bad news?'

'It's my divorce papers. It's so much longer than I'd expected that I'd forgotten about it.'

'Isn't that good news, though? I mean, that's what you wanted, right?'

'Yes, of course. I don't know; it's just taken me by surprise. I wonder if Michael's received the same documents from his solicitor?'

'Why don't you go and ask him? So you're a single woman now, eh?'

'Not for another few weeks. I guess I should go and see Michael.'

'No probs. I'm not going anywhere, so if Simon wakes up, I'll give him his bottle.'

'Thanks, Maddy; I won't be long. Give me a shout if he needs a nappy change.'

'Oh, I think I can just about cope with that. Now be off with you. Hey, and good luck.'

'I don't think it's luck I need this time. Maybe a bit of courage might be useful.'

Emma walked up to Simon's room and knocked lightly on the door before going in. Michael put his newspaper down and stood up. Simon was sitting up in bed with pillows behind his back and head, fast asleep.

'Hi, Em. We had an early breakfast this morning, and Simon said he felt tired, so he's just having a rest. I'm sure he won't mind being woken, though.'

'Like father, like son. That's exactly what Simon's doing now in the office. No, I won't wake him; it's you I've come to talk with anyway.'

'Oh, okay. Have a sit down – what's it about?' Michael picked up another chair and put it next to his.

Emma wasn't sure how to start the conversation. She was getting on well with Michael now, better than in a long time. She also couldn't put into words how grateful she was to him for all that he did for Simon.

'I've just had a letter in the post. It's from my solicitor.'

'Ah yes, I should have guessed. Mine came late last week.' It was impossible for Michael to hide his dejection. 'It appears we're officially single in six weeks and a day. Is that your understanding?'

Emma had been looking into Michael's eyes but now diverted her stare towards Simon, who was still sound asleep. She studied her wedding ring, twisting it absentmindedly. She'd moved it to the middle finger of her right hand a long time ago.

'Yes, that's what it looks like to me.'

Michael noticed what she was doing and looked down at his own ring, still sitting on his wedding finger.

'I know it's taken much longer than I thought, but … Well, strangely, it feels very sudden to me. I'm not sure I can explain it. Did you and Simon have a date in mind?'

'It's been a while since we talked about it. I must admit, it hasn't been the first thing on my mind these past few months.'

Michael attempted a brave smile which Emma awkwardly returned. A moment passed, and then she moved her hand and put it on Michael's.

'I'm sorry the way everything's turned out for you. Were you really upset when Victoria left? Or was it you that left her? Sorry, that's very rude of me, and none of my business.'

'No, no, not at all. Of course it's your business. It was honestly a relief, though it didn't feel like it for all of half a day.' He laughed at himself, and Emma was transported back to the young Michael; the self-deprecating one who was happy to make a fool of himself with the residents. She stared at his silver-grey hair. It hadn't changed in twenty years and surely wouldn't for another twenty.

'She didn't even wait for the ship to start taking in water, let alone sink. *Abandon all decks – middle-aged ladies with Jimmy Choo stilettos first,*' he said, putting his hands to his mouth in the shape of a loud hailer.

Emma giggled and put her hand to her lips. 'I'm sorry; that's mean of me. I shouldn't laugh.'

'Oh, but you should. The woman's a caricature of herself. She'd actually left the flat within a couple of hours of hearing I'd been sacked. I went out on the lash to drown my sorrows, and by the time I'd got back, she'd gone. Not a trace of her anywhere. Wellll, apart from the smell, obviously.' Michael grinned and chuckled to himself.

Emma smiled too. This was the man she'd married a lifetime ago, and she couldn't remember the last time she'd

237

seen him. In the comfortable silence that followed, she racked her brain to try and remember when that last occasion was.

It hit her. It was the time they went to Oxford. The beautiful flowers she'd received and the way it made her feel about him. Realising it was madness to consider Simon when she should be with her husband.

Then the note. The note meant for Julie. Written with the lack of affection which befitted a recipient he'd only ever spoken to once before.

It was one of life's crossroads. One of thousands people came to, stopped, made a decision, then took the path they thought best for them. Some were trivial, most were moderately importance, and a few were vital. This was a critical junction, and someone had turned the signposts around.

It had changed her life forever, and there was no going back.

'Penny for them. The future or the past? You're definitely not in the present, Em.' Michael was still smiling at her, but there was a little concern on his face.

'Oh, it's nothing. Sorry, just daydreaming – I must be tired. I'm just a bit confused, that's all.'

'Anything I can help with? I'm a great listener.'

'I know you are, but I don't think it's a very good idea. In fact, it's a very bad idea.'

Michael's grin disappeared, and he looked at his hands on his lap. This time it was he who touched his wedding ring. He sighed and looked up again.

'Where did it all go wrong? No, that's not fair on you. Where did *I* go wrong? Was it when I went down to London or was it something I said or did? Tell me, Em? Please? Before we're divorced? Before you marry Simon?'

Michael heard the words but couldn't believe he'd spoken them. He'd promised himself he'd ask Emma these questions before it was too late, though in his heart he knew it was too late a long time ago. He was worried that if he looked in her eyes, he'd already see the answer he was dreading to hear, but he couldn't stop himself.

Emma's voice caught as she tried to speak. She knew tears weren't far away.

'It wasn't your fault.' She bit her lip. 'It was my fault. Everything. It was all my fault.'

Michael swallowed hard. He didn't understand what Emma was saying but didn't want to interrupt her.

'It's true that when I saw less and less of you, it was tough. But you had to follow your career, I knew that. And I could have followed you down to London, but I chose not to – it was me who made that choice.' Emma couldn't look into Michaels's eyes as she continued.

'We drifted apart naturally, but it was still my decision. Then I didn't hear from you for a while, and the bond wasn't as strong. Simon came to live here and, well, I couldn't help myself.'

Emma could see she was hurting Michael. It was the last thing she wanted, and she could feel the tears forming at the back of her eyes. He went to touch her, but she held her hand up.

'Wait, let me finish. You sent me some flowers before we went to Oxford. They were beautiful – do you remember that?'

'Yes, of course. I went to a florist in London and wrote you a note. I wanted you to see my thoughts in my own handwriting. I'd been an idiot after that surprise weekend went wrong, and I wanted to apologise. I wanted to start again – try and start all over again.'

'You sent flowers to Julie as well. And a note.'

'I know I did. I'd been terribly rude to her and … Oh, God … You didn't get angry or jealous because I sent Jul…'

Emma grabbed Michael's arm. 'No, of course not. Don't be stupid.'

Michael was confused and distraught. He didn't know how to hide it, and his eyes moistened as well.

'So why were you so cold to me when I arrived at Orchard and on the drive to Oxford? And the whole weekend? I've played it over and over in my mind – that weekend was when we fell apart. That was the end of us. Why? What did I do?'

'You did nothing. I told you – it was me.' Emma started to sob. She took a tissue out of her pocket and held it to her face as Michael stood up and put his arms around her, resting his chin on her head.

'It's okay, Em. It's okay. I love you. I still love you. I'll love you forever.'

Michael was facing the bed as his arms were wrapped around Emma's shoulders. Tears of his own were falling onto her hair.

His eyes opened and focused on his friend's face. Simon was staring back at him, creases in the corner of his eyes as he gently smiled.

21

Tuesday 02 October 2018

Michael had been deeply shocked by the previous day's incident with Simon, which he'd chosen not to mention to Emma. He'd noticed that when she kissed Simon just before leaving the room, he appeared to be sound asleep again.

His attempt to gently wake Simon after Emma was gone had proved fruitless, though Michael was convinced his friend was faking sleep. He told Simon he'd be back before lunch and went off to catch up with some paperwork.

They had lunch together in the room, and it was as if nothing had happened. Simon was neither lucid nor confused – a state Michael was seeing more of these past few weeks.

The following day, the weather had improved considerably, and they managed two circuits of Simon's old track after lunch. It was the first time Michael had heard mention of running for a long while.

'I used to run here. I used to time myself. Good fun.'

'You were famous for running here, Simon. Everyone knew you used to run, and run very fast too. Do you want to run now?'

'No point. I wouldn't beat my record.'

The walks were where Michael now had most discussions with Simon. The exercise caused an extra flow of blood to the brain which seemed to encourage the interaction.

'Emma told me you used to run twice a day, and every run you'd complete six laps. She said you'd accurately mapped out the circuit to be a mile, so that means you ran …' Simon interrupted.

'Twelve miles every day. I timed every run.'

'That's a lot of exercise. If I ran one single lap, I think my lungs would burst.' Michael chuckled to himself. Neither of them looked at each other during these talks. They just walked and looked straight ahead, enjoying the scenery and the peacefulness.

'My father's lungs burst.'

'Really? Was he a runner like you?'

'No, a smoker.'

'Oh. I'm sorry.'

It was always Simon who decided where they walked and how far they went. Most of the time recently it would be on his original running circuit, but whichever route they took, it always ended up by the car park entrance. When Simon had enough fresh air, he'd continue straight across the tarmac to the main door instead of veering off into the grounds again. At this point, it was rare for him to talk any further, and they'd head up to the room where Jamie was on hand if Simon needed help with his shower. It was a routine, and routines were now very much the fabric of Simon's life.

They were in the room and Michael was about to buzz Jamie to come and take over, when Simon stood rigidly by the foot of his bed and gasped.

He was staring at the wall. A large framed picture had been hung up which dominated the room. It was a photograph of Emma and Simon in the Botanic Garden.

It took Michael's breath away as well. It was a stunning image of happiness. A beautiful woman with pure love in her eyes stared directly at anyone who looked at the photo.

His woman.

Her head rested on the chest of a handsome, smiling man who was no longer here.

Michael was moved and hurt, turning away to hide the heartache showing in his face. He went to the bathroom and turned the shower on, making sure the temperature was just right. When he came back, Simon hadn't moved; he stood there, completely transfixed by the image, his face vacant, and his mouth hanging open.

As Michael moved nearer to his friend, he could see the tears running down his cheek. For once, the carer was at a loss – he didn't know what to do or say. He sat down in the chair where yesterday he'd comforted Emma as she wept, and put his head in his hands.

A few moments later, he went back to the bathroom and turned the shower off. Michael left the room quietly, leaving the door ajar.

Simon had still not moved – had not even blinked.

*

Am I crying because I'm sad? Sad is when Mum died. When Dad died. When I didn't run my race in under forty minutes.

Forty is how old I am. Maybe I'm not anymore. I was forty. And I've been every number under forty as well. But I don't know how many numbers above forty.

I've been thirteen and that was the best. I was a teenage. That's not the word, but it's nearly the word. I wanted money for my ... For when I was 13. For a bike with racing handlebars and ten gears. Ten gears were only really five and a half gears – the extra gears went in between the main five gears. But ten gears was ten gears. Not five gears.

I got money for my thirteen. Mum and Dad gave me five pound notes. They sellostuck them together so they looked like a toilet roll. A roll of money. To buy my bike.

I crashed my bike. A car hit me. Dad took me to the care home. I hurt my head and my leg and my stummy and Dad cried. And all the king's horses and all the king's men, couldn't mend my bike again. I cried. That is sad. This picture is sad. It looks happy but it's sad.

I was seventeen – that was the best. I learned to ride a car. Then one day I had to stop. That is sad. That is what sad means.

That picture is sad but the man and lady are happy. It makes me happy sad.

Why is my friend in my room sad? I like the lady in the picture. I love the lady in the picture. Why is my friend going? I love my friend.

I saw them love each other. I saw them hug. I saw them talk. It makes me smile. Happy sad smile.

They are they and I am me.

I don't know my name. I don't know any name.

I like this picture. I like that lady and I know her name. But I can't 'member.

Her name is … I ran forty minutes and thirty seven seconds.

I was forty. Her name is …

Her name is happy sad.

*

'It's a stunning picture, Em. Took my breath away. It's still taking Simon's breath away now, actually. In the Botanic Garden, right?'

Emma felt herself colouring a little. She wasn't quite sure how she wanted to share this with Michael, but she'd accepted that the conversation would probably crop up after she'd had the photo put in the room.

'Yes, the Botanic Garden. A while ago now. Just a selfie that turned out better than I expected. A lucky shot.' Emma busied herself tidying papers she didn't recognise, in an office that no longer felt her own.

'It's more than that. Much more than that. It's the most incredible photo I've ever seen of you. I've got some nice ones of us in the Maldives – both times – but nothing like that. Do you still have our wedding album?'

Emma was beginning to feel trapped and awkward. She tried to calm herself.

'Yes, of course I have. Why do you ask?'

'Oh, no reason really. It's just that however hard you look in that album, I don't think you'll find something as special as the photo in Simon's room.' Michael looked down at his feet, then panicked at how Emma could take that.

'Oh, I didn't mean to say that our wedding wasn't the best thing that ever happened to me. Sorry, not that at all. I just meant that however hard I tried, I don't think I could ever give you what you had with Simon.' He put his head in his hands. '*Have*. What you *have* with Simon. Oh, Christ, Emma, I'm so sorry.'

The baby had woken up and began to cry.

'I have to feed him. Can you go and tell Simon I'll be up to see him in an hour?' She moved to the door. 'Julie, can you call Maddy? Let her know the office is all hers again, please?'

*

'Look who I've brought to see you. Simon, this is Daddy. Daddy, this is Simon.'

'Hello. Who's this lovely baby? What's your name? Is it a boy or girl?'

Emma put an arm around Simon and held the baby so he was between them both.

'This is your son. He has the same name as you – Simon. He's named after you. Do you remember?'

'Of course I do. Hello, Simon Michael.' He put his hand gently around the baby's head and kissed him on the forehead.

'Do you like the picture? Jamie helped me put it up; I love that photo.'

'I had a good look at it. You look beautiful. I wish the picture were just of you.'

'Thank you, sweetheart.' Emma kissed him on the lips. 'But the reason I look so happy is because I'm next to you. Without you it means nothing.'

'That means it's me in the photo – I wondered about that. When I look in the mirror, I don't see that man. I don't like the feeling it gives me. You make me happy, and I make me sad. Can you make it so it's just you up on the wall?'

'It's the same you, Simon. I loved you in the picture, and I love you now. It's the same person, darling.' There was a lump in Emma's throat.

'No, it's not. You're beautiful, but I can't remember your name. What's your name?'

Emma wanted to cry with frustration and sadness. She wanted to beat her arms on his chest and drum out the poison from his body and soul. She remembered how he'd tricked her when they first met, pretending he couldn't remember her name. It was less than a year and a half ago. It was too fast, and it was so unfair, and she wanted to die. She wondered if she'd trade her own life for his question to be a joke again.

'I'm Emma, and this is baby Simon.' She held him up again to Simon's face, but his interest had waned in his son. 'And I'm going to marry you very soon.'

'Married? Am I married?'

'No darling, you're not married, but you can marry me. I hope you'll marry *me*.'

'Are you married.'

'No ... Well, yes ... But I soon won't be and then ...'

There was a light tap at the door, and Michael walked in.

'Hello guys, am I disturbing you?'

Emma was startled and flushed. 'No. No, not at all. We were just looking at the photo, weren't we Simon?' She looked at Simon, but he was staring at Michael now, a smile beginning to appear.

'Are you married?'

Michael's eyes widened, and his mouth opened involuntarily. 'Well, I guess I am, but just for a few more weeks.'

'Why?'

'Why? Errr, well we're getting a divorce.' Michael could feel his armpits start to sweat. The baby was starting to fidget in Emma's arms.

'Why?'

'Ummm, because that's how it's worked out.'

'Sad. Who are you married to?' Simon was still smiling which made it all the more awkward for Michael. He loosened his collar from long lost habit. The last time he'd worn a tie was when he wore a suit, and that felt like a thousand years ago.

Emma was now looking intently at Michael whilst still trying to pacify her child.

'Errrr, I'm married to Emma here.' He nodded at Emma who immediately looked away.

Simon's smile grew until he was beaming from ear to ear. 'Perfect. Lovely. Is that your baby?'

'No, of course not. Why don't I come back and see you later? Oh, unless you're doing something with Emma and baby Simon.'

'Simon Michael.'

'*What?* Sorry, I mean pardon?'

'Baby's name.'

Emma looked at Michael as the baby started to cry. She could tell he needed his nappy changing. 'That's his name. I have to go. Simon, will you come and see me after dinner?'

'Do you have a photo of you and Michael? Can I have that one? I don't want this one here.' Simon went to pull the frame off the wall, but Michael stepped in and gently put a hand on his arm.

'Don't worry Simon; I'll get that sorted later. Shall we go and do something else for now?'

Simon stared into Michael eyes, all traces of the smile now gone. He looked at the hand on his arm, then back at him.

'Stay married.' He shrugged the hand off his arm, walked around the three of them and out of the door, shutting it forcefully behind him.

The couple stared at each other, the baby now crying loudly. 'Jesus, Em, I'm sorry. What was that about?'

Emma opened the door and left Michael in the room on his own.

*

Simon had wandered down towards the main lounge opposite reception. Julie was surprised to see him on his own.

'Hello Simon, everything alright? Where's Michael gone – want me to call him?'

Michael was walking quickly down the stairs. 'It's okay, Julie. There you are, Simon. Fancy watching a bit of telly in the lounge?'

Simon looked at Michael and then back at Julie. 'He's getting married. Isn't that happy?'

Julie frowned through her smile and looked at Michael.

'Ah, well that's not quite right, Simon. You see, Em ...'

But Simon had interrupted him loudly with an aggressive tone of voice.

'That's *right*!'

He turned and walked purposefully away to the lounge, settling himself down by a large table in the corner of the room. It was an area where residents could draw or paint whenever the mood took them.

Michael looked sheepishly at Julie and shrugged. 'He's a bit confused at the moment - getting the wrong end of the stick.'

Julie folded her arms. 'That's not such a difficult thing to do, especially where you're concerned.' Her patience had finally run out, and she'd been itching for this for a long time.

Michael was puzzled. He'd been getting on well with Julie lately and was convinced any remnants of the past were well and truly behind them now. They certainly were for him.

'I'm not sure I understand. Is there a problem?'

'Well, not if you're Michael Lowry, it seems. I'm sure there's absolutely *no* problem at all in that case. But if you're the one he hit on, *then* stood up, *then* unceremoniously dumped, *then* pretended nothing had ever happened, I'd say , yes, there probably would be *a problem*.' Julie made bunny ears with her fingers as she delivered the last two words, which felt oddly satisfying. Michael's growing confusion and gaping mouth were strangely satisfying as well.

'I'm not quite sure what you're talking about, but I hardly think it'a the place to be having this sort of discussion.'

'Don't you pull fucking rank on me again, you *prick*! How dare you. Simon owns this home now, and you're a nobody. You're just a member of staff like the rest of us.'

Michael put his hand on Julie's elbow and tried to steer her towards the front door.

'Get your fucking hands off me! I'm not your *sexy gorgeous woman* now.' The bunny ears had appeared again, and Michael knew he was dealing with the maddest person in the home at this moment.

'Hey guys, would you like to use this office?' Maddy had come out of the office and was standing behind reception.

The two of them turned towards her in unison, then turned back to each other again.

Michael had now gone from confused to rather angry. 'What the hell are …'

Maddy's voice was louder and more authoritative this time. 'What I meant was, you'd *like* to use the office.' She moved to one side of the door and waved them both in, much like a policeman waving on the dawdling traffic. Julie grabbed her jacket from behind reception on the way into the office.

'I don't know what the hell you're talking about, Julie. Okay, fair enough, guilty, I stood you up, and I'm really sorry for that. I've thought about that many times and felt terrible. I mean it – truly terrible.'

'Awwww, boo hoo. Need a tissue, do you?' Julie's anger had ramped up to incandescent as the pent-up frustrations of fifteen months spilled out of her.

'Hey, now wait a minute. Just remember it was *you* who started it. I'm just a normal guy, and if a much younger attractive woman starts falling all over me, well, I'm hardly going …'

'Are you *mad*? Are you completely fucking *insane*?!'

'Certainly not, but it looks like I'm in a room with someone who clearly is.'

'Well, you know what you can do with your *special wet kisses*? You can stick them up your own arse!'

'You're psychotic. And what was all that provocative nonsense you gave me in the toilets at that pub in the Cotswolds, eh?'

Michael was puffing up with indignation as Julie took the note out of her pocket and slammed it on the desk.

'I suppose you're going to pretend you didn't write this then, eh?'

They both stopped talking, their eyes moving from each other to the piece of paper.

'Read it then, you shit. Get out of that one. Bastard.'

He picked the letter up gingerly by one corner, as she folded her arms again. Julie watched him scan the words to the bottom of the page.

'Cat got your tongue?'

'What are you doing with my wife's note?'

'What? *WHAT?*'

Then both their faces slowly and simultaneously drained of all expression and colour as they continued to stare at each other in horror.

Julie was the first to break the silence.

'Oh fuck.'

Michael, stuck for a reply, was equally economical with his response.

'Oh dear.'

The silence was deafening at reception. Maddy opened the office door and walked in.

'Oh boy.'

Julie walked sheepishly back to her desk behind reception, and Michael walked the other way, towards the main door and the sanctity of his own quarters. He passed Simon who was looking intently at photos of all the staff mounted on a plastic screen, their first names written underneath the pictures.

'Hello, Simon, alright?'

'That's you.'

'Yup. That's the one.'

'Michael.' Simon's finger moved across the plastic display to the manager's photo. 'Emma.'

252

'Right again, old buddy. Want to do anything? Another walk if you like? I could do with some fresh air, actually.'

'No. I'm painting.' Simon turned and walked back to the lounge.

*

Maddy picked up the letter on the office desk, folded it, and put it in her pocket.

'I'm just going to see Emma for a few minutes. I'll be back soon.'

Julie was doodling on the back of an envelope – a series of daisies with what looked like barbed wire connecting them all up. She stopped and looked up.

'I'll have to leave. This is the most embarrassing thing of my life. I just want to crawl into a hole and hibernate until nobody remembers me.'

'You'll do no such thing. You're a highly valued member of the team, and we'll all be much worse off without you. Call Pauline and get her to cover for you, then go and have an hour's break in the canteen.'

The baby had been fed and was back in his cot and sound asleep.

'Sorry Emma, but I need to hand this over to you. I overheard Michael saying it was yours. I haven't read it, of course. I think it might be a little contentious; Michael and Julie were having a big row.'

Emma took the note but already knew what it was. A cursory glance confirmed her fears.

'Oh, Lord.'

22

Wednesday 03 October 2018

Julie called in sick the following morning. She wouldn't have been able to put in a full shift without falling asleep, at least that's what she told herself. The truth was that it made her feel physically ill just to think about bumping into Michael or Emma.

She'd spent the first part of the night wondering if it was all a terrible mistake, and the second half realising it *was* all a terrible mistake. Even in the privacy of her bedroom, Julie's face glowed as she thought about her behaviour after first reading the note.

She'd seen the two bouquets, for God's sake. Was she really too thick to realise Emma had got the notes mixed up? Was it ignorance or just pure desperation, though? How long should it take to find a man? Was she *that* ugly?

At 3.30 in the morning, she'd gone to the fridge and dug out a bottle of cheap Cava. She wasn't a big drinker, and it had been in there for ages. Perhaps she imagined Michael and her would have a drink at her place after their first date. The thought produced a mixture of nausea and depression.

She grabbed a glass tumbler from the cupboard; using one of her two Champagne flutes would have made her want to cry. And why did she have two glasses anyway – wasn't one enough? Did she ever imagine in her wildest dreams that there might be someone else to share a bottle of bubbles with in her flat?

She teased the cork out of the cheap bottle, and it made no noise whatsoever; not the slightest sound. The irony actually made her briefly chuckle. She filled the tumbler to the brim but no head rose to spill over the edge – the drink was void of all effervescence.

Pouring the liquid down the sink made her think of Australia. Julie had been there as a teenager with her parents. The uncle they stayed with had told her water swirled down the sink or toilet in the opposite direction to England. She didn't believe him, but he dragged her mum and dad into it, and they'd both swore blind it was true.

For some reason, whenever she thought to Google it, she stopped short. It was almost as if she didn't want to find out it was a myth. What definitely wasn't a myth was the mechanic her mum had been seeing prior to their big trip. She went off with him for good a couple of months after they were back, and Dad wasn't over the moon about that.

So even her mum, who hand-on-heart wasn't as attractive as her, could still manage multiple relationships with guys. Yet her pretty daughter, aged 31, was already well and truly on top of the scrap heap. Even that was bigging herself up – *buried* in the scrap heap was much nearer the mark.

'You sure you're okay, Julie?' Maddy was genuinely concerned.

'Yeah, I'm fine. Just didn't sleep very well. I've never done this before, and I'm sure I'll be back tomorrow.'

'I know you haven't, sweetie, and that's what worries me. It's no problem, but promise to call me if you need anything?'

'Sure, and thanks. See you tomorrow.'

Maddy made a mental note to phone Julie during the day. She had no idea of the exact details of yesterday's fracas, but she wasn't stupid.

*

Michael had resisted alcohol for the whole evening. He'd messaged Jamie to ask if he could put Simon to bed tonight, citing an abundance of paperwork he needed to catch up on. Then he'd sat in his armchair staring at the blank screen of a television, wondering what a different place the world would be if Emma had received the note meant for her.

At midnight, his resolve was weakening. He opened a kitchen cupboard and stared at the unopened bottle of gin. There were two large bottles of tonic water standing next to it. He knew the ice was in the fridge, and he could dispense with a slice of lemon on this occasion.

He unscrewed the top, sniffed the liquid, and memories came flooding back. Bars on aircraft, perfectly manicured women in uniform, the never-ending Californian sun, the never-ending meetings, and the never-ending bullshit. The embarrassment of Penny, young Susie fawning all over him at the office, the overpowering smell of Victoria's perfume, being kicked out of his own apartment, his parents, the Liverpool of his youth which had gone just as surely as the love of his life.

He couldn't remember the words, but it was an innocuous enough note, he was sure. And that was where the problem would lie. He'd always, always written emotional notes to Emma, ever since they'd first met. She'd have read that letter of almost formal apology, and her mood would have darkened. The rest was history – down a pathway of no return.

It would make no difference now if she knew what had happened; all the damage had already been done. There was no winding back the flirting with Julie and the affair with Victoria. The hatred he'd displayed to his special friend – to her partner, her fiancé.

If he couldn't have Emma, he wasn't sure he wanted to carry on. To be so close to her and not be with her was becoming an agony that was going to destroy him. He put the bottle to his lips. The tonic and ice weren't needed on this occasion.

*

Emma wondered if the baby was ever going to sleep through the night. If someone could have shared the duties with her, it would be so much easier. She was so tired by the morning that work seemed an impossible dream to her. She refused to use any of the carers' hours to look after him, so he had to be with her at all times.

The residents loved to see the baby, but there was only so much she could do of that – Orchard was a residential care home, not a nursery. More than anything, she worried about her fiancé. Her one wish was to be married to him, but Emma knew the speed of his decline would prevent that now. The vows would be beyond his capacity, and there would be no one who would marry them, whatever arrangements he'd previously made with his solicitor.

She pulled the ring off her middle finger and studied it. The inside was engraved – *'Forever yours, Michael.'* Emma could no longer read it clearly even with her reading glasses on, but she knew what it said; remembered what it meant to her when Michael had pointed it out. She placed it on the table, next to the album she'd fetched from her apartment that morning. She hadn't looked at these photos in a long time.

The memories were so clear. The wedding gown – still the most expensive item of clothing she'd ever bought, now gathering dust in the loft of her parents' home. She looked so different now, but Michael had hardly changed.

Their families and friends, all brought together in one place for one day, never to be repeated. A special woman in a group photograph, then one of Emma and her giggling together on the same page. It was Lisa, who would have been about the same age as her now. She was in the final stages of Simon's illness at that time, yet the split second in time captured her only as a vibrant, happy woman. She'd passed away less than three months later.

Sadness engulfed her, and she closed the album. This disease crawled and stretched its poisonous tentacles around a sufferer's loved ones, just as surely as it did in the victim's own brain. Suffocating and extinguishing the love and the life of all who came into contact with it.

If she were in Simon's position now but could think with clarity, what would she want for herself? How would she conduct herself in what life remained, and what would she want for her loved ones?

She absentmindedly picked up the ring and put it on her wedding finger as she sought the answer to an unsolvable question.

*

Simon had remained in the lounge long after all the other residents had retired to bed. Nobody was in reception as he wandered to and from the activities table to the notice board. It was unnecessary as the front door was always locked after eight o'clock; anyone wanting to come in after then would ring the outside doorbell. Jamie had been into the lounge to turn the television off at 10.30 and gone to make Simon a mug of hot chocolate.

The two men sat at the table, and Jamie told him about the arrangements for Christmas. Maddy had already booked a band and a DJ, with firm plans for the appearance of Father Christmas and reindeer on Christmas Eve. As Simon continued studiously with his artwork, Jamie shared with Simon his belief that it probably wouldn't be actual reindeer, but more likely donkeys from the nearby sanctuary. Simon didn't offer an opinion on the subject, so Jamie moved on to the weather.

According to the carer, it was definitely going to be a white Christmas this year.

Simon stopped working and looked up at him. 'Snow?'

'For sure. If I were you, I'd get a bet on it now. I checked online today, and you can get odds of five-to-one if it snows on Christmas Day. The weathermen say it's going to be getting really cold soon, and we're in for a freezing winter.'

'Winter freeze?'

'You betcha, Simon. We'll be fine, though – it's always warm and snug in here. Do you want me to take you up to bed now? Take your hot chocolate with you? It's nearly eleven o'clock.'

There was no reply – Simon had a tongue stuck out of his mouth and was concentrating on his creation.

'I'll keep coming back every half hour. You tell me when you're ready for bed, and I'll take you up. There's no rush. There's never any rush in this place, mate.'

Simon wasn't aware of Jamie leaving the room.

The carer had completed his duties before midnight and sat at reception so he could keep an eye on Simon through the lounge doors. Eventually, he appeared to be packing up his things, and Jamie helped him upstairs with a folder, some brushes, and a small pot of green paint.

'No problem with painting in your room, buddy, but what do you think about getting some sleep now and starting again in the morning?'

'Busy.'

'OK, Simon, you're the boss. Press the buzzer or pull the cord if you want any help with anything, okay? Do you want me to get you into your pyjamas now?'

'No. Busy. Goodnight. Thank you.'

*

The weathermen hadn't been wrong. From the unseasonal warmth of a sunny autumn day, an overnight storm with gales from the north had brought a taste of the Arctic winter the meteorologists were predicting. The temperatures had plummeted.

Jamie's overnight notes had shown there was little unusual activity to report. It mentioned that Simon had stayed late in the lounge doing some painting and had carried on in his room until the middle of the night. Jamie had put his bedroom lights out at 2.45 a.m. He'd not been displaying any signs of agitation or excessive confusion, and in Jamie's opinion, it would simply lead to a later breakfast than normal.

Michael had spotted Emma in her office with Maddy when he walked past for breakfast just after 8 a.m. He was nursing an almighty hangover which paracetamol had yet to help. He was hoping to grab a croissant and get back to his room without being noticed, but Emma had seen him walking past and called out.

'Michael, can we grab a coffee together if you have a few minutes?'

'Oh, sure. Canteen or main dining room?'

'Here in the office if you like? Maddy's just about to go on her rounds.'

'Okay, I'll just grab a couple of croissants and see you in a minute.'

This was not what he needed. He'd had a shower but was sure he still stank of alcohol. He'd probably managed less than three hours sleep and hadn't bothered to shave yet. He'd thrown a parka over his old jeans and sweatshirt to battle the coldness on the way from his place across the car park, and probably looked like a tramp.

Michael had seen the nightshift email report, and Simon's predicted late breakfast was a blessing. He planned to be properly dressed and hopefully nearly sober by the time he went to see him at 9.30, when he hoped he could face a normal breakfast with his friend.

'Are you alright? Are you going down with something?'

'I'm fine. Wellll, fine-ish. Late night – storm kept me awake. I guess you slept through it as normal?' It was an unintentionally intimate comment that only the alcohol could have produced, and he bit his tongue to control himself.

'I didn't, actually. So you went into town last night?' Emma was more than familiar with Michael's appearance after too much to drink.

'Is it that obvious? I feared it might be. Do you want to meet up later, after I've got my act together and had breakfast with Simon?'

'No, it's fine – as long as you don't feel too rough? I thought you were on the wagon?'

'Yeah, I was. I'll be jumping back on it from now, too. Just had a bit of a slip. Stupid of me, and I'm cursing myself.'

'What triggered it?'

Michael sighed, and his cheeks puffed out. He definitely wasn't ready for the croissant yet. 'It's a long story. A very long and boring mixed up story.'

Emma put the note on the table in front of him. 'Would it have anything to do with this?'

Michael looked at the piece of paper he'd been holding in his hand in this very office only yesterday. His alcohol-fuelled paleness quickly changed to bright beacon red.

'Oh shit. That wasn't quite how I imagined confronting you with this.' He was grateful Emma interrupted him; he really wasn't sure what to say.

'As I said to you in Simon's room, this is totally *my* fault. It's nothing to do with you. Oh, Christ, is that why you've been drinking? Tell me it's not.'

'Wellll. Yeah, maybe. A little bit. But that's it – not a drop more.'

'Oh, Michael, I'm so sorry. I feel even worse than when Julie showed me the note.'

Michael looked at Emma as things began to fall into place. A wave of nausea hit him, and he thought he might throw up.

'Em, I'm going to have to be very rude and rush back to my room. Can we meet up in Simon's room at 9.30? I should be okay to face breakfast then. He'll be up late today.'

'Yup, I saw the notes from Jamie. Okay, but don't worry if you can't make it. We can meet up later if that works for you. I'd like a chat.'

'Me too. I'll see you later.'

He did his best not to run out of the office.

*

Desperate to do something to lift his hangover in the next hour, Michael had gulped down two double espressos from his machine. He knew time was the only real cure, but that wasn't an option. He soaked his face and hair with cold water in the sink and stared at the image in the mirror. The whites of his eyes were bloodshot, and he now had a pale grey complexion.

This couldn't happen again, and he swore to himself it wouldn't happen again. He'd said that before more than once, but he hoped this time was the last. He needed to change his life, and it needed to start now.

Michael looked out of the bathroom window at the grounds beyond. Everywhere was saturated from the storm, but at least it had stopped raining. It felt bitterly cold, but he'd warm up. He pulled his parka and one of the two sweatshirts off, then swapped his jeans for a pair of summer shorts. He only had one pair of trainers which he was already wearing.

Michael tried to remember the last time he'd run a mile; definitely not since school and probably not then either. He'd never been interested in athletics – all his running was done on a football pitch. Even then, goalkeepers weren't renowned for the ground they covered during a match.

He stopped halfway around Simon's circuit to be sick, wondering at one point if he'd ever draw a full breath again.

The second half of the course was considerably slower, but at least he'd completed what was rather obviously his very first mile run.

Stumbling into the shower and getting dressed as quickly as he could, it was only when looking in the mirror on the way out that he realised he hadn't shaved. Ten minutes later, he was knocking on Simon's door. It was Emma who opened the door to let him in.

'Now that's quite a transformation. Where's the Michael I saw an hour and a half ago?'

'Oh, he's gone forever. Well, at least I hope he has. Hello, Simon, I heard you were up late last night? Jamie said you'd been painting? I didn't know you were an artist – is it good?'

Simon smiled.

'He wanted to wait until you were here before unveiling it.' Emma linked her arm in Simon's and kissed his cheek.

Michael turned around and noticed two white pillowcases hanging over the canvas photo Emma had given him. He could tell it was the same picture as the exposed light brown frame was identical.

Simon took his arm out of Emma's and turned to Michael, moving him nearer to her. When they were close enough, he put Michael's arm around Emma's shoulders. He stepped towards the wall and turned to them.

'Are you ready?'

There was a huge grin on his face like a child on Christmas morning. Emma and Michael were both feeling a little awkward in their designated positions, but they sensed this was how Simon wanted them to remain.

'Three, two, one, dah daahhhh.' He pulled the pillowcases theatrically out of the way, and Michael's and Emma's faces froze in unison.

The canvas had been completely transformed. Where Emma had been relaxing her head against Simon's chest with his head just above hers and a background of grass, she was now entirely on her own. He'd very skilfully and effectively removed all trace of himself with a blanket of painted grass. Her face continued to beam out of the photograph.

Next to her face, Simon had stuck a small separate painting on top of the canvas. A perfectly symmetrical heart covered most of the art paper, again beautifully painted to show light reflections as if made of mercury. Within the heart, three further images had been pasted. The two smiling head and shoulders staff photos of Emma and Michael from the board in reception, and the scanned black and white image of baby Simon as a foetus between them.

'Very good?'

As they continued to stare, both speechless, Simon moved behind them and put his arms around the couple.

'Very good.'

23

Thursday 04 October to Thursday 08 November 2018

An extraordinary development had taken place in the past four weeks. After Michael's initial vomit-inducing run around Simon's circuit, he'd attempted the same feat again the following week. Without the alcohol in his system he was no longer sick, and although he found the last part tough, he'd managed to avoid slowing down to a walk.

The weather was continually hovering just above or just below freezing in what looked like becoming the coldest winter in many years. The daily walks he and Simon took were becoming intermittent because Simon refused to wrap up in winter clothing. Michael had offered him his own gear which would have been fine – both men were of almost identical build and height – but Simon would have none of it.

Michael had raised the subject the following day, but with a slight twist.

'Simon, I've just started trying to run your course. I'm hopeless, but yesterday I managed to finish one circuit without stopping to walk. You're a great runner – would you be prepared to coach me? I'll never run as fast as you, but can you show me how to run better? You can put your tracksuit on, and we can have a workout in the gym to get warm, then go for a little run together. Will you help me, Simon?'

It was difficult to know what Simon was thinking nowadays. He may say nothing but understand everything, and other times he'd reply but make no sense. By this stage, Michael liked to think he knew his friend better than anyone. From the way Simon was staring into his eyes, Michael was certain he'd been understood.

Simon nodded and went to his wardrobe. A single tracksuit hung there on its own, nestled amongst twenty or so redundant coat hangers. He pulled the top over his sweatshirt, took his jeans off, and then put the rest of his tracksuit on.

'Ready.'

They went down to the gym, and Michael set up the running machine for Simon. With no effort, he ran for twenty minutes without breaking into a sweat.

Michael turned the machine off. 'I don't know how you do that. I'd have collapsed ages ago.'

Simon laughed and touched Michael on his shoulder – it was the first physical contact he'd made with him in months.

'You go. Try. Not fast.'

Michael set the machine at a slower speed, almost a fast walk, and got on. He jogged slowly as Simon watched him intently. After a minute, Simon moved to the side of the machine and put his hand under Michael's chin, pushing it higher. He lifted his head, and Simon nodded and continued to study him.

He moved in front of the machine and held his hands straight, just as Michael was doing. Then he curled the fingers into a very loose fist. Michael did the same, and Simon nodded again and smiled. The connection was deeply moving, and Michael wanted to get off the machine and hug the man.

His breathing was becoming a little laboured now, but as he was thinking about getting off the never-ending road, Simon's hand moved over the big red stop button and tapped it.

Michael had been running for ten minutes and was sweating from head to foot.

'Phew, thanks for that. I guess we go outside and run now, do we?'

Simon nodded and walked out of the gym.

At the end of the car park where the circuit started, the two men stood together and looked at each other. Simon held up Michael's left wrist so the watch was in front of him.

'Ah, good point. You want me to time this, right?'

Another nod, then 'Go.' Michael started off, and Simon let him go ahead. For the mile, he stayed glued to Michael but never in front of him.

When Michael staggered back to where they started from some time later, he bowed down and put his hands on his thighs, fighting for breath. Simon grabbed his wrist again and looked at the watch.

'Leven mins forty.'

Michael started to cough and spat a couple of times. 'We need some water. Well, I do at any rate. Let's go to my flat.' As he was talking, he heard a scuffle on the ground. He looked up to see Simon sprinting off down the track.

'Hey. Hey, Simon. Come back.'

The man had gone, and there was nothing Michael could do. He was so exhausted he could hardly move, such was his lack of fitness. He thought to go back across the car park and call for help, but praying his instincts were right, he waited.

Simon appeared a few minutes later, and this time there was a little sweat on his face.

'Hey buddy, you had me worried. Why di...'

But Simon had lunged for Michael's wrist again to stare at the watch.

'Six twenny. Bad.'

He strode across the car park with Michael following, still trying to find his breath.

*

The photographs of Michael and Emma had been replaced on the staff board. The two which Simon had pinched for his masterpiece still remained on his painting for all to see.

Michael found it awkward to look at the picture, and Emma found it downright impossible. She'd occasionally asked Simon if he'd take it down, but he was adamant; it was going nowhere. Because of this, she'd try and meet Simon in her rooms whenever possible, but he was now spending so much time in his own room that it meant seeing even less of him.

She wondered if it was possible he could have planned it this way, then scolded herself for being ridiculous. Simon was well past anything of that complexity. On a rare occasion when he'd had lunch in the main dining room with Michael, she'd joined the two men.

'What would we do without Mr Patel, Em?' Michael was stuffed after his roast lamb and couldn't manage a dessert. He was also aware that his run would be coming up in a couple of hours. There was no way of avoiding it, however full he felt – it was now a daily ritual, and Simon would be devastated if they didn't run.

'Well, we'd stop eating like kings, and I'd probably start to lose weight, but I'm still having a fruit salad. Will you have some fruit, Simon?'

Simon had been grinning for most of the meal, though had said little. He appeared to be delighted to see Michael and Emma together. 'Yes. Please.'

Michael stood up. 'I'm going to finish that review; the accountants are in next week. I'll see you in your room in about an hour, Simon. Then off to the gym and the track.'

'Good.' Simon nodded and touched his wrist. Michael was never without his watch, but Simon always became anxious of its proximity before a run.

'I'll report to you in my tracksuit and watch in an hour, coach.' He'd managed to buy the exact matching tracksuit as Simon's online – something that had thrilled the man when he saw Michael in it for the first time, and every time since. Every day he'd marvel at the coincidence and say '*Same tracky, same tracky.*'

Michael saluted Simon and winked at Emma as he left the table.

Emma leaned across their table towards Simon. She knew already what would happen, but she extended her hand anyway and smiled.

He stared at her hand but made no move to make contact. He hadn't touched her in a long time, and the coldness killed her. She moved her hand back and rested it on the table.

'Simon, there's something I want to say to you. It's so important to me, and I want you to understand. Will you look at me while I talk to you? I'd like that.'

He was staring at his glass of water and didn't lift his head. It was how things had deteriorated between them, but however illogical, she chose to believe it would change back again one day. Today may be that day if she was careful and gentle enough. The man in front of Emma owned her heart and soul.

'Listen to me, darling. Today is a big day. Today I can apply for my official divorce from Michael. Once that's done, we can try and get married. Even if that doesn't happen, I can be with you properly. It's what I want; I love you.'

Simon lifted his head and looked into Emma's eyes. His face was expressionless, and it was impossible to tell what he was thinking or even if anything was registering.

He shook his head twice then looked back down at the table again.

Emma could go no further until she'd said this. It was something she felt compelled to tell him, even though it went against all her training.

'Simon, I believe you know exactly what you're doing. You're the most selfless person I've ever known, and you've purposely denied your love for me because you know our time is limited. You'd go through any amount of pain if you thought it might spare me some of my own. Even though your heart may be bursting with pain, you've pushed me and Michael together and pretended that's what you want.'

Emma was trying to gulp back tears, but they were dripping down her face.

'You're even prepared to give your son away and deny the love you surely must have because you believe it'll be better for him. I can't allow this Simon. I *won't* allow this. I want you for every minute we have left.'

He lifted his head again, but this time his face was wracked with pain and misery. As he looked at Emma, tears started to form in his eyes. He stood up and moved to her side of the table, put his hand on top of hers, and squeezed. When she looked up into his face, he was crying.

He leaned down and kissed her head, then left the dining room.

*

With Simon's help, Michael had begun to feel better about his running and was now much less fatigued during and after their sessions. As soon as he'd managed to achieve a time of less than ten minutes for the mile circuit, the following day Simon had made him run around twice.

What had started out as an idea to get Simon back into running was now becoming Michael's favourite part of the day. It also bewildered him that Simon had the capacity to remember recent occurrences when short-term memory was always catastrophically affected in his advanced condition.

Doubling the distance had left Michael panting for some time after the run, but Simon, using mostly body language and the occasional word, had kept him lapping the circuit twice on their daily runs.

A week had gone by before Michael managed the two miles in just under twenty minutes. As before, the following day Simon had pushed him to run an extra lap, by which time Michael realised the eventual goal was to complete the three miles in less than 30 minutes.

He'd been fifteen seconds over the half-hour mark on their last run, but today the weather had taken a turn for the worse. The temperature was minus-two Celsius and predicted to fall as low as minus-six overnight. It seemed unlikely to him that the target would be achieved in the near future.

Simon was already in his tracksuit when Michael arrived.

272

'Sorry I'm a bit late. Shall we go down to the gym and get warmed up? There won't be too much light left by the time we're finished today.'

In their gym workout, it was normal for Simon to go on the running machine first while Michael did some stretching. Then he'd take his turn on the machine while Simon watched him. The speeds had increased considerably since they first started, and he felt much more comfortable now.

Today, the routine was broken when Simon wouldn't go on the machine. He motioned for Michael to start running on it but wanted his watch first. He secured it on his wrist and watched it constantly as Michael built up a sweat. At one point, he leaned across the machine and increased the speed a little; something only Michael had controlled in the past. It was to be a day of firsts, and the carer was amazed at his patient's lucidity.

'Stop. 'Nuff. Running now.'

By the time they got to the start of the course, it was beginning to get dark. This was definitely the coldest day of the winter so far, and smoke was billowing from both their mouths. They'd normally set off with Michael noting the time on his watch while standing beside his silent coach, always with the second hand approaching the 12 – Simon was insistent on that.

With Simon wearing Michael's watch this time, he took up position half a dozen paces in front of him.

'Ready. Steady. Go.' Simon bolted off at a quicker pace than Michael could remember, but he kept up with him. The distance between them remained constant as they completed the first circuit. Michael couldn't remember running this fast ever before and instinctively looked for the time on his bare wrist.

'Eight mins forry. Hurry.'

Michael couldn't believe it. He'd knocked over a minute off his best lap. Maybe Simon wasn't reading the watch correctly.

The pace remained constant, and Michael could feel tightness in his chest building. His breathing was faster too but nothing compared to a month ago. He felt good and could feel a rhythm; the gap to Simon wasn't widening, and the second lap was up.

'Seveneen thurry five. Hurry. Push.'

The rhythm was getting more ragged, and the breathing was harder. His head was dipping so he held it up again, just as Simon had taught him. The feeling was agonising, yet fantastic. He was starting to gulp air now.

'Push. Push. Come. On.'

Michael could see the car park in the distance, the tarmac and cars lit up by sodium lamps. Sweat was getting in his eyes, and he wiped his face.

'Go, go, *go.*' Simon peeled to one side and slowed, letting Michael overtake him. His eyes were glued on the watch.

'Yes. Twenny six mins fiffy eight. *Yes!*'

Michael fell on the ground by the side of the tarmac, his body screaming for air and rest. It was probably a rubbish time compared to reasonable athletes, but he'd run his guts out and felt proud. More than that, he felt a huge warmth and affection for his friend.

Simon stood next to him and clapped his hands, his face glowing with delight. He put a hand down to Michael and squeezed his arm, and the two men looked at each other.

Then both laughed. It was the first time Michael had heard Simon laugh in so long that he'd forgotten the noise. He stood up and put his arm out to shake hands, but Simon ignored it. Instead, the coach embraced his pupil.

'Well done. Good. Keep run every day.'

'Of course I will. Try and stop me now. We'll keep doing this every day, and with you as my coach, I'll be in the next Olympics. Now *that's* what I call a plan.'

Simon stood back, and his eyes blazed into Michael's. The elation and the laughter had gone, and his expression was now one of almost sadness. He broke eye contact and extended his hand. Michael went to shake it but then saw his watch dangling from Simon's fingers.

'Yours. S'cold now. Good bye.' He turned and headed back to the home. Michael followed but knew not to bother him – the silence was never uncomfortable between them. He saw him back to his room, but Simon didn't turn around or say anything else, closing the door behind him.

Michael stared at the number on the door, displayed in large brass digits. He thought about the person who lived in room 30, and how very much he'd miss him when he was gone. Simon Carter was a truly remarkable human being.

The two men had never broached the subject, but he knew how much Emma meant to Simon, even now. He loved her with a purity that Michael could never hope to reach or emulate.

At that moment, Michael believed he'd give his own life if it could save Simon.

He turned away and walked back down the stairs. Julie was at reception in deep conversation with the Major, who was explaining how it was quite impossible to play knock-out whist without an ace of diamonds. It was most distressing because it was his own pack of cards which he'd carried all over the world during the war and kept with him at all times ever since.

Julie knew this was a deck of cards barely a month old and supplied by the home, but that was certainly not the point.

'Don't worry, Major; I'll have a look later and find it for you. For now, I know just where there's a brand new pack of cards. You go and sit back down with Raymond, and I'll bring them over to you.'

The army veteran thanked her and wandered slowly back to the lounge.

'Hey, Michael, you look shattered. Has Simon been working you too hard?'

'You could say that, but nothing a ninety-minute shower and twelve hours of kip won't sort out.'

'Alright for some. How is he, anyway? Probably didn't even break out in a sweat, eh?'

'Well, I have to admit you were right. He sure isn't ready for a wheelchair yet, that's for sure.'

There was a split second of uncertainty from Julie, then they both giggled at the distant memory.

'Be off with you Mr Lowry, before it costs you another bunch of flowers.'

Michael raised his hands in self-defence and walked to the entrance. He turned back at the door.

'I'll tell you what, Julie, that man's a saint. We're all in the presence of a saint.'

24

Thursday 08 November 2018

A member of the kitchen staff had been to see Simon a little before six o'clock with the dinner menu, just as she did with all residents who chose to have an evening meal in their rooms. She knew what he'd have, but the routine was important. There were always two choices of starter, main course, and dessert, and Simon would have soup, fish, and fruit. He'd often say nothing and just nod at her suggestion, but this was what Emma had instructed the staff to serve when he didn't offer any decisions himself.

Simon was still in a tracksuit and sitting at his desk. He seemed to be writing something, which seemed most unusual to Laura. She couldn't remember the last time she'd seen him reading or even watching television in his room, and rather presumed writing would be beyond his capabilities at this stage.

She tried to glimpse if it was just scribble or actual words, but he put his arms over whatever he'd been doing. It reminded her of a schoolboy in an exam and made her smile.

'Writing love letters to Emma, eh? That's really lovely. Wish my old man would do that. I think the last time he gave me a proper kiss was after we'd said our vows in the church.' Laura cackled with laughter which provoked a cough. It was the chesty rattling cough of a smoker that Simon knew only too well. He looked at her and assessed she was somewhere in her fifties. His father had died of lung cancer in his sixties.

'Stop smoking.'

The woman was momentarily taken aback, but it wasn't for long. Laura wasn't the best listener and could talk for England.

'How did you know? You're right, though. I've tried so many times, and then something ruins it. After a meal or when I have a few drinks, that's the worst time. I wish I could give it up for good, love. I even tried that vaping malarkey. Oh, and those patches too. All rubbish – I just need the right frame of mind and the right incentive. I said to my hubby the other day; I said Frank, you know ...'

'You'll die.'

The silence lasted longer this time. Laura turned to walk out of the room. In a little world of her own, she'd forgotten to ask Simon what he wanted for supper.

'Soup. Fish. Fruit. Thanks.'

She turned around with her mouth open, but for once, no words came out. This was the first time she'd heard Simon verbally choose his dinner for at least a couple of months. He was looking at her with what appeared to be a mischievous grin, but that seemed more than unlikely.

'Okay dear. I'll see you tomorrow. You take care now.'

Simon lifted a hand and pointed a finger at her. 'No cigarettes. You'll die. Bye-bye.'

*

Most unusually, it was Orchard's star chef who presented Simon with his tray of food that evening. Mr Patel's hat fascinated Simon.

'It's Michael's idea and a very good one. From now on, every Thursday evening I'll be delivering dinner for all our residents who wish to eat in their own rooms. There's a good few people I never get to meet, and he wants everyone to know everyone at Orchard. He wants us to be like a big family. He's a good man, that Michael.'

'Very good man. Can I use your hat?'

'Aha. You're not the first person to admire my hat. Do you want to try it on? Give me your phone, and I'll take a photo for you. Oh, hold on, do you have a mobile phone?'

Simon looked at him and shrugged.

'That's okay, I'll take it on my phone and send it to the boss. Emma can show you it later. Here you go; I'll put it on for you.'

As Mr Patel held the phone up, Simon put a hand next to his face and waved.

'Excellent. I'll send that to Emma tonight, and you can have a laugh when you see it tomorrow.'

'No. But thank you. Good hat.' Simon bent his head towards the man, and he took his chef's hat back.

'I've had this hat since I became a chef, Simon. God willing, I'll have it until I retire. It puts the food on my family's table, so to speak. It's called a ...'

'Toque.'

Mr Patel's eyes widened. 'How did you know? I mean, how come you ...'

'Toque Blanche. One hundred folds. One hundred eggs.' Simon's eyes sparkled as he looked at the bewildered chef.

'I … I have to go and feed the five thousand, Simon. Their meals must be piping hot. I hope to see you again very soon. Come down to the dining room tomorrow, maybe? We'd all like that. We all really miss you.'

'Can't. Sorry. Bye-bye.'

*

Simon had emptied all his food into a polythene bag and placed it in the bathroom bin. He wasn't hungry, and it would not assist him in any way. Leaving it on the tray untouched would also have been problematic; his solution was the correct one.

Pauline had come to his room after seven o'clock to collect all the trays and offer tea or coffee. It was turned down in favour of water.

'Fancy one of my regular tea drinkers turning me down. Shame on you, Simon.' She smiled and rubbed his shoulder. Pauline was a delightful woman, and one of his favourite carers.

'It's brass monkeys out there tonight, darling. Ice all over the place. You sure you don't want something warm? I can get you a hot chocolate if you like; it's no bother.'

'No. Water good. Thanks.'

'Okay sweetheart. Jamie will be up soon with your pills. Do you want the television on?'

'No. Bye-bye.' He turned to face her and held out his right arm to shake hands.

'You want to shake hands, love? Awwww, bless. Come here – give Auntie Pauline a hug. I'm the Orchard hug machine.' She opened her arms and moved towards him. She was in her mid-sixties and the oldest member of staff. There wasn't a resident or colleague who didn't adore her.

Once Pauline had gone, he sat back at his desk and continued to write. He couldn't remember where his reading glasses were and it was all a blur, but he'd only get one shot at this. He slowly and laboriously penned each capital letter – joined-up handwriting was impossible for him now.

Twenty minutes later, Jamie knocked at the open door and walked in.

'Only me, Simon. Just your tablets to take.' He passed Simon the little plastic beaker and watched him swallow them.

'Good man. You coming down to the lounge tonight or staying in your room?'

'Sleep.'

'Okay, mate. I heard about your running today; Michael told me all about it. He's over the moon – you're one amazing coach, dude. Do you want me to help you get into your pyjamas?'

Simon shook his head. 'Thanks. Bye-bye.' He stuck out his right arm, and Jamie took it, turning the hand so it pointed upwards.

'Try it this way, Simon. It's how sportsmen shake hands, and you're sure one of them.' They linked palms and thumbs, and both men grinned at each other.

'Have a good kip, mate. I'll pop my head in later tonight. Seeya.'

'Bye-bye.'

Jamie passed Emma in the hallway as he pushed his drugs trolley to the next room.

'Hi, Emma. Simon was just telling me he's tired; thinks he'll go to sleep soon. Must have been that epic run he had today. Did you hear about it? Michael smashed his personal best by miles.'

'Wow, sounds good. I'm sure I'll hear about it soon enough. I'm a bit shattered myself, so I'll see you tomorrow, Jamie. Thanks a lot.'

Emma walked into Simon's room and found him lying on the bed in his tracksuit. The main lights were out, and there was just a dim glow from the bedside lamp.

'Hello, sleepy, Jamie tells me you had a good run with Michael today?'

Simon sat up, and Emma moved next to him on the bed, leaning her head against his shoulder. She was surprised and delighted when he put his arm around her. At last, a genuine display of affection from her lover.

'Tired. So tired.'

'I know, love. Want me to get you into bed? It's so cold outside tonight; I've never known a start to winter like it.'

Simon shook his head. 'Need shower. Then sleep.'

'OK, darling. Hey, our son is getting better at sleeping. Last night he only woke once; if that carries on, I'll get back to work again soon. Will you come and see us tomorrow after breakfast?'

'Simon Michael. Kiss him f'me. And cuddly.'

'Sure I will, but you can do that yourself tomorrow. Tell you what, I'll bring him up here before you get out of bed in the morning, and we'll all have a big family hug. Would you like that? We'll come and wake you up, okay?'

Simon stood up. 'Need shower. Hug me?'

Emma was taken by surprise and overjoyed – she'd seriously begun to wonder if they'd ever truly hold each other again. She stood up and moved close to him, then folded herself into his arms.

Simon didn't want to let go. This was the best feeling he'd ever had. Right here and right now. This togetherness – this now-ness.

He smelt his lover's hair and inhaled deeply. Images flashed by at light speed as a few of the faltering trillions of synapses briefly allowed lost neurons to make fleeting connections with each other, firing sparks of dying memory.

Why couldn't now last forever?

The love was overpowering him, and it couldn't last a second longer.

It mustn't.

'Shower.'

Emma hadn't moved when Simon turned around to her at the bathroom door. The eyes were the ones that had so profoundly affected her as she'd first looked into them - deepest azure blue, shimmering with light from an unknown source.

'I will love you frever and frever.'

And then he closed the door.

*

Simon sat under the shower. The cold had taken his breath away at first, but his body was gradually acclimatising to it. It was time.

He towelled his face and hair dry but let his body drip. Leaving his T-shirt, underwear and socks on the floor, he then put just his tracksuit and trainers back on.

Simon always slept with two pillows. When dawn arrived through the curtains, he'd use one of them to cover his eyes. It was a habit he'd maintained since a boy at boarding school. He hated that life so much that he wanted to blank out his world for just a little longer, if only by a couple of minutes.

On a shelf at the top of his wardrobe were two further spare pillows. They'd remained untouched since he moved into the room and were still in their individual protective covers. He pulled them down and pushed both under the covers of his bed along with his own two, then pulled the blanket and sheet up to the headboard against the wall.

He looked back from a distance, then plumped the pillows and made a few adjustments. Satisfied with his work, he pulled three pieces of paper out of the drawer of his bedside table and put them in his pocket. His skin was still damp and cold against the inside of the tracksuit. Looking around one last time, he turned the bedside light off and walked out of the door.

At reception, Julie had nearly finished her shift and was tidying up the desk. In her diary, she'd placed an envelope marked '*The Major*', containing an ace of diamonds. She'd found it down the side of the armchair Raymond had been sitting in.

'Hey, Simon, what's up? Want me to organise some tea for you in the lounge?'

'Want to run.'

'It's a bit late for that now, isn't it? Besides, it's freezing outside – you'd catch your death out there. How about I call Michael or Jamie and see if …'

'Gym. In gym. Run machine.'

'Ohhhhh, okay. Here, let me go down with you and put the lights on. Just leave everything on when you're finished, and Jamie will sort things out, okay?'

They walked down the corridor beside the lounge and down a small flight of steps. She unlocked the door and turned the lights on.

'There you go. Want me to wait while you get started? I can call Jamie if you want?'

'No. Thanks. Fine.' Simon stepped up onto the track and set the machine in motion. It defaulted to the slowest of slow walking paces. He dialled the speed up and started jogging.

'You look great when you run, Simon. You look like you're floating. If I had a go, I'd be knackered in two minutes.' She giggled, and Simon looked at her and smiled.

'Bye-bye. You are special.' He waved from the machine, and Julie waved back, blowing him a kiss.

*

This was when he was at his most relaxed. Running for the pure joy of it. He thought he could probably run on this rubber road for the whole night without getting tired. Maybe he could run forever, permanently suspended in the now?

He started to feel warmer and instinctively knew it was time to stop, though he couldn't quite remember why. The reason was swimming in the periphery of his consciousness as he pressed the stop button and dismounted the machine. Looking around the gym, he saw the door he'd come through with Julie and started to walk towards it, but something wasn't right. It wasn't what he wanted or needed to do.

He turned slowly and studied the room until his eyes came to rest on the fire door. The door they used to go outside when he went running with his friend. He walked over to it and pushed the bar handle.

A blast of icy wind enveloped him, and Simon cowered and shivered. He pulled on the handle to shut the cold out but stopped short. As he faltered, neurons battled for control of his movements. The natural instinct to shun the cold and seek the warmth was being blocked by a deeper-seated desire.

He pushed the door wider, and the wind took it, flinging it wide open against its hinges with a clatter. As the bewildered man felt icy spots of rain spatter his face, he slowly stepped outside. With the sharp coldness came the clarity, and he ran into the welcoming darkness of the trees beyond.

*

Michael had fallen asleep in front of his television. The exertions of the day had been wonderful but exhausting. As he drifted off, he was thinking what he could get Simon as a gift, for all the help and encouragement he'd given him this past month. Something he'd really appreciate. It would be difficult, but Michael was determined to find something. Maybe they could go to an athletics meeting in the spring if Simon was well enough.

Emma fed baby Simon for what she hoped would be the last time before he woke again in the very early morning. As she held the bottle to his lips, she told him that tomorrow was going to be a special day. They would go and see Daddy and wake him up with a kiss each – one on either side of his face. Then they'd all have one big snugly hug in bed, just as it was meant to be for every family.

Julie was tickled pink by Simon's compliment. He was now a man of few words but always a gentleman and such a good-looking guy. He was her absolute favourite resident, and she'd tell him so tomorrow when she saw him. She was five minutes late leaving work and in a rush to get to her second evening-class. A girlfriend had confided in her that it was often a great place to meet new people, and the man taking the Italian Cooking for Beginners course had definitely been flirting last week while helping her knead the pasta dough.

Jamie had finished his nightly medicine rounds earlier than normal and nipped into the staff canteen for a quick coffee. He had a brief chat with Mr Patel who told him what an extraordinary man the owner of Orchard was. Did Jamie know if Simon used to be a chef?

No, Jamie was sure he'd been an accountant all his working life, and a very successful one at that.

Then that was amazing because Mr Patel had never come across anyone outside the catering industry who knew the correct name for a chef's hat, let alone why and how it was originally made.

Jamie wondered if Chef had been at the sherry bottle after dinner.

The far-fetched yarn had caused him to miss Julie before she left. He knew why she was off promptly, though; there was apparently the potential for a first date in yonks. She often asked him why she could never get a man, yet he'd been blissfully happy with the same one for years, and he'd always shrugged – he didn't know the answer to that one.

He looked behind her desk, but there were no notes for him on the observations list – just an envelope for the Major in the main diary.

Laura had been soaked while running to her car at the far end of the car park. Settled inside and out of the freezing wind, she leaned over to the glovebox to grab her packet of cigarettes. She placed one thankfully between her lips and produced a lighter from her bag. The interior of the car illuminated as the flame appeared, but as she drew it towards the end of the cigarette, she stopped. Simon was right – it was going to kill her. The flame wavered as slivers of wind found their way through gaps in her old car.

It *was* going to kill her. Of course it bloody was. She snapped the lighter shut, pulled the cigarette out of her mouth, crunched it in her hand, and threw it on the car floor, then did the same with the half-empty packet.

'God bless you, Simon,' she said to herself as she drove out of the car park. Her headlights picked up movement in the grounds, and she momentarily stopped the car. It was someone in a tracksuit running in the freezing rain. Michael must be off his head. A lovely guy, but he must be bonkers. Laura drove out of the home.

*

By nine o'clock, there were no residents left in the lounge. Half an hour later, Jamie was wandering along the bedroom corridor of his floor to make sure nobody needed any further assistance with anything. Walking past room 30, he listened at the door. There was no noise; not surprising after running in the freezing weather with Michael today. Simon was probably asleep the moment his head hit the pillow.

His final room checked, he made for the stairs. Chef's story about Simon was playing on his mind. It was nuts. Not knowing why but following the instinct which had seen him become a carer of rare talent and ability, Jamie walked back to Simon's room. He listened again and then lightly tapped on the door. There wasn't a sound. He frowned and shook his head. Turning the door handle as quietly as he could, he opened the door wide enough to pop his head in.

The room was in darkness, but the hall lighting allowed him to see enough to put his mind at rest. Simon was sleeping the sleep of the dead.

*

It was incredibly cold and very wet, the gale force winds slicing through him. Simon put his hands into the tracksuit trouser pockets. He'd forgotten the photos until he felt them. The full moon gave the illumination he needed to see the three most important people in his life, but the icy rain wet the pictures immediately. He put them back in his pocket and sought shelter.

By now he was soaked, and his teeth were chattering. Wandering through the woods, he crossed his running course, clumps of grass rising either side of soil tightly compacted by a million footprints. He veered off the track and into the darkness again, where the moon was unable to penetrate through the blanket of trees. It gave him some respite from the incessant rain, but he could get no wetter.

Over a thousand metres from the home, he came to the end of the property. Ruddy and pocked brick walls standing some twelve feet tall formed a corner of the estate. Halfway up against one wall stood a lean-to corrugated iron roof held up by two sturdy wooden poles buried deeply into the ground. The structure had been there for decades, and the roof was rusty and holed, offering the chopped and stacked firewood only a modicum of protection.

Simon moved under the roof and sat down, his back resting against the wood. Within minutes, the lack of movement was dropping his core body temperature. He was tired and closed his eyes.

Sometime later, fitful dreams of the woman he loved were interrupted by a growing heat in his body. He couldn't comprehend why he was so hot when it was so cold. Unzipping and removing his top, he bundled it up and put it behind his head and neck, which were stiff from the unforgiving logs. He slipped further down into a more comfortable sleeping position, crossed his legs, and put his hands in his pockets.

Bringing out the photos again, he held them up in front of him, one at a time. They were creased and tatty by now, but only slightly damp. Each had a note on the back; it was his own handwriting, but he couldn't remember writing it.

The image was of a tiny baby, surrounded by a blurred white and grey background. The shape of the child was clear against the dark bubble it lay in.

On the reverse, '*BE HAPPY ALL YOUR LIFE*'.

A close up of a grey-haired man smiling. Almost laughing. A wicked sense of humour in his eyes, but a loyalty too. Someone to trust.

He turned the photo over – '*LOVE THEM ALWAYS ~ 6 LAPS/40m 37s ~ BEAT IT*'.

The woman he'd dreamed of looked back at him. Beautiful and perfect, gentle and kind, compassionate and his. He slid further down to get more comfortable. He still felt hot, but so very tired too. So, so tired.

'*NO TEARS. NO REGRETS. MY HEART IN YOURS. FOREVER*'.

Simon's woman looked back at him as his eyes closed.

25

Friday 09 November to Thursday 20 June 2019

Simon Junior had woken once at 2.45 in the morning, but only for a nappy change. Emma could nearly do this in her sleep, and what had once taken ten minutes now took a couple. She jumped back into her warm bed, but a chill shook her deep inside. The wind and rain had subsided, but the light of the moon showed a layer of snow and ice everywhere.

The baby cried again three hours later, and this time it was hunger. She wondered about feeding him up in Simon's room, but the harmony she hoped for would be better achieved with a sated child.

It was a little before 6.30 when she walked up the stairs to Simon's floor with their son. It was still dark outside, and Simon would definitely be asleep unless there'd been a problem during the night.

Carrying the sleeping baby in her arms, she opened the door quietly and moved to the bed to switch the bedside lamp on.

Rising panic moved up her throat as the pillows gave way to her hand. She turned the room lights on and called out his name, running to the bathroom. She pulled the red cord in there, and moments later, Jamie was in the room.

He looked at the bed, and his face drained of colour. 'Christ, where is he?'

The panic in his mother's voice had woken Simon, and he started to cry.

'When did you see him last? Oh, my God, where is he, Jamie?'

'I checked on him mid-evening and once during the night but he was, well, I didn't realise. Oh, Christ.'

Fear had spread across Emma's face as she scanned the room and the baby cried. Her eyes had already moved past the altered painting when she stopped and looked back again. The three photos stuck on the picture. Gone.

'Check the dining rooms on all the floors. I'll check the main one and the lounge, and everywhere else I can think of. Come down to reception and meet me when you've finished. He has to be somewhere in the building.' She said the last part with more conviction than she felt.

Running through reception in her dressing gown, she saw one of the kitchen staff in the dining room.

'Rosie, please can you take Simon to my room and put him in his cot. Just try and calm him down if you can – we've lost Simon. He wasn't in the canteen or kitchen, was he?'

Emma already knew the answer to her question. She scanned the dining room as Rosie took the struggling baby, then ran to her office. From there she went to the lounge and then downstairs to the swimming pool. Two minutes later, she approached the door to the gym. Light was coming from under the door, and her hopes momentarily soared.

Back at reception again she dialled Michael's extension. The groggy reply changed instantly.

'Okay Em, calm down, he can't be far. Have you checked everywhere inside?'

Jamie was back at reception now and shaking his head at Emma.

'Everywhere apart from the resident's rooms, and I can't do that yet.' Dawn light was just beginning to seep through. 'There's something else, Michael. Those photos he stuck on the picture in his room? Of you, me, and Simon? They're gone.'

'I don't get it. He was fine when I left him yesterday afternoon; we'd had a great time.' As Michael was talking, he was throwing clothes on himself. 'Can you go and check his room again and look for his tracksuit? It's just about the only clothing he has apart from a couple of T-shirts and sweatshirts.'

Emma instructed Jamie to check for the tracksuit. 'I'll get some gear on and see you at your place in five minutes.' She put the phone down and ran to her rooms.

Jamie was at reception when she got back. Dismal grey light was filtering through the dense clouds outside.

'The tracksuit's gone. I'm coming with you — it's all my fault. I can't believe I thought a bunch of fucking pillows was Simon.'

'Stay here. Some of the residents will already be up. Wait for whoever's on reception to arrive at eight o'clock, and then you can help. Hopefully, we'll have found him by then.' Emma ran out of the front door.

Michael was waiting outside his apartment when Emma arrived. It was dry, and there was hardly a breath of wind, but the coldness was almost incapacitating.

'I'm going to run around his track. Can you head through the trees towards the outer wall? If he's not on the

293

course, I'll head to where you are, and we'll go around the perimeter wall to the main gate.'

As Michael curved towards and around the car park, the sound of Emma's voice calling Simon had faded. He passed close by Laura who was getting out of her car.

'For heaven's sake, Michael, do you ever sleep or do you just run all night and day?'

'I'm looking for Simon – he's gone missing. Did you see him on the street on the way here?'

'Oh, Good Lord, have you been looking for him all night? Is that what you were doing last evening? I'd only seen him a short while before that.'

'I don't understand.'

'I saw you running through the woods in the freezing rain last night just after eight o'clock.'

'What? That wasn't me. I don't ... Oh shit – go inside and call an ambulance now, okay? It's an emergency.'

He turned around and headed in the opposite direction, running as fast as his body would allow him. He was hoping to pick up Emma's voice again but could hear nothing.

As he cleared the trees, he could see Emma kneeling down in the distance under a dilapidated metal roof.

He could hear the sobbing before he reached her. Emma's forehead was pressed against Simon's frozen face, her arms around his shoulders and chest.

*

The funeral had taken place thirteen days later in the parish church, less than a mile away from Orchard. The coroner's verdict was death by misadventure, the cause of death, heart failure. Every member of the care home not on duty was in attendance, and Emma's mother and father sat with her and the baby, while Michael and Maddy sat on her other side.

She'd given the photograph of Michael to him the day after discovering Simon, and they'd wept together as she showed him the other two pictures. The day after, Emma moved down to the apartment in Cambridge with the baby, but despite every offer from Michael, she didn't want any company.

Emma had taken a call from him each evening, but the conversations were limited to the home and its residents. If he raised any other subject, she'd tell him she had to go and look after Simon, and the call was terminated.

Maddy had been to see her a couple of times a week, taking provisions for mother and baby. After every trip, Michael was keen to hear the news, but there was little to talk about. It appeared they weren't leaving the apartment.

The only visitors apart from Maddy had been the cleaning lady once a week plus a visit from the doctor to check on a persistent cough Simon was suffering from. Emma admitted to her friend that she'd been prescribed Prozac while he was there examining the baby. Maddy was surprised and concerned that Emma had chosen a home visit rather than go to her doctor's surgery; it was so out of character.

A week before Christmas, Michael had broached the subject.

'The decorations here are wonderful. Julie organised everything with the maintenance guys, and they've all done such a good job. Don't spend Christmas Day on your own, Em. Everyone here is desperate to see you. Apart from anything else, a lot of the staff have bought presents for you. They'll be so disappointed not to see you.'

Michael felt guilty for using such a reason to get Emma to agree to visit, but he'd use anything if he thought it might work.

'Let me pick the two of you up on Christmas Eve and come and stay until Boxing Day. Then if you want to go back home, I'll take you back then. Would you consider that? There's not a day goes by when the residents don't ask how you are.' He could hear the sigh down the line.

'I don't know, Michael. I just feel so tired all the time.'

'Well, how about I look after Simon for some of the time? Especially night time – I can do all that so you have a full night's sleep. You'll feel so much better.'

'I don't want him away from my side. I can't leave him with you overnight – I just can't.'

'I didn't mean like that, Em. I'll get a put-you-up bed for the lounge, then when he wakes, I can carry him from your room and feed him or whatever until he's asleep, then put him back in his cot next to you. I'd love to do that for you; for Simon.'

There was no audible sigh this time, but the silence didn't bode well.

I really don't know. I'm more comfortable here on my own with Simon. I don't know if I can face anybody at the moment. I'm sorry, I need to go and feed him now.

'Wait, please – just one minute. Please will you think about it, if nothing else?'

'Okay, I'll think about it. I have to go now.'

'Em, apart from everyone here missing you, I miss you even more. I miss you so much.' Michael's attempt at hiding a crack in his voice had failed.

'Goodbye, Michael.' She was gone before he had time to reply.

Maddy was going to see Emma again tomorrow. Maybe he'd go with her this time.

*

'Here we go, sweetheart. And this is from Audrey – she said if it's a bit too big for him, she'll knit another one.'

Maddy passed Emma a tiny mid-blue jumper with a kitten on the front and a puppy on the back. 'I think she's suggesting you and Simon think about getting a pet. I think it's a lovely idea.'

Emma held the top up and admired it – it was the first time Maddy had seen her smile in weeks.

'That's so kind of Audrey, bless her. We could never have a pet here, though. Too small for a dog, and if the cat got knocked over on the road, I'd never forgive myself.'

'I meant for Orchard. They'd have a great life and bring a lot of joy.' Maddy looked at Emma, but she turned away, busying herself with the groceries.

'There's something else I want to tell you. No pressure at all, but I brought someone with me. He's in the car now. If you don't want him to come up, that's fine with him. Maybe you could go down and say hello? I'll look after Simon and put the stuff away.'

Emma froze. 'I … I can't see anyone – not yet. It's too soon.' She turned around and looked at her closest friend. 'I'm sorry, but I just can't. It's Michael, isn't it?'

'Yes. He wants to see you so much, but he'll understand. He told me he's trying to persuade you to come back for Christmas, just for a couple of days. Have you thought about that?'

'I've thought about it, but I'm not ready yet. I don't want to see anyone yet – only you.' She moved to Simon's cot and looked at him sleeping.

'Sit down love, Simon's fine. I'll put the kettle on.'

They sat in silence for a few minutes, the untouched coffees sitting in front of them. Maddy knew she was crossing a line, but something had to be said.

'Simon would want you back at Orchard. If he knew how you were conducting your life now, he'd be very sad. He bought the place for you and your son. Honour his wishes, sweetheart. Come back home – if not today, then for Christmas. Please?'

Emma was still looking into her lap as tears fell onto her jeans. Maddy moved to her and held her tight, then Emma opened her arms and held on to her friend fiercely.

'It's not fair, Maddy. It's just not fair.'

*

On Christmas Eve morning, the doorbell sounded in Emma's flat. She was expecting it and knew who was there but couldn't get rid of her nervousness. She buzzed Michael in, and a moment later, he knocked on the door.

'Hello, Em.' He kissed her on both sides of her face, and they walked into the flat. 'And hello, Simon. Wow, you're bigger than the last time I saw you. What have you been feeding him on?'

'Oh, the normal, but his appetite's bigger now.'

'Well, he looks fantastic. You both look fantastic. Are you packed and ready? Let me grab your bag.' Michael looked around the living area. There didn't appear to be any luggage there, so he walked towards the main bedroom.

'Oh, it's in the spare bedroom.'

'Ah, okay.' Michael walked into the room, and it was immediately clear this was where Emma was sleeping. He was almost certain he knew why she chose to sleep here.

The two photographs were propped up against a wooden casket sitting on a chest of drawers opposite the bed. They faced the other way so only the writing was showing. Still creased and exactly as she'd found them, now leaning against Simon's ashes.

He wasn't aware she'd walked into the room.

'Oh, I'm sorry. Just looking for your bag – here we are.' He took her small suitcase off the bed.

'You've done exactly the same as me. I've put the photo you gave me in a frame, but with the writing facing outwards.

'Oh. I see.'

'Not that I could ever forget, but I want to always be able to see the two things he asked me to do. Do you remember what he wrote?'

'Yes.'

'One of those requests is going to be next to impossible, but you can be sure I'll give it my best shot. Without Simon, though, it's so daunting.' They looked at each other across the bedroom.

'But the other is an absolute certainty for the rest of my life. Ready to go?'

*

Emma was profoundly touched by the kindness of everyone. She found it hard to admit to herself, but she knew the last month had been a big mistake. It was the worst period of her life, and the last thing she needed was solitude, but she didn't want anyone to see her like that.

Within hours of being at Orchard, she knew she'd come back home. And Maddy, as always, was right. It *was* what Simon would have wanted. When Michael asked her what time she wanted to leave on the 27th, she told him she'd stay a little while longer and see how things panned out.

He was overjoyed and couldn't hide it; didn't want to hide it. He held Emma and hugged her; whether she cared to acknowledge it or not, it felt good. She closed her eyes, rested her chin on his shoulder, and pictured Simon in her mind. She saw the creases in the corners of his vivid blue eyes, and he was smiling, nodding his approval.

And she wept yet again.

After New Year, when helping put all the decorations away, Emma felt a strong urge to get back to work again. Not just part time as she'd been doing since her baby had come along, but the shifts she used to put in. In order to do this, she needed someone to help her look after Simon. Michael had been marvellous with the baby, and she could already see a bond growing, just as it had between him and Simon this last year.

She could see that Michael was behaving as if the child was his own. He'd always wanted to be a father, and now he was playing out that role. But there was someone else who the baby seemed to adore, and it appeared the feeling was mutual. Julie spent all her spare time talking and playing with him, and it wasn't long before Emma was relaxed and happy with this development.

It gave her much more time to dedicate to the residents. For the first time in an age, she had the freedom to see and talk to everyone who lived at Orchard, just as she'd done in the past and for so many years previously.

She built her routine up again, and things really did seem to get a little easier – a little less painful. Michael and Maddy would have a working breakfast with her in the main dining room on weekdays, and Maddy was finally taking things a little easier, having weekends off.

Julie applied for one of the few staff accommodation rooms when one came up, and now lived at Orchard. She no longer had need of the flat she was renting, but Emma insisted there should be no charge for her studio apartment at the home because of the amount of time she was helping with the baby.

Although Michael hadn't asked Emma out to dinner since she'd come back, they regularly ate meals on their own in the evening, or with Julie, who always had the pram right next to her. As the days grew longer and winter gradually disappeared, Michael could be seen running around the grounds every day, twice a day. The course was being used again. The running machine was also being used for something other than slow and gentle walking.

On Valentine's Day, Emma received a card in the post. There was no chance of identifying the handwriting on the envelope because it was typed, but inside it became apparent immediately.

'The first part is the easiest and most pleasurable of my life.

The second is soooo tough though!

But, I have a milestone to report - I broke the 50-minute barrier yesterday!

Please will you come out to dinner with me tonight to celebrate? A table is booked ...

Yours forever,

A Secret Admirer x

Emma sat at the desk in her office and smiled. Then she read the card again – and she was still smiling.

*

It had been a lovely meal. Emma had sent only one text to Julie to see how Simon was, and the reply was a big thumbs-up emoji and a kiss. Michael had insisted she have a glass of Champagne, and he wouldn't accept no for an answer. However, he'd stuck with sparkling water, claiming he was in training. Emma was truly relaxing for the first time since she'd lost Simon.

Over coffee, Michael had raised the subject of their Decree Nisi. He was adamant that he wouldn't apply for the Decree Absolute, though he would of course agree if that's what she wanted. Emma admitted that she hadn't given it a thought, and Michael said he'd take that answer all day long.

He tried to capture the smile she gave him in his mind. Michael's sole ambition now was to get Emma back home without letting on how much he loved her and ruining everything. Patience was a virtue, but God, it was difficult.

*

The Valentine's meal seemed to have changed something in the way Emma thought and felt. She'd forced her heart to harden during her month of solitude in Cambridge, determined she never wanted to look at or be with another man again. To think otherwise was to cast a slur on her relationship with Simon. It had taken until now for her to relax her guard enough to know that the world moved on, regardless of what happened within it.

Simon's wishes that his place be taken by Michael was abhorrent to her. During her exile, she'd felt betrayed and demeaned as if she were some possession to be passed around. But it was only Simon's acceptance of his situation and her denial of it. That was the only difference. He was so much stronger than her, and she felt ashamed at her weakness, and the extra pressure she may have put him under towards the end of his life.

She accepted Michael's invitations to dinner, and by the summer it was becoming a weekly event. Though none of the staff or residents ever said anything, she sensed an acceptance of her situation. Perhaps it was wishful thinking, but at times she felt as if some were willing her and Michael to get back together again.

Emma had suffered a setback when she'd gone on an outing with a group of residents to the Botanic Garden. Michael and Maddy had gone with her, and he'd known this was a big test for Emma. She'd come through it by avoiding the areas she remembered going to with Simon. The little sunken rockery would have broken her heart, and it was all she could do not to run back to the minibus at one stage.

That night, Michael had come to Emma's room and asked if she would email him the photo of her and Simon in the Botanic Garden. A week later, she'd gone back to her quarters after a long day and seen the framed canvas photo hanging on the wall of her lounge. It had left her struggling to breathe. The phone had rung moments later, and she'd answered – it was Michael. If it were okay, he'd like to come and see her now.

*

He put his arm around her as they stared at the photo. Nothing was said for there was nothing either could say. Then they turned to each other, and he held her wet face in his hands, and they kissed. Gently, tenderly, and for a long time. Then he let her go and wished her a good night's sleep.

And she knew she loved him again.